# "DID YOU MISS ME?" HE ASKED.

He was smiling, but his gray eyes were serious, and Margo knew that whatever happened now was up to her.

Before she could make a lighthearted response, a white heron rose from the water and flew into the trees. The sky was filled with streams of coral cloud, and the air was tinged with the scent of roses and the ghosts of old love. How could she lie?

"Yes, I missed you."

He'd forgotten how honest she was. Niell caught his breath as he saw the sunset reflected in her clear eyes. For the space of a heartbeat they looked at each other. Then he drew her into his arms.

Their kiss cut through pretenses and mere words to something buried so deep within her as to be imprinted in her DNA. Amid a jumble of sensations, Margo remembered everything about the taste and texture of Niell's lips. Her mouth opened under his, welcoming the sweet invasion of his tongue.

Warm honey seemed to flood through her veins as she felt his hands stroking her bare arms, scattering jewels of fire across her skin. His hands slipped down over her back, stroking up over her hips and ribs to the proud mounds of her breasts before rising again to cup her face.

"Margo, I want to make love to you." His voice was rough with need.

# LAURA JORDAN
# Roses At Dawn

**ZEBRA BOOKS**
**KENSINGTON PUBLISHING CORP.**

ZEBRA BOOKS

are published by

Kensington Publishing Corp.
475 Park Avenue South
New York, NY 10016

First Printing: December, 1992

Printed in the United States of America

*To*
*Donna and Tom, who are lucky in love.*

# Chapter One

Blue, graying blue, lavender, rose, and almost-purple red—Bussey Hill looked like one of Grandma Beth's patchwork quilts. That and the scent of the lilacs made her think of a spring day in West Virginia. Margo sucked in warm May air and closed her eyes.

She could almost hear her grandfather pruning the old lilac bushes by the front porch. . . . But that was as far as Margo got before something butted her in the thigh. The next moment a furry muzzle pushed against her hand and, snapping open her eyes, Margo blinked at the golden retriever by her feet.

"Now where did *you* come from?"

The dog's coat was so glossy that it practically glowed. He was wearing tags, one of which said BRUNO, and when Margo began to rub behind his ears, he wriggled with pleasure.

She looked about her. It was Lilac Sunday, and all of Boston seemed to have come out to the

Arnold Arboretum to admire the flowers. People were strolling about, alone or in groups, but no one appeared to be looking for a lost dog.

"Who do you belong to, baby? Never mind, we'll look together." Margo undid her belt and pulled it through the loops of her jeans, then slipped it under the dog's collar and fastened it.

They started down the hill together. Margo hadn't realized how much she'd missed having a dog padding beside her. "Whoever let you go must be driving himself nuts trying to find you," she murmured.

That was when she spotted the man. He was tall and had dark, windblown hair, and though he wore jeans and a sports shirt, Margo noted that he carried a briefcase under his arm. He was walking too fast to enjoy the lilacs and was holding a leash in his hand.

"Are you looking for this dog?" Margo called.

The man stared up the hill at Margo and then came jogging up. At the sight of him, Bruno wagged his tail and gave a deep-throated bark of recognition, then began to leap about the new-comer.

"Where did you find him?" the man asked.

"It was more like he found *me*." Margo watched as the newcomer hunkered down and attached the leash to Bruno's collar with strong, competent hands. "How did you lose him?"

He glanced up, and she caught a glint of light gray eyes as he adjusted his sunglasses. "I was reading, and he was on his back, fast asleep. To give him some slack I stupidly unleashed him. Never mind the sweet talk," he added sternly as the retriever began to lick him all over his face. "I'm not buying ice cream for any four-footed con artist."

Bruno barked excitedly.

Margo laughed. "I don't think he believes you."

"Thanks for heading him off at the pass. Barry would have killed me if something had happened to Bruno." Getting to his feet, the man held out a hand. "I'm Niell Kier."

Margo decided that she liked Niell Kier's handshake. It was strong without being overpowering and as direct as his smile. She also liked the way he carried his six feet of broad shoulders and hardmuscled lean flanks with the assurance of an athlete. His face was strong-boned, square-jawed, and deeply tanned. His expensive-looking sunglasses rested on a proudly aquiline nose.

"I'm Margo Sanders. So you don't own Bruno?"

"I'm just the dog-sitter." She liked his voice, too. It was deep, softened, and shaded with humor. It was the kind of voice, her grandfather would have said, that was easy on the ears. "Bruno belongs to Barry, my old college friend. My schedule's too crazy for me to own an animal, but I enjoy having one around sometimes."

"I know what you mean."

Niell watched in approval as Margo bent down to rub Bruno's ears in a gesture of farewell. With her thick, shoulder-length fall of auburn hair and her peach-bloom skin, she looked as wholesome as an advertisement for Ivory soap. The neat plaid shirt she wore tucked into her jeans showed off a figure that was slender yet rounded in all the right places.

"Do you own a dog?" he asked to postpone her leaving.

"I wish. My landlord doesn't allow pets, unfortunately. Some of the people in our apartment complex own cats on the sly, but my roommate's allergic to them." Margo drew in a breath that was almost a sigh. "I discovered that last year when I found a stray Siamese. Her former owners had declawed her, so she was defenseless and scared to death. I'd have loved to keep her, but Naomi had an allergy attack and I had to give her away."

"That's too bad."

"Lady Hamilton was the most—" Margo broke off to smile ruefully. "Sorry. I'll talk your ear off about animals, if you let me. And speaking of animals, now that you and Bruno have found each other, I'll let you get back to your reading."

She had, Niell noted, a terrific smile. It revealed a single dimple in her chin and caused her mouth to curve in a way that he could only describe as delectable. He considered the briefs he had yet to read, then dismissed them. He'd get his homework done tomorrow on the plane.

"Will you join us for an i-c-e c-r-e-a-m first?" he asked. "I'm spelling it so that Fur-ball here won't go ape. He lives for the stuff."

He slid off his sunglasses as he spoke, and his gray eyes — almost silvery against his dark skin — smiled down at her so that smiling back felt natural.

"Who am I to deny a dog anything?" Margo said. Then she added, "There's usually an ice — I mean, a you-know-what vendor up by the Jamaica Plain gate."

They began to walk down the hill again, the retriever padding happily along beside Niell. "You obviously know your way around here," he commented.

"It's one of my favorite places."

"Really?"

"You should see it when the forsythia is out in April, or later in May, with the flowering cherries and crabs and azalea. And in July, when most gardens look wimpy and uninteresting, the purple loosestrife grows rampantly in the meadow over there."

"I'll take your word for it."

He smiled, but Margo was serious. "You shouldn't do that. Come see for yourself and you'll be surprised. Ez — my grandfather — used to say that a garden was one of God's finest inventions."

"*My* grandfather hardly realized gardens existed." There was a touch of amusement in Niell's deep voice. "I take it you agree with Ez, though."

"I should. I'm a landscape designer."

Margo broke off as her shoulder brushed

11

against Niell's. It was only an accidental touch, but there was nothing casual about her reaction to it. It felt, Margo thought, as though goose bumps were prickling along her skin. *Warm* goose bumps.

"So you design gardens?" he asked.

"Gardens and grounds and parks and whatever I can get my hands on. I work for Alloway Landscapers, and right now we are beautfiying the grounds at a nursing home. It's a challenge because we want to give an illusion of space and privacy in a very small area."

He nodded. "What else have you done?"

"It's not so much what I've *done* as what I'd like to do someday. I'd love to create atmosphere with foliage rather than flowers—it's been done successfully in New York at the Central Park Conservatory Garden—and I'd like to design a prairie garden with windflowers, or create a frankly European look as Warren Manning did in the Midwest back in 1916." Margo's tone turned reverent as she added, "And then there are the beautifully spare Japanese gardens, like the one at the Ginkakuji in Kyoto. Now that's beauty that will *endure.*"

When she tipped back her head like that, sunlight darkened her hazel eyes to amber, and he could see a scattering of freckles on her nose. There was determination and drive under Margo's warmth and softness, and Niell liked that. She wasn't just an attractive woman. She had substance and body, like a truly fine wine.

12

"If I ever want a garden," he promised, "you'll design it."

Before she could thank him for his vote of confidence, Bruno went wild. They had reached the exit to the arboretum, and the retriever had spotted the ice-cream truck. He danced on his hind feet, barking and whimpering, while Niell ordered three vanilla-chocolate cones. Then, flattening himself on his belly, Bruno devoured his own cone in a gulp and begged for more.

Niell surrendered his cone and positioned it between Bruno's front paws. The expression of pure bliss on the dog's face made Margo laugh.

"He looks like he's died and gone to heaven. You're a pushover, Niell. I bet Bruno waits to have you sit for him."

She sat down on a grassy bank to enjoy her own ice cream. Niell joined her. "I don't do it often," he confessed. "Barry caught me between trips. Most of the time I'm on the road."

So he was a salesman. With that voice and that smile he had to be a success. "What's your route?" Margo asked.

"It varies. Tomorrow at this time I'll be in Athens."

"Athens!" Margo turned to look wide-eyed at him. "What do you do?"

"I'm with Grenville, Simons, and Kier, a law firm." Offhandedly he added, "We have several overseas clients, and I'm usually delegated to take care of them."

"I'd kill for a job like that."

There was a dab of ice cream on her upper lip, and Niell felt an almost irresistible urge to run his thumb lightly over that soft curve. Or, even better, to lick the sweet smudge away.

His body's frankly visceral reaction to that notion surprised Niell. Lusting after a woman met by chance wasn't usually his style. Generally he was in perfect control, but today his normally acute reasoning powers seemed fogged. It took an effort just to concentrate on what Margo was saying.

"Where else do I travel? Istanbul, Paris, London, Rome . . ."

Margo put her hands over her ears. "Stop, I can't stand it. I'm pea-green with envy, Niell. I'd give anything to study English gardens firsthand. And the Villa d'Este in Tivoli—" She stopped as an incredible thought occurred to her. "Don't tell me that you haven't even gone to the Villa d'Este?"

"Hey, I sometimes stay in a country only for the day. There's no time to sightsee."

"No excuse, counsellor. To be near one of the most beautiful gardens in the world and not even go to see it is . . . it's criminal."

He threw up his hands in a gesture of surrender. "Give me a break, Ms. Sanders. Until now I didn't even know this Villa what's it existed." Margo groaned. "Tell you what I'll do for you. I'll be in Rome on Wednesday—No, Thursday, I'll do my darndest to get out to Tivoli and look around. Then I'll give you a report."

He had meant it as a joke, but she took him seriously. Her eyes glowed like warm topaz, and her cheeks bloomed with enthusiasm. *"Will* you?"

Her undisguised pleasure was irresistible. "I'll make a point of it," Niell vowed. "I'll call you as soon as I get back."

On the point of blurting out her phone number, Margo stopped short. Her roommate, Naomi, who was worldly and city smart, had warned her never, never to give her number to a stranger.

"I don't care how good-looking the man is," Naomi had lectured. "You're not in Taylor, West Virginia, now, Margery Ann Sanders. This is Boston. There are some really perverted dudes out there."

But Niell Kier hardly looked like a pervert. Margo compromised by giving him her work number at Zach's and watched as he unsnapped his briefcase, took out a gold pen, and wrote it in a slim black leather book.

"I'll phone you," he promised.

His smile transformed his strong face, making it even more incredibly attractive. The warm, lilac-scented air seemed suddenly to become motionless, to surround them in a golden chrysalis. It was as if they were both suspended in time and space.

Margo forgot about Naomi's stern warnings and smiled right into Niell Kier's silvery eyes.

"I surely hope you do," she said.

\* \* \*

"Is *this* the man you met in the arboretum?"

Warily Margo looked down at the copy of *Newswatch* magazine that Naomi had plunked down on the kitchen table in front of her. A photograph of Niell Kier looked sternly up from the page. He was dressed in a dark suit and was getting out of a black limo. With his shades and that briefcase he appeared slightly sinister.

"Why?" she demanded. "What's he done?"

Naomi folded her arms and rocked back on her high heels. She was tiny—no more than five feet in her heels—but her air of assurance seemed to give her stature. *"That,"* she exclaimed dramatically, "happens to be one of the most successful young corporate attorneys in the country. His firm is exclusive *and* expensive. Capital Es, Margo. I know because his firm handled that merger between us and Wilston Computers."

"No fooling!" Margo exclaimed.

"A list of his clients would read like a page out of Who's Who." Naomi paused. "And you didn't give him your phone number."

"Will you listen to yourself? You're the one who told me not to give out my number, for Pete's sake. Anyway, I gave him my work number."

Naomi rolled her eyes and mimicked, " 'Hello, you've reached Zach Alloway Landscapers. If you want to talk business, leave your name and number. If you want to sell me something, forget it.' Niell Kier's going to be charmed by *that*."

It was her turn to clean up after supper, so

Margo rose from the table and carried the dinner plates to the kitchen sink. She yelped as the hot water hit a new blister. For the past few days she'd been helping Zach set posts for a lattice-screen fence, and her hands were wrecked.

"What I'd like to know," Naomi continued, "is why you work for a flake like Zach in the first place. You leave Taylor and your grandparents to put yourself through the Rhode Island School of Design, and when you finally get your degree in landscape design, you waste yourself on Alloway Landscapers. You could do a lot better, Margery Ann."

Naomi always used Margo's full name when she wanted to hammer in a point. Diplomatically Margo kept her peace. She knew that her employer and her roommate rubbed each other the wrong way. They saw every issue from diametrically opposed viewpoints, and the last time she had been unwise enough to leave them alone for five minutes they'd got into an argument over local politics. Naomi had told Zach that his attitude toward life was that of an aging hippie, and Zach had called Naomi, who was a certified public accountant employed by a large electronics firm, a mercenary corporate flunky.

"You ought to have your own firm or at least be working for a *big* landscaper," Naomi went on. "Then you could be helping to design a fabulous garden for Mr. Moneybags instead of planting petunias at the Carlton Nursing Home."

Margo smiled. "The residents enjoy petunias."

"Seems to me you had a great design worked up for that nursing home but that Zach vetoed it," Naomi accused. "You need to stand up for yourself, Margery Ann."

A trace of regret crept into Margo's voice. "Zach and I discussed my design, but he didn't go for it. Zach's still the boss."

"Meaning that if you were in charge, you'd do things differently." Margo said nothing, and Naomi ran a hand through her fashionably short, dark hair and leaned back in her chair to survey her friend. "You'd also be a lot better off financially if you were the boss. Zach Alloway has the business sense of a gnat."

Margo couldn't argue the point but said, "Even so, he can teach me a lot." Naomi mumbled under her breath. "No, really. Maybe he isn't a businessman, *and* yes, many times I think we could do things differently on a job. But he's a real craftsman."

Margo finished washing up, stacked the dishes, and picked up a dish towel, disclosing a small stack of envelopes and flyers. "I didn't know I had mail."

"Sorry, I forgot to tell you. Seriously, Margo, you have to think of yourself. You want to be your own boss, make heaps of money, and get out of this rat race. Then you can have a gorgeous place in the country and bring home all the stray dogs and cats you want—"

18

"Oh, my God," Margo exclaimed. She slumped back against the sink and stared blankly at the letter in her hand. "She's dead," she whispered.

Naomi sat bolt upright. "Not your grandmother?"

"What? No, not Grandma Beth. It's Miss Lattimer. You know, the old lady who adopted Lady Hamilton, that Siamese cat I found but couldn't keep." Margo turned her blank gaze to her roommate as she added, "The letter is from Miss Lattimer's attorney. He says that I'm mentioned in her will."

Naomi's eyes were round. "Do they say what you inherited?"

"No, they don't. It's so sad, Nao. Miss Lattimer was such a spry old lady. I enjoyed meeting her and talking on the phone with her. And she was so nice to call and tell me about Lady Hamilton's kitten. I meant to drive out to Carlin to see her . . . and now it's too late."

"Don't start with the guilt trip," her roommate counselled. Then she added, "I just had a horrible thought. Supposing she left you her cats? I remember she had about ten of them."

"Three." Margo thought of the tall, angular woman with the iron-gray hair and direct sky-blue eyes who had answered her ad about her foundling Siamese cat. Miss Lattimer had been so feisty and independent that it was hard to think she was gone. "Don't worry about the cats," she told Naomi. "At least not until Friday. That's when the

19

will is being read."

Margo worked hard for the rest of the week to clear the decks for Friday, and the end of the week saw her driving toward Carlin. Margo's sole means of transportation, an aged and temperamental Chevy, developed a shimmy when it went past fifty. The ride to the Berkshires that normally took three hours had lengthened to four by the time she reached the town of Carlin.

From Miss Lattimer's description of her hometown, Margo had pictured it to be a small, laid-back place nestled at the foot of the Berkshires. The mountains were a breathtaking as she'd imagined, but Carlin wasn't at all what she'd envisioned. Far from being a quaint, backwoods spot, it was one of the most expensive-looking communities Margo had ever seen.

The town boasted fine old houses and mansions set on two-acre tracts of land. Lawns were manicured; gardens were precise and colorful. Even the air seemed more rarified. As she drove down the pristine streets, it occurred to Margo that only someone like Niell Kier could afford to live here.

The shopping mall where she stopped to ask directions had an exclusive look. "Rupert Brooke's office? Well, certainly," exclaimed the smartly dressed saleslady Margo approached. "It's down the road in the center of town. Let me point out the direction to you."

Margo noted the subtle change in the saleslady's manner when she saw the battered pickup. She concentrated on the woman's directions and was soon drawing up to the curb beside a neat Cape Cod cottage, whitewashed to within an inch of its life. The gleaming brass nameplate, topped by a huge bronze door-knocker, announced that she had reached Rupert Brooke, attorney-at-law.

Inside, the office glowed with fine old wood and Hepplewhite furniture. It was soundless except for the tick of an aristocratic grandfather clock. The clock announced that Margo was several minutes late for her appointment, and she apologized profusely to Mr. Brooke, an elderly, balding personage with rimless spectacles and a nervous habit of clearing his throat.

He said, "Not at all," in a way that made her positive that she had been keeping him away from more important affairs. He then cleared his throat and asked, "Before we begin, may I ask how you are connected to the late Miss Lattimer?"

"She adopted my cat," Margo explained.

An apprehensive look flickered momentarily in the lawyer's eyes. "I see. Which, er, cat would that be?"

"Lady Hamilton. I found her lost in Boston, and since I couldn't keep her myself, I advertised for a home for her."

"And Miss Lattimer answered your ad."

"Yes. There were others, but Miss Lattimer *really* wanted the cat. She had a forceful personality

21

and the gentlest hands." The lawyer nodded slightly. "She said she wanted her as a companion for her male Siamese, Lord Nelson, whom she described as old and mean. I guess he got on well with Lady Hamilton, though, because they had a kitten together. Miss Lattimer called it Traffy — short for Trafalgar." Margo paused. "That's all there is to it, Mr. Brooke. I can't understand why I'm to be a beneficiary."

"*The* beneficiary, Ms. Sanders."

"Please?"

"If you will give me an, er, minute, it will become clear to you." Mr. Brooke opened a file, drew out a document, straightened his tie, cleared his voice, and began to read.

Far from having matters grow clearer, Margo felt her sense of unreality increase. "I'm not sure if I understand this," she interrupted. "Did you say . . . did you say that Miss Lattimer has left her *entire* estate to me?"

Mr. Brooke did not crack a smile. He did not look congratulatory or pleased in any way. "She has."

Dark spots had begun to dance in front of Margo's eyes. "But . . . but why sh-should she — "

"The estate comprises her house on Peachtree Lane, her grounds, and all that they contain. There is also a small bequest over which you are to be the executrix. The bequest is for the, er, cats." Mr. Brooke paused. "Before I go further, I should point out that the will stipulates that in order to inherit, you must provide a home for the cats. Since the male feline would hardly take kindly to being relocated, this means that you would perforce have to, er, reside at Lattimer House."

Margo raised a hand to clutch her reeling head. "What I can't understand is, why should she leave me her estate in the first place? Surely, a relative—"

"She had no living relatives and few friends. She was," Mr. Brooke added primly, "something of an, er, eccentric. In fact, she and her neighbors had an, er, running battle over the years."

"Because of the cats?"

"Er . . . in part. Miss Lattimer's neighbors take pride in their estates."

"And Miss Lattimer didn't?"

"The best way to explain is by taking you to see the, er, estate itself." Mr. Brooke rose to his feet. "We will go in my car."

Margo was too confused to make polite conversation, and Mr. Brooke did not initiate any. In silence they drove through the center of town and onto a side road that, like the rest of Carlin, was flanked by elegant homes, each set on a manicured and landscaped property.

A particularly fine garden brought Margo out of the fog that enveloped her. "The Amberlys have won the Carlin Garden Club's horticultural award several years' running," Mr. Brooke replied to her queries. "And over there you have Mrs. Sheridan's lovely home. Mrs. Sheridan is the president of the,

23

er, Carlin Women's Group." He paused significantly before adding, "And here is, er, Lattimer House."

Miss Lattimer's house—*her* house now, Margo thought, fuzzily—was a large colonial set back some distance from the road and shaded by a clump of silver spruce. Behind the trees Margo glimpsed a large fountain.

"It's lovely," she enthused.

Mr. Brooke maintained an ominous silence, and Margo soon saw why. A closer look showed that the trees shading the house were old and in desperate need of trimming while the house itself looked like an aging beauty gone to seed. Its paint was peeling, windows had been broken and replaced with tape and cardboard, and fallen shingles littered the ground.

The garden was in even worse shape. With a sinking heart Margo noted that weeds were choking out beds of roses and lilacs. An herb garden had been all but obliterated by crabgrass, and the fountain was green with mold.

Mr. Brooke cleared his throat. "You can see why the lady's neighbors were not happy with the way the property looks."

"Some work would have to be done," Margo agreed. "But I think that—"

The lawyer interrupted. "Unfortunately, Miss Lattimer's, er, bequest is very small. It barely covers the land tax. I feel compelled to tell you all this before you agree to abide by the terms of her will."

He was warning her not to take on more than she could handle, and from his point of view he was right. Walking around, Margo could see how much work the estate needed, and such work would cost money, which she didn't have. Naomi would be the first to agree with Mr. Brooke, but then Naomi hadn't seen the house. She hadn't fallen in love with its clean lines, or seen the sweet-scented lilacs and rosebuds bursting out of the weeds.

The house had great charm. Darn it, it had potential! "Where are the cats now?" Margo temporized.

Mr. Brooke sniffed. "After Miss Lattimer passed on, we attempted to move them to an animal shelter. The male cat clawed everyone who came within reach. The female evaded the animal officer and hid. Finally our secretary agreed, er, to come and feed the cats once a day. It was not," the lawyer added, "an ideal situation but the best we could do."

"Then they've been left alone for more than a week," Margo exclaimed. "The poor creatures must feel abandoned. Do you have the key with you, Mr. Brooke?"

The lawyer produced it. As Margo fitted it into the lock of the front door, he cautioned, "I'd be careful if I were you. The male animal is dangerous."

As he spoke, Margo swung open the door and blinked into the dimly lit interior. Out of the shadows glared a pair of blue-green eyes.

"Lord Nelson?" Margo wondered.

An ominous growl answered her, and now she could see the cat. He was huge and mean-looking. His back was humped, his tail whipped back and forth.

"All right," Margo told him. She kept her voice calm and friendly as she added, "I'm not here to hurt you, Lord Nelson. I'm not even going to touch you till you want me to. But if I'm to take care of you, we have to at least coexist. What do you say?"

The cat yowled—Margo had never heard such a noise before—and spat. Out of the corner of her eye, Margo saw that Mr. Brooke had retreated several steps. "Be careful," he repeated. "That animal is vicious. It should be, er, destroyed."

"He's frightened and confused," Margo snapped over her shoulder. "You would be too, if—" She broke off as something soft and sinuous landed on her back.

Her scream sent the lawyer scurrying to take refuge behind a juniper bush. Lord Nelson uttered another yowl and leaped back into the shadows. Margo, poised for flight herself, suddenly realized that the soft something that had landed on her neck was emitting a rumbling sound. In fact, it was purring.

Raising both hands, she scooped a soft, pliant body into her hands. Sapphire eyes stared unwinking at her out of a tawny mask, and a warm brown nose sniffed curiously. "Hey, there, Traffy," Margo exclaimed.

The young Siamese yawned delicately, showing his pink gums. He studied Margo for a moment, then reached out a velvet paw to touch her cheek. "Hey, no problem, I like you, too," she said, grinning.

"Miss Sanders?"

She turned and saw the little lawyer hovering behind the junipers. *Her* junipers. And next to it was *her* moldy fountain, and *her* overgrown garden which surrounded *her* house.

The sense of unreality that had shrouded Margo lifted like morning mist. In its stead came a sense of rightness and almost blinding joy.

"It's all right, Mr. Brooke," she called happily. "Come and meet Traffy. He's the youngest of *my* cats."

# Chapter Two

"It's a disaster, Margery Ann. An absolute, complete, dyed-in-the-wool disaster."

Naomi stuck her hands into the pockets of her size-four jeans and rocked back on her heels. "No way should you even touch this place with a ten-foot pole," she continued. "It would cost a fortune to put this eyesore right, and a fortune you don't have."

"Tell me about it." Margo poked her toe at a shingle lying among the weeds. Before driving with Naomi out to Carlin this morning, she had checked her bank balance—a depressing experience, to say the least.

Now that her earlier euphoria had faded, she could see the amount of work that was needed to transform the Lattimer property into something that didn't assault the eye. She knew that Naomi was right, that she should walk away from Miss Lattimer's bequest, but even so . . .

28

Margo looked up at the house again. If she squinted her eyes, the grisly reality of the place fuzzed over, and she could visualize not what was but what could be. With a new roof, several coats of paint, new windowpanes — correction, make that new windows — and gutters, the house would look a lot better.

"It used to be a beautiful old house," Margo mused aloud.

"My advice is to tell that Brooke type you want out of the bequest. You need to go on to other things. Better things." Naomi turned to give her friend a lopsided grin. "I know you don't want to hear any of this, but you didn't bring me out here to make nice. You brought me here so that I could tell you the tru — the tr —"

Naomi broke off to sneeze violently. "One of your darn cats is sneaking up on me," she accused.

There was a tawny streak among the greenery nearby, and Trafalgar poked his face out from behind a tangle of weeds. He closed his blue eyes lazily, yawned, and then flopped on his back and commenced batting the air.

If she refused the bequest, what would happen to Miss Lattimer's pets? She might be able to find homes for Lady Hamilton and Traffy, but even if he were willing to relocate, nobody in his right mind would adopt Lord Nelson. So far the old curmudgeon hadn't even let her get near him but prowled around the premises like a deposed dictator.

Naomi sneezed again. "Don't let that critter near me," she snuffled.

"I'll put him back in the house." Margo went over and scooped up Traffy. As she did so, she noted the cat had been lying on a sundial hidden by the weeds.

She knelt to study the sundial. It was shaped like an old-fashioned rose with a stylized butterfly at the heart. Margo ran her fingers over the finely chiseled petals and noted that a name had been carved into it.

"J. Lattimer, 1789," she read aloud. "Nao, look, one of Miss Lattimer's ancestors must have carved this."

Naomi cautioned, "Don't start getting sentimental, Margery Ann. Taking on this place would be crazy."

"She'd be crazy not to," rasped a voice behind them.

Naomi frowned as Zach Alloway came strolling down the overgrown garden path toward them. In contrast to Naomi's designer jeans, well-fitting jacket, and spotlessly clean sneakers, Zach was in his usual working uniform: muddy boots, threadbare denims barely held up by an old belt, and a flannel shirt rolled up to the elbows. An ancient Red Sox baseball cap sat well back over his longish blond hair. His lantern-jawed face, bisected by a drooping mustache, was glowing with enthusiasm.

Naomi regarded the newcomer with impatience. "What's *he* doing here?" she demanded.

"I asked Zach to come and give me his opinion of the place," Margo explained. Then she added, "I didn't hear your pickup, Zach."

"And you can usually hear *that* heap of nuts and bolts a mile off," Naomi interjected.

Ignoring Naomi, Zach focused on the house. He crossed his arms over his narrow chest, tipped back his baseball cap, and pronounced, "She's something else, Margo."

Margo felt warmth wash through her. She'd caught in Zach's voice the identical emotion that she was feeling. "She could be beautiful, couldn't she?" she whispered.

"Are you two nuts?" Naomi interrupted. Turning to face Zach squarely, she added, "Pardon me, but it looks as if we're talking major repairs here. Margo can't even afford to keep up her subscription to *Gardens Beautiful* magazine."

Still ignoring Naomi, Zach said, "She's got good bones from what I can see from the outside, Margo. And the garden has possibilities. Were you thinking of keeping that retaining wall over there . . . and maybe trimming back those rhodies over by the fountain?"

Margo nodded eagerly. "Definitely. And, Zach, the view of the Berkshires from over here is incredible. Come take a look."

Traffy jumped clear of Margo's arms and darted off as Margo and Zach walked through the garden, deep in conversation. Naomi followed, bristling.

"I like it, Margo. It *feels* right," Zach said at last. "And the house shouldn't be too bad to fix up. It just needs a new roof and replacement shingles and a new coat of latex paint. Good-quality latex paint is as good as oil-based. Better for ecology, too."

Naomi finally got a word in edgewise. "While you two are planning *House Beautiful*," she quipped, "the insides of this place are probably dying of house rot."

"Can we go in?" Zach asked.

Margo nodded. Though she had respect for Naomi's hardheaded common sense, she trusted Zach's instincts, the reason she had asked him to come and look at Lattimer House before she gave Rupert Brooke her decision.

The kitchen door was stuck. "Did you have any trouble finding the house?" she queried Zach as she struggled to push the door open.

"Nope, just followed the map." Zach strode into the dark kitchen and peered about him at sagging shelves and peeling wallpaper. "Needs some work here," he conceded.

Margo watched Naomi shudder as she saw the vintage refrigerator and a stove so ancient that it was almost an antique. And the next room—the dining room—was hardly better. Someone had painted the paneling a hideous pink, and some of the windowsills had rotted through.

Naomi began to sneeze as Zach strolled about, knocking on walls and peering at flooring and windowsills. "Panneling's in good condition," he commented. "This house has sound bones. And these are beautiful hardwood floors. You can't get this kind of oak anymore."

"Some of the floor has to be redone," Naomi countered. She walked past them into a large room off the dining room, obviously a living room. "This place is a firetrap!"

Stacks of newspapers, books, and magazines were stored all around this room. More newspapers were piled high on a coffee table that stood dispiritedly between two dingy overstuffed chairs. A fireplace, the focal point of the room, was large, shallow, and built into a rock wall. Some of the rocks were chipped, while others were black from years of use.

The place smelled of mildew and neglect, and Margo's heart sank. Naomi's assessment was probably more realistic than Zach's, she thought. To get this house in shape would cost a fortune.

Zach stamped over to the fireplace, knelt, and looked up. "Give me some newspaper," he commanded.

Margo handed him one of the hundreds of newspapers, and Zach twisted it into a spill, took a match from the fireplace, and lit the paper. He held it up the chimney, and the flame whooshed up bravely. "Fireplace isn't blocked," Zach reported triumphantly. "Draws well."

Naomi muttered under her breath.

"Some people just think they know it all," Zach said huffily.

"And some people don't know anything," Naomi retorted at once. "Wake up and smell the coffee, why don't you? This building should be condemned."

"Heard about a man who bought an old house, tore out the insides, redid it from the ground up," Zach said. He was speaking to Margo, but he kept his eyes on Naomi as he added, "That man now has got a half million dollars' worth of property—"

"Which he probably spent in refurbishing costs."

Zach chewed one end of his mustache. His blue-green eyes narrowed under sandy brows. Slowly, as if speaking to the village idiot, he continued, "Like I said, he has prime property because he had the sense to see what everybody else didn't bother looking at. That's what I call vision and instinct."

"I call it trouble," Naomi snapped. Hands on hips, she advanced toward Zach. "And if you weren't so mule-headed, you'd admit that."

Margo interposed hastily, "Maybe we should take a look at the second floor."

Stalking toward the staircase, Zach paused to run his hand down the bannister. "Good old oak," he remarked.

"Probably worm-eaten like the rest of this place." Naomi sounded nasal as she climbed the stairs after Zach. Margo followed them both, torn between a desire to laugh and a growing need to knock their heads together.

"Careful at the top of the stairs," she called. "The ceiling's low."

She broke off as she stopped at the landing. Here a window seat nestled against tall arched windows, and a book was still lying between faded pillows. Generations of Lattimer children had probably played on that seat, and Miss Lattimer herself must have sat down here to read and look out onto the rose garden. From the window Margo could see the garden — not as it was but as it could be.

"Bedrooms are a good size," Zach was saying. "Closets are pretty poor, but people back in those days didn't think about closets. Bathroom — you'll need work here, Margo. And the electrical system is probably knob-and-tube wiring. You'll have to call in an electrician to change all that."

"Translation," Naomi put in, "she'll need a lightning bolt to come and set fire to the whole place."

Zach turned on her. "What is *with* you?" he snarled. "Why do you have to be dang-cussed negative about everything?"

"Because there's nothing to be positive about," Naomi retorted. "You can't see the forest for the trees. Who's going to help her tackle the work and expense of rebuilding this place? You?"

There was the sound of teeth grinding. "Yes, I am. I'm not one to leave my friends in the lurch. Not like *some* people I could mention."

"Look," Margo exclaimed, "that's not necessary. I didn't invite you here to ask for handouts. I just wanted—"

"And you're saying *I*'d let my friends down?" Naomi growled.

"Why aren't you offering to help her instead of making those cracks about everything?" Naomi opened her mouth, but Zach would not allow her to talk. "You know Margo loves this place. Loves it deep in her bones. That bequest fell into her lap as if it was meant to be."

Naomi rolled her eyes. "Now we're getting metaphysical."

"As if it was meant to be," Zach repeated coldly. "Way I see it, Margo was meant to have this house, and she should keep it. It's got potential, and the grounds could be something else. I'll work on it along with her in my spare time—at no cost to her."

They were almost nose to nose. It didn't take any imagination, Margo thought, to picture electricity sizzling between them. It was always that way when Naomi and Zach squared off. Like tinder and flint, they set off sparks.

"I care about Margo just as much as you do," Naomi was spluttering. She was so infuriated that she ran agitated hands through her short dark hair and rumpled it wildly. "I just don't want her taken for a ride. I'd help her any way I could."

Zach's lips curved up in a sneer. His mustache tilted at a provocative angle. "Prove it."

"That's enough," Margo cut in. "Thank you both for your input. I'll think of all you said and make up my mind one way or another. And, Zach, you're really generous, but if I do decide to keep the property, I won't let you work on it — not for free, no way. I absolutely mean that, and — What's that?"

A hideous yowl came from a corner of the master bedroom, and a shadow seemed to leap out of the greater shadows. The next moment Lord Nelson, eyes glowing green-blue fire, leaped for a window ledge, missed, and disappeared into space. There was an awful screech.

Zach swore. Naomi began to sneeze uncontrollably. Margo ran to the window and stared out in horror, then saw with relief that the cat had skittered down the trunk of a tree. He had landed on the ground just feet away from a portly man and a thin, rawboned woman who were walking up the driveway.

"Get away! Get!" the man shouted as Lord Nelson arched his back and spat defiantly. "Get away, or I'll —"

He caught up a stick lying nearby and brandished it. "Don't do that," Margo called down. "Don't hit him, please. Just stay where you are, and I'll be right down."

Ignoring Naomi's loud predictions that her roommate was about to be sued by the neighbors, Margo ran down the stairs and hurried out the front door to meet her visitors. The man was wearing a three-piece suit. The woman had on a ratty pair of overalls and an ancient green sweater.

"Ah, hello," Margo began. "Lord Nelson, cut that out. Behave yourself, you wretched cat. I'm sorry," she added as the large Siamese prowled off, "but he's sort of upset. He just fell out of a tree."

The woman sniffed loudly. The man said in a loud voice, "I'm Evan Amberly, and this is my wife, Emma."

Margo recalled the palatial home and the magnificent grounds. She recalled Mr. Brooke saying that the Amberlys had won the horticultural prize in Carlin several years in a row.

"Hi, I'm Margo Sanders." Margo smiled at Emma Amberly, who did not smile back. Margo's apprehension increased as she saw the woman look about the weed-infested garden.

"We heard that you'd inherited the Lattimer place," Evan Amberly boomed. "The long and short of it is that it's a crying shame how run down it's gotten."

Once again Margo nodded. Behind her she could feel her friends stiffening to attention. Zach stepped forward to stand beside Margo and announced, "It'll be a fine property once Margo gets done with it."

The Amberlys ignored Zach. "Luckily," Evan Amberly boomed on, "the condition of the estate doesn't affect the real value of the property. Land in Carlin is at a premium, as I'm sure you've heard."

"Our property," Emma Amberly declared suddenly, "has been assessed for over a half million dollars."

Margo didn't know what she was expected to say except, "Aha."

Traffy came strolling by, his tail high. He glanced at the Amberlys, crossed over, and investigated Evan Amberly's pant leg. Mr. Amberly looked down askance at the cat, and his wife sniffed once again and commented, "A shame and a disgrace about Miss Lattimer's cats. She did let them run wild. What's going to happen to them when you sell the property?"

"But I haven't decided to sell—" Margo was beginning, when Evan Amberly interrupted her.

"The long and short of it is that we're here to make you an offer for the property," he shouted. "A generous offer, if I may say so. We're prepared to give you a hundred and fifty thousand dollars for the place."

Behind Margo Naomi sucked in her breath. Margo asked, "Who is 'we,' Mr. Amberly?"

"Why, some of the neighbors." Margo watched Evan Amberly seem to swell with importance as he added, "The Caforths and the Martinsons, the Van Wycks, the Gordons, and the Sheridans. They elected me as their spokesman." He paused to let the string of names sink in. "Perhaps you don't know, Margo, but in Carlin we're particularly proud of the appearance of our houses. Miss Lattimer was difficult about some things."

"Stubborn," his wife corrected. "She was as stubborn as a mule."

"The long and short of it was that we weren't on the best of terms," Evan Amberly said. "A few of us — her neighbors, you understand — tried to make her realize that neighborhoods have to cooperate, but she didn't see it that way. We *know* that you'll have more sense."

The patronizing note in his voice got her back up. Without looking at Zach, Margo felt him bristling, too. Naomi said in a stage whisper, "A hundred and a half is peanuts for the house and land."

Evan Amerbly frowned. "The house is useless," he pronounced. "It has to be razed. Then the ground has to be completely replanted. You see, we'd make this common land between all our houses. A landscaper to replant this eyesore will cost a mint of money. The long and short of it is that considering the expenses we'll incur, ours is a generous offer. But we *may* go up to one hundred and sixty-five thousand. That's our last offer."

Traffy gave one more sniff at the Amberlys and then darted off. With her eye on the dancing figure Margo said, "I'm a landscape designer, and I understand all you say about expenses."

"Then you'll sell?"

"No," Margo replied. "Even if I were willing, I couldn't. The bequest states that I must make a home for the cats. Besides, this house has real historical value. Miss Lattimer wouldn't want it torn down."

40

With a thrill of surprise Margo realized that she'd made her decision. Actually, it hadn't been hard to make. "Of course," she went on, "I intend to clear the grounds and fix up the house. It'll be beautiful when I get through with it."

"And when will *that* be?" Evan Amberly asked sarcastically. "The long and short of it is that it's not over till it's over," he added in an ominous tone. Then, followed by his wife, he marched down the driveway.

"Pompous old goat," Zach growled.

For once, Naomi didn't argue with Zach. Instead, she said slowly, "Margery Ann, I don't blame you for telling that chowderhead off, but I thought you were going to think it over."

"She's done her thinking," Zach exclaimed before Margo had a chance to reply. "And like I said, I'm going to help her. It'll be an awesome house when we're done, and the neighbors can go eat grass. That, my friends, is the long and short of *that*."


She had counted fifty shingles on the ground. If she found another one, she would scream. "There can't be a shingle left on the roof at this rate," Margo muttered.

"Yo, Margo, you want to bring those bags down here? I've got to get to the dump before noon."

Wearily Margo dumped a wheelbarrow full of debris into a large garbage bag and tamped it

41

down. Then, straightening her back, she looked down the driveway to where Naomi was fastidiously raking what seemed like ten years' worth of leaves from under the trees. Across from Naomi, Zach was loading his pickup with newly pruned tree branches.

"The spruce trees are in bad shape," he commented as Margo lugged her bag over. "Old lady Lattimer really neglected the yard something fierce."

There were at least twenty bags full of debris in the pickup and more on the driveway where Naomi was working. "I hope the town dump agrees to take all of this," Margo said worriedly.

"You have a permit, remember?" Zach tossed another garbage bag into the bed of his pickup. "We're making a dent, Margo, really making a dent."

She wasn't so sure. In spite of several days' work, Miss Lattimer's yard looked as overgrown as ever. The only exception was the so-called rose garden, which she had attacked first. Now with weeds, bittersweet, and honeysuckle vines cut back, the rosebushes looked scraggly and sick and the sundial lay among the ruins like a grave marker.

Two weeks ago it had all seemed so easy. That was when Margo had packed her bags and, with her friends' help, moved into Lattimer House. Buoyed with enthusiasm, she had plunked a sleeping bag down on the creaky bedstead in the master bedroom, cleaned up the refrigerator and prehistoric stove as best she could, and taken up residence.

Then she'd sat down and drawn up her plans for her house and property. She'd sketched in everything as she wanted it to be and made watercolor drawings of various views of the grounds. Zach had warmly approved, and even Naomi agreed that Margo's ideas were excellent.

"But," Nao had pointed out, "it's still going to take time and money. A big capital M, Margery Ann."

Though Margo still did initial site visits for Zach, she now prepared the actual plans in Carlin. This gave her time to work on her own house. Since time and cash flow were limited, Margo elected to attend to the yard first. She devoted every waking moment to cleaning, clearing, and cutting back, and to ferrying weeds, brambles, debris, and branches to the town dump in her pickup.

She'd hoped that the neighbors would see that she was making an effort and pull in their horns, but so far there was no hope of that. Margo waved at a white Lincoln Continental slowly cruising by the house, but the immaculately coiffured middle-aged matron behind the wheel ignored the greeting.

"Friendly type," Zach commented.

"Friendly isn't the word." Margo sighed. "That's Mrs. Sheridan, the president of the Carlin Women's Group. She came up to me at the post office, introduced herself, and wanted to know when I was moving out."

Zach glowered after the departing car. "Don't worry about those fools," he advised. "You can't change ignorant people from thinking ignorant."

A mail truck had pulled up at the end of the driveway. Naomi put down her rake and went down to meet it. "You got one letter," she commented as she brought the mail over to Margo. "Looks like a bill from the town."

Margo opened the official-looking envelope and gasped in dismay. "They can't *do* this."

"Who's doing what?" Zach demanded.

"The selectmen say that they've been notified by the planning board and the zoning commission that my house is a public nuisance."

"Here, let me see that." Zach snatched the letter from Margo's hand and stared at it. "This is unbelievable. Says here that if you don't clean up the mess, the town will take over Lattimer House. What's the matter with these dang-cussed ignoramuses, anyhow? Can't they see you're trying?"

Margo sat down on one of the overstuffed garbage bags and looked wrathfully at the Amberlys' house. Through the boxwood hedge that separated their properties, she caught sight of Emma Amberly climbing about a slope at the back of the house.

"The Amberlys must've complained," she said

through gritted teeth. " 'It's not over till it's over,' remember?"

Naomi put a small hand on Margo's shoulder. She said fiercely, "Who are they to tell you what to do?"

"According to this here, the town has been trying to get Miss Lattimer to clean up her act for years," growled Zach. "They say that's why they're giving you—Cripes, Margo, nobody can clean up this place in a month."

The three stared at each other in mutual distress.

"It's the least of my problems," Margo groaned. "If I get evicted, what'll happen to the cats?"

"You need a lawyer," Naomi replied decisively.

Margo felt a rush of affection for her friend. Instead of rubbing in the fact that she'd told Margo not to take the old house, Nao was rallying to the cause.

"I could call Mr. Brooke," she began.

"No, not him. He's a townie and probably in cahoots with the Amberlys." Naomi frowned for a moment, considering. "Call Niell Kier."

Margo blinked in astonishment.

"He'd be perfect, don't you see?" Naomi urged. "His firm's the best. And it's so exclusive that just having him represent you would carry weight with the snobs around here. Besides, you guys know each other."

"I met him one time. That certainly doesn't

mean I know him," Margo protested. "He probably wouldn't even remember me."

But she remembered *him*. The image of a tall, dark-haired man with eyes like gray smoke and a lazy smile took shape in her mind. For a second the memory was so vivid that Margo felt herself actually surrounded by the scent of lilacs. But then reality returned.

"Big, jet-set-type lawyers *cost*, Nao. There's no way I could pay his fee."

"I could lend you the money," Naomi offered at once, and Zach proclaimed that what he had was at Margo's disposal.

"Hey, what are friends for?" Zach wanted to know. He gave Naomi a look of rare approval. "I like the idea of Margo getting together with this Kier. A good cooperation mouthpiece would make mincemeat out of the selectmen *and* the zoning commission."

"I tell you, I can't afford him. Besides, he's probably out of the country. The time I met him he was flying all over Europe."

"He's back in Boston," Zach said. Encountering Margo's astonished look, he looked sheepish. "He called me last week to ask for your phone number."

"He phoned you and you didn't tell me?"

Zach hesitated, and Naomi exploded, "That's the most irresponsible thing I ever heard. Didn't I tell you, Margo? Giving Niell Kier this chowderhead's phone number had to be the worse move of your life."

"Who are you calling a chowderhead?" Faced by two pairs of outraged eyes, Zach took refuge in bluster. "Did I know the guy was a friend of yours? I thought he was a salesman or bill collector or something." He paused. "So, okay, I messed up. I'm sorry. But it proves that Kier hasn't forgotten you. You should call him, Margo—"

"After you told him to get lost? And besides, there's the question of his fee. I'm not going to borrow money from either of you," Margo added firmly as both her friends started to argue. "That's out, so forget it."

"Then what are you going to do?" Naomi asked.

"I'll go and call Mr. Brooke. Seems to me he keeps office hours on Saturday mornings. Maybe the town is just blowing smoke and can't really evict me."

The telephone in the kitchen was almost as ancient as the rest of the house. It crackled faintly with static when in use. Margo listened to the static and then to the lawyer, who said that he had been on the point of leaving his office, cleared his throat several times, then let it be known that he could not help her.

"You see, I am also the Amberlys' attorney," he explained primly. "Since he is one of your abutters and involved in bringing the complaint against you—Well, you see my, er, difficulty. It would be a conflict of interest."

He paused. "I will say this. You should, er, retain another attorney, Ms. Sanders. The matter, er,

47

is not to be taken lightly. No, not at all."

Margo felt her already heavy heart sink steadily down to the floor. "So what you're telling me is that I could lose the property?"

"It's highly possible," Mr. Brooke told her. "The town's zoning commission has been, for many years, attempting to, er, have Miss Lattimer comply with town regulations and codes. Miss Lattimer was a longtime resident of Carlin and, er, managed to forestall all demands. She knew a great many people and slipped through the legislative cracks, so to speak. But you—"

"But I'm an outsider and have about as much of a chance as a snowball in summer," Margo said as she hung up the phone. What Brooke meant was that her goose was cooked unless she got herself some legal help, and fast.

Without legal help she'd never be able to buck the powerful lobby in town. The question was, how was she going to get the money to engage a decent attorney?

Margo sat down at the scarred kitchen table. In the first week she'd been there, she'd scrubbed the kitchen cabinets till they glowed and shored up the shelves and lined the cupboards. She'd stripped off the old fly-specked wallpaper and painted the walls a lovely celery-cream color. She'd fixed the windowsills and washed the windows and hung lacy white curtains that blew in the spring wind.

"It's not fair," Margo muttered.

The old saying was wrong. It *wasn't* better to

have loved and lost than never to have loved at all. If she'd never seen Lattimer House, she'd undoubtedly have gone through life wistful but still hopeful. Now Margo knew that she'd almost attained what she wanted, and that want would stay with her forever. Even if she could afford a house somewhere someday, she'd always yearn for this old place and the garden with the rose sundial carved by some long-forgotten craftsman.

Margo turned to look at Lady Hamilton, who was sitting on the windowsill, peering hopefully outside. Lady Hamilton was the world's greatest scairdy-cat. She didn't even venture outside without Lord Nelson around to protect her.

Once lost and frightened, Lady Hamilton had come to consider Lattimer House her home. Traffy and Lord Nelson were her family, her security. As for Lord Nelson himself, he'd rather die than move anywhere else—and most probably he would.

"Not fair," Margo repeated, and at the sound of her voice Lady Hamilton crept up and timidly rubbed her head against Margo's hand. The act revitalized Margo's fighting spirit. Cats couldn't fight city hall—but she could.

She wasn't going to knuckle under to strong-arm tactics. No way. She was going to give the Amberlys and the Sheridans and the zoning commission a run for their money. The question was, how would she accomplish this?

She heard a bump on the kitchen door. Proba-

49

bly her friends had come to see what Brooke had said, she thought.

"You have to push hard," she called to them. "You know how the darn kitchen door sticks. . . ."

Her words trailed away as the door swung open. "Hello, Margo," Niell Kier said.

# Chapter Three

To say she was surprised didn't even begin to scratch the surface. In that first speechless moment Margo wondered if she were hallucinating. But he looked remarkably solid standing there in jeans and a flannel shirt with a fisherman's knit sweater thrown over his broad shoulders. When she drew in a bracing breath, the air was tinged with the subtle scent of his cologne.

"N-Niell." By drawing another deep breath, she managed to control the shake in her voice. "This is a, ah, a surprise."

"I'm sorry I didn't phone you before coming out here," he apologized. "I tried to get in touch with you as soon as I got back from London, but I had some trouble locating you."

"I heard. I'm sorry about that. I should never have given you Zach's number."

"We had an interesting conversation before he hung up on me." Margo winced. "Fortunately the next time I called I connected with his assistant, who told me that you'd inherited an estate and moved to Carlin. After that, it was simple detective work."

Niell shut the door behind him and walked over to shake her hand. When his cool firm hand clasped hers, warm prickles of awareness awoke beneath her skin. Margo forgot the entire frustrating day as she exclaimed, "I'm sorry about your encounter with Zach, but I'm glad you tracked me down."

He'd phoned Margo mainly because he'd promised to do so, but when Zach had brushed him off, finding her had become a challenge. Now looking down at her open, eager face, Niell was glad he'd made the effort. Deep down he'd wanted to see this woman again.

He thought he'd remembered Margo Sanders, but now he realized that the mental picture hadn't done her justice. He hadn't properly recalled the color of Margo's hazel eyes, which could warm to amber when she smiled, and his memory hadn't quite captured the soft curve of her mouth. Even the weeds and leaves that were caught in her hair gave her a certain style.

And her candor was a refreshing contrast to the mental games he'd been playing last week in London with the Herris Company officials. "I really wanted to see you again," he told her.

The conviction in his voice nudged Margo's internal thermostat up a few notches, and the expression in his eyes did the rest. Her cheeks felt warm, and she had the horrible suspicion that she was actually blushing.

She was only a kid from Taylor, West Virginia, for Pete's sake. Things were happening much too quickly for her. Margo hastily backpedaled and focused on the one thing she'd remembered him saying.

"When did you get back from London?" she asked.

"Last Friday. Before that I was in Rome—with a detour to Tivoli."

Her eyes widened. "Did you really go to the Villa d'Este?"

"On my last day in the country," he said. "You were right—it's quite a place. I took some photographs that are being developed right now."

Before Margo could comment, the kitchen door was once more assaulted, and Naomi burst in, announcing, "Zach's taking the last load of junk to the dump. I say he should leave the stuff on the town hall steps and let those fools—"

She broke off and stared at Niell. "Oh, I'm sorry. I was in the back with Zach, hauling out stuff for the dump. We thought the BMW belonged to one of the rotten neighbors."

Margo performed introductions, and since Naomi was for once in her life tongue-tied, she added, "Naomi's helping me clean out the yard, Niell. Since I last spoke with you, Lady Luck smiled on me—sort of."

"I heard the good news from Alloway's assistant. But what's all this about the town hall? Are you in some kind of trouble?"

"Yes," Naomi replied instantly.

"No." Margo frowned at Naomi. "It's nothing. Just some small-town red tape."

"Perhaps I can help," Niell offered. "I specialize in red tape."

Behind Niell's back, Naomi was gesturing wildly. Ignoring her friend, Margo said, "No, really, I can handle it. I'd rather hear about the Villa d'Este."

"I'll tell you all about it when you're not so busy." Niell broke off as Zach trudged past the kitchen window lugging a wheelbarrow full of debris. "Right now it looks as if you could use some help."

"You can say that again," Naomi exclaimed. "You see—"

"Zach's calling you," Margo interrupted. Naomi didn't budge. "Let's give him a hand, Nao," Margo continued. "I'll be back right away, Niell. Don't go away."

Reluctantly Naomi followed Margo outside where she exploded. "Are you certifiably insane? The best lawyer in Massachusetts asks you if you need help, and *why* aren't you going to tell him about your legal troubles?"

"I explained to you why. If you breathe a word to Niell about the zoning commission, I'll never speak to you again." Margo softened her tone. "Nao, please do this my way."

Naomi shook her head in baffled futility. "I don't understand you," she said at last. "The man's willing to help you, darn it. Why can't you let him advise you?"

"Only if I can pay for the advice." Margo realized she sounded stubborn, and by Naomi's lights she no doubt was acting like a fool. But Naomi was a pragmatist who figured that people had to be opportunists to get ahead whereas the grandparents who had raised Margo had given her a different set of rules. A person worked hard, dealt squarely, was loyal to friends, and never tried to use people.

"Promise me you won't say anything to Niell," Margo begged and when Naomi nodded unhappily, she gave her friend a quick hug. "Thanks. It's bad enough that I'm using all of yours and Zach's weekends. I won't involve Niell, too."

"Seems to me he's already involved," Naomi pointed out.

Margo followed Naomi's gaze and saw that Niell had emerged from the kitchen and was hauling bags of debris down the driveway. "What are you doing?" she called as she caught up to him.

"Getting the next load ready for your friend with the pickup." Niell dumped a barrel of shingles down next to a pile of bagged leaves. "We figured that he could make one more run before the dump closes if I got everything here ready for him."

Margo's heart sank. Zach had surely told Niell about her hassles with the town. "Did he say anything?" she hazarded.

"Just that he'd be right back." Niell lifted a trash can full of rocks and bottles, and easily carried it down to stand beside the others.

"There's no need for you to do this," Margo protested. "If you'll come back into the house, I'll make you some coffee."

He shook his head. "I don't mind yard work. I haven't had much exercise lately."

"Can't you think of better ways of getting exercise?"

And looking at her, he could think of a few right off the bat. Hastily Niell pushed the inappropriate thought away and reached for a bag of leaves at the same time Margo did. Their hands brushed, their fingers entwined. The silky warmth of that brief clasp invaded Niell's system like a shot of straight-up bourbon.

Why was he looking at her like that? Margo looked around for Nao, saw that her friend had pointedly retreated to the other end of the property, and added hurriedly, "I remember your telling me that gardening isn't your thing. And this isn't even gardening."

That much was for sure. When Alloway's assistant had explained to him that Margo had inherited property in Carlin that needed work, Niell had imagined her pruning a few bushes or scraping paint off the side of the house. Knowing something of the exclusive Berkshire town, he'd formed a picture of Margo's new inheritance in his mind.

The reality of Lattimer House was light-years from that imagined property. Margo had inherited a disaster. Niell looked around wondering how anyone could possibly have let things get so out of hand without the neighbors having apoplexy.

"It's a royal mess, isn't it?"

She was looking at him with that direct hazel gaze, and Niell knew he couldn't lie. "Yes," he said, "it is. Your neighbors must have petitioned the zoning commission to bring this place up to snuff."

"Zach has a big mouth."

"He didn't say anything. He didn't have to. It's pretty obvious." Niell lugged another bag of trash down the driveway. "Want to tell me the details?"

"Look, you didn't come here to—"

"How long did the town say you had to clean all this up?"

Margo gave up. "A month," she admitted. "But if I could improve the looks of the estate, they might give me a break."

"I'd like to take a look at the letter they sent you—if you'll let me."

There was real interest in his quiet voice. Realizing that to refuse would sound churlish, Margo led the way to the house. A cat dozing on a flat gray rock looked up sleepily.

"Which one is that?" Niell asked. She told him. "So Trafalgar must be the son of the cat on the windowsill—the Siamese you rescued, Lady Hamilton," he said. "Is there a Lord Nelson?"

She was surprised at his keen memory, but then most things about this man were out of the ordinary. "There sure is. He's prowling about somewhere sharpening his claws and fangs." Margo pushed the kitchen door, which refused to budge. "Oh, blast this fool thing," she said with a sigh.

She was so close to him that Niell felt suddenly surrounded by some light floral scent she wore. It came to him that he'd thought of Margo Sanders more often than even his conscious mind had realized. The flowers in the Herris' conference room . . . the flower seller at King's Cross . . . a brilliant, sunny day in Rome . . . all had reminded him of Margo.

No wonder he'd taken the trouble to run her to earth. With some effort Niell focused on the fact that Margo was still struggling to open the kitchen door. "Let me," he said, adding as they entered the kitchen. "Now where's the letter?"

Lady Hamilton had decided to lie down on the selectmen's ultimatum. Margo extricated the document and handed it to Niell without comment. As he took it, their hands brushed again, and the shadow-touch made Margo's skin act as if she'd rubbed up against static electricity.

*Enough, already.* "So, what do you think?" she asked. Briskly, she hoped.

"That there's much more bark than bite here," he replied. "I doubt if they'll proceed with this if you can demonstrate that you're trying to get the place cleaned up. You're doing that, so the powers that be should be satisfied."

"But? I take it that there's a 'but'?"

"Unfortunately, yes. The neighbors can still harass you. Though the town may be reluctant to haul you into court and take the house from you, the neighbors can make your life miserable. It says here that the neighbors have made an offer for the property. How much did they offer?" She told him. "That's far below the market value of property in Carlin."

"I know it is. Anyway, by the terms of the bequest, I couldn't sell. According to the will, I have to provide a home for these cats, and Lord Nelson wouldn't take kindly to moving." She took back the letter as she added, "Thanks for the input, Niell. I'll go and talk to someone at the town hall on Monday and show them the plans I've drawn up for the estate. Maybe I can convince them that it'll be the kind of place that Miss Lattimer would have been proud of."

In spite of her troubles, she spoke with enthusiasm and determination. She would be pretty hard to resist, Niell thought, but unfortunately small-town bureaucrats usually were about as flexible as concrete.

"Could I look at those plans of yours?" he asked.

"Sure thing. Wait, sit over here." Margo ran into the other room; a moment later she returned with several sketches, which she spread on the kitchen table before Niell.

"Here are several views of the estate," she explained. "This is a view of the gate, the driveway, and the western side of the house. This one's a look at the eastern view, and here's the northern view."

The sketches in front of him were colorful and imaginative. Niell looked from them to the grim reality he could see beyond the window. He didn't say anything, but Margo saw the skepticism in his expression.

"Let me explain it in stages," she continued. "Let's start with the north view. Over here by the house flowering crabs and maple and blue spruce will give color and foliage in the spring and fall."

"What's this over here?"

"I'm leaving the old retaining wall there mainly to define space. Near it I mean to plant low shrubs—mostly greens and grays. I don't want anything to interfere with the view of the mountains."

With Margo bending over his chair so that her silky hair brushed his cheek, Niell was finding it hard to concentrate. Her sunlight-and-flowers scent was intoxicating at this distance. When he shifted in his chair, one soft breast pressed against his back for a millisecond.

He was behaving like an adolescent, Niell warned himself. Aloud he said, "This can't be that wreck of a fountain that I saw on the east side of the house."

"That's what it'll look like when it's been cleaned up. Because the east side is pretty run down, I want to put in a rock garden. There are tons of rocks around here, so that'll be no problem. And by planting artemesias, veronica, and astilbe, I'll be able to establish a feeling of intimacy."

Margo stopped speaking as she realized how close to him she had been standing. Talk about Freudian slips, she thought.

"How would you do that?" he was asking.

"Make it secluded. You know, sort of private." Under the pretext of presenting a third sketch, Margo shifted her position to a more prudent distance.

"Here's a sketch of the west side. The walkway to the house will be bordered with perennials and annuals. And here is the rose garden. You may have seen it when you came up to the house."

If she meant a decrepit spot full of mangy bushes, he'd definitely noticed it. Dubiously Niell looked at Margo's drawing of a large area full of blooming roses that clustered around what seemed to be a sundial.

"Zach and I've talked it over, and freely admit it'll take more than a year to get things to where I want them to be. But in a way, that's good. Landscape designers aren't always given the luxury of *time*. I want to see how my land looks in all seasons so that it can be naturally beautiful."

Enthusiasm had transformed the hazel of her eyes to a warm amber. Her face fairly glowed. Margo believed in her vision and in herself, and perhaps that belief was getting to him, too, because Niell found himself actually seeing possibilities in the Lattimer estate. He looked back at her sketches and noted that even though he knew nothing about gardens, he felt that there was a sense of rightness about what she had done.

"I'm impressed," he told her.

He meant what he said, and her spirits soared. If she could convince Niell, perhaps she'd have some luck with the town fathers.

"The estate as you envision it will be an asset to the neighborhood," he continued. "I know we can get them to pull in their horns."

Reluctantly Margo shook her head. "I'm not asking you to involve yourself in this, Niell. I'd never be able to afford your fee, and I'm not going to start my life in Carlin riddled with debts."

Most people he knew would have been conniving to get free legal advice from him. Niell was intrigued more than ever.

"You're right," he observed equably. "You probably couldn't. On the other hand, I'm not offering you advice for nothing. Remember that I told you that if I ever wanted a garden designed

I'd come to you?"

Was he proposing a barter? Margo asked doubtfully, "Do you want a garden designed?"

He leaned back in his chair and looked up at her. She was standing very straight with her hands locked behind her back, her shoulders squared. Her mouth was firm, but she couldn't keep the wistfulness out of her eyes. Watching her, Niell had to war with a totally illogical need to put his arms around her and tell her not to worry, that it was all going to work out.

"I'm suggesting you start a landscape design firm of your own," he told her. When she blinked at him, he added, "The timing's right, Margo. My advice is to form Sanders and Company right now and let any work you do on your own estate be your advertisement."

The thought was provocative. But, Margo hastily reminded herself, she'd have no time to work on anything except her own grounds. How could she even consider starting a new venture?

However, when she told him this, he said it didn't matter. "You wouldn't have many takers in the beginning, anyway. But if Sanders and Company can fix up the Lattimer estate, people are going to be very, very impressed." Niell gave the sketches before him an appreciate tap. "Your work will speak for itself."

The word brought Margo back to reality. "Zach should be back from the dump by now," she exclaimed. "Thanks for the advice and the vote of confidence, Niell. Someday I hope to do all that."

" 'Someday' won't get you anywhere. Make that today." Niell stood up and looked down at Margo. "You've got a winner here, Margo."

Margo frowned. Niell's words seemed to lead her past her present problems and show her how she could turn misery into victory. And wasn't it her dream to have her own landscape design company and create gardens of outstanding beauty?

"Don't you see it, Margo?" Niell urged softly.

He wasn't touching her, but Margo felt the connection to him, anyway. It was as if her vision and Niell's ideas had somehow touched each other in a way that amounted to more than mere physical contact.

She said the words to herself: Sanders and Company, landscape designers. Then she looked at the drawings on the kitchen table.

"You really believe I can do it," she murmured.

"So much so that I'm proposing to be Sanders and Company's legal consultant. For a share of future profits. Naturally, we'll draw up an agreement here and now and your friends can witness it."

Under the spell of his suggestion, Margo allowed herself to daydream. She imagined the Amberlys and Mrs. Sheridan shaking their heads over the transformed Lattimer estate. She pictured herself and Zach in business together and the phone ringing off the hook asking for the services of Sanders and Company.

"But none of this can happen if you let the town fathers get the better of you," Niell reminded her.

She didn't answer, but from the rapt look in her eyes, he guessed that she was succumbing to the idea, even accepting it. Her lips were parted as if she could almost taste success.

The curve of those rosy lips was an unconscious invitation. The need to put his arms around her and pull her to him was so strong as to be almost visceral.

"So, what do you think of my proposition?" he asked. "Are we in business?"

His voice was deep and persuasive, and Margo blinked rapidly, fighting for a toehold in reality. What Niell suggested could happen. She could *make* it happen. But first she needed to get the zoning commission off her back. And she would have to talk to Zach to see how he would feel about working for her rather than the other way around.

"Yes," Margo replied. Then she added sternly, "Yes, we are. But once Sanders and Company gets on its feet, the first thing I do is pay you what I owe."

His eyes touched her lips, lingered there. "I'll count on it," he promised.

* * *

Zach paused on his way up the stairs to push back his Red Sox cap and squint up his nose at the ceiling. "Not bad," he allowed. "You're doing okay, Kier—for a Sunday carpenter, that is."

His voice held grudging approval, and Margo stopped in the act of spritzing water on the living-room walls. "That's high praise," she commented.

"You mean, keep it up and someday I'll make the grade?" Niell wondered drily.

It was no secret that Zach was torn between his gratitude to Niell for what he was doing to help Margo and his inborn suspicion of anyone who hauled in a six-figure salary. Those misgivings had been apparent from the moment he'd been called on to witness the agreement between the new president of Sanders and Company and the firm's legal consultant. Though Naomi had gladly signed, Zach had studied the contract as if it were a minefield of hidden loopholes.

"Give him time," Margo advised. "Yesterday Zach went so far as to say that it was decent of you to offer us a hand on your days off. He also said that if you ever give up being a high-powered corporate attorney, you could make it as an apprentice painter or carpenter."

"What he meant was a gofer, but I'm flattered, anyway." Niell watched her as she went back to the painstaking task of removing the mildewed wallpaper from the living-room wall. With her hair slicked back and tied in pigtails that stood

66

out on each side of her head, she looked about eight years old. There was a drop of paint on the tip of her nose, and spackle had hardened on one ear. Not even on that golden day at the arboretum had he ever seen her so happy or so content.

"I read someplace that you should steam wallpaper off," he told her.

"Not this stuff." Margo peeled a strip of paper off the wall. "Look at this gunk on the walls. Want to give me a hand scraping it off?"

As Niell descended the ladder and picked up a scrub brush, rain spattered against the windows. Since he'd had some time off the past week, he'd volunteered to help Margo. Zach had often come up to help in the early afternoon, and even Naomi had taken Friday off to assist in the yard work.

They had planned a working weekend, but bad weather had driven them inside to do interior work this Saturday. Naomi, allergic as ever, had refused to set foot inside the house and had remained in the Boston apartment she'd once shared with Margo, but Niell could hear Zach hammering upstairs and whistling tunelessly to himself.

"At least we aren't listening to any wrangling today," he commented. "I'm curious. Do Zach and Naomi ever agree on anything?"

"Who, those two? Nah," Margo replied. "Zach's a yellow-dog Democrat. Naomi's a staunch Republican. She believes in CDs and blue-chip stocks that pay her nice solid dividends. She likes her new Toyota Camry and her time-share on Martha's Vineyard. Zach can't hold onto a single dollar because he's always giving it away to somebody or sending a donation to some far-out cause. He says pink, she says green. Neither one was put together the same way."

As Niell began to scrub the wall, Margo had the fleeting thought that she liked the way *he* was put together. He was wearing jeans so worn that they clung to his lean hips and hard thighs like a second skin. His spackle-splashed shirt displayed the play of muscles in his arms. And the painter's cap he'd jammed on his head still let her admire the way his dark hair curled slightly at the nape of his neck.

She forced herself to focus on what he was saying—something about opposites attracting. "I don't think it holds true all the time," she remarked doubtfully. "My late mother and father were about as opposite as they come. What one liked the other hated. They didn't fight like Zach and Nao, but I remember a lot of thick, cold silences. They definitely did *not* complement each other." Margo paused before adding soberly, "They were killed in a car accident when I was nine, but if they'd lived, I have a feeling they would have split up."

Niell watched her work. "You went to live with your grandparents after your parents' death?" She nodded. "Were they opposites, too?"

"No way. They were childhood sweethearts and have known each other all their lives." Margo smiled fondly as she thought of them. "Actually, when you consider it, Nao and Zach have a lot in common. They both come from poor families, for one thing. Nao had to wear her cousin's old clothes, and Zach was the youngest of seven kids. He told me that he never had a bedroom—used to sleep in the hall on a folding cot."

"Really."

Something in his tone alerted Margo to the fact that she'd lost Niell. His background was light-years away from fold-up cots and cast-off clothing—and, for that matter, from a small, ranch-style house in Taylor, West Virginia.

Yet for all his privilege, Niell worked well with his hands. He'd learned so quickly that even Zach had been amazed.

"You're frowning. Am I doing something wrong?" Niell was asking.

"No, you're fine. I'm just wondering why you're doing it at all. And I don't buy that bit about your having nothing better to do with your days off. You could be playing sports or . . . or going through photographs of your trips or something."

"If that's a hint that I still haven't shown you my photos of the Villa d'Este, I have to admit I totally forgot to pick them up. I'll bring them by soon. As to why I'm, ah, scraping gunk off the walls, I'll have you know I'm conducting research. Being a participant in the restoration work will make me more convincing when I get in front of the Carlin town fathers."

She laughed.

"So don't believe me. Actually, I enjoy working with my hands. When I was a kid, my grandfather used to make cabinets."

"Really? Was that his profession?"

Niell shook his head. "He founded the Kier Investment Corporation," he explained. "Grandfather would work at least twenty-six hours a day with his mind, so it relaxed him to do things like painting his own house."

Niell began to sponge down the wall. "My father was different. He relaxed by reading the *Wall Street Journal*. He believed that men were defined by their work."

"The Yankee work ethic," Margo murmured.

"I suppose. But it wasn't just work for the sake of work," Niell said. "What's most important is to set your goals and go after them."

"Meaning that you like to win."

"If you don't win, you end up a loser." Niell's tone was matter-of-fact.

Margo glanced sideways at him and saw his concentration as he worked, the firm line of his cheek and jaw. She believed that if Niell Kier ever really wanted something, neither hell nor high water would stand in his way.

They reached for the sponge at the same time, and their hands clasped. It was a casual mistake,

Margo knew. There wasn't any reason for the sudden leap of her pulse. She started to pull her hand away, but then Niell tightened his hand on hers, and the contact wasn't casual anymore.

Her heart hammered as she turned to look at him. The expression in his eyes made her catch her breath. The color of his eyes had changed to smoky gray. Margo felt as if the glue that held her joints together was starting to loosen, as if her muscles were weakening. She racked her brain for a witty comment to lighten the mood, but her brain appeared to have turned to oatmeal.

Static electricity seemed to be circulating through her veins, invading her bones, waiting for something unknown and wonderful to begin. Just waiting.

Niell tried to catch his breath but couldn't find it. Her lips were soft as if they were expecting a kiss. The air felt almost sulfurous, ready to ignite. One touch, and the fire that simmered just under their skin seethed into life. He hadn't the slightest idea why Margo affected him that way, but at the moment that didn't matter. He reached out to draw her into his arms.

There was a bumping sound upstairs and then Zach's voice cussing the hammer he'd dropped. Niell realized that he was leaning forward, arm extended. Margo was looking at him uncertainly, and Niell mumbled the only thing that swam into his abnormally fogged brain.

"You have glue on your nose."

Automatically she raised a hand and rubbed her nose. The everyday gesture seemed to restore some kind of normalcy, and her mind began to function again. Time to retreat and regroup.

"I think this is ready for the new wallpaper. I'll go get it," she volunteered.

Margo swung to her feet, relieved to find that her knee joints still worked. She wasn't fooled by Niell's obvious lie. He'd meant to kiss her back there.

That wasn't what bothered her—it was her reaction to him. For Niell, a few days of working with her was a diversion, a change from his usual high-pressured life. For her, it *was* life. For Niell, convincing the Carlin zoning commission was a challenge. For her, it was the whole nine yards. To Niell, a kiss probably meant a few moments of pleasure, perhaps even a goal to define and achieve.

Thinking of what it would mean to her made Margo weak in the knees again. To steady herself she walked to the living-room window and looked out at the drowned north side of the house.

"Drat!" she exclaimed.

Niell looked up abruptly at the change in her voice. "What is it?"

"Evan Amerbly's out there gloating."

Niell got up to come over and stand behind her. Together they watched Evan Amberly. Encased in a raincoat and holding an umbrella over himself, Amberly kept shaking his head.

"He knows I'm watching," Margo continued heatedly. "He's reminding me about the zoning commission. And the other neighbors aren't any better. Mrs. Sheridan told me that *most* people in Carlin only take one load of trash to the dump a week."

She broke off as Niell turned and walked out of the living room. "Where are you going?" she called after him.

"To do my job." Niell pulled on a bright-yellow slicker that belonged to Zach and strolled out into the rain. Margo ran after him and stared out the kitchen door as he approached Evan Amberly and extended a hand.

Even from this distance, Margo could sense the local man's extreme reluctance to shake Niell's hand. Then a change occurred. Margo watched in astonishment as her neighbor stiffened almost to attention.

"What's going on?" Zach had come downstairs and was peering over Margo's shoulder at the figures in the rain. "Are my eyes going bad or is Kier bringing that dad-blasted jackass to the house?"

Margo doubted her own eyes as she watched Niell escorting Amberly to the back door. "Be careful of the door," Margo could hear Niell say. "It sticks."

Dripping and not at all conciliatory, Evan Amberly walked into the kitchen. He gave Margo a sour look. "Ms. Sanders," he said coldly, "your

73

attorney tells me we have something to talk about. Have you changed your mind about selling your property?"

Zach glowered.

"Of course not," Margo replied annoyedly.

Niell said briskly, "As I explained to you, Mr. Amberly, Grenville, Simons, and Kier is representing Sanders and Company. As Ms. Sanders' legal counsel, I felt I should introduce myself to the neighbors who are the most affected by the changes that she plans for her property."

At the mention of Niell's firm, a reluctant awe began to dawn on Evan Amberly's face. No matter how badly he wanted Margo gone, Amberly didn't want to appear uncooperative to Niell, whose photo had appeared recently in *Newswatch* and whose firm was one of the finest in the region.

"I've heard of your firm," he admitted. "What, ah, what changes were you talking about, Mr. Kier?"

With a sweep of his hand Niell spread out Margo's sketches on the kitchen table. Margo looked on and listened in amazement as he then outlined what was to be done.

"Of course, being as knowledgeable as you are about real estate, you'll know that these changes not only will raise property values but will also make Peachtree Lane a landmark in Carlin. The rock garden on the east side of the house, for instance, will be at least as beautiful as anything seen here in the Berkshires.

Margo watched Evan Amberly's jaw work as Niell went on cataloguing the changes to the estate. "But . . . but how long will these changes take?" he asked weakly. "Miss Lattimer was talking about making improvement for years. The long and short of it is that nothing ever came of it."

"Miss Lattimer is not an issue here." Niell smiled pleasantly as he added, "However, since you mention her, you of course know that Miss Lattimer was a descendant of Micah Lattimer, who conspired with the Shays' Rebellion in Pittsfield and later fought with General Washington?" Amberly looked bemused. "I'm surprised. Many people hereabouts believe that Lattimer House is a historical landmark and shouldn't be tampered with. Silas Rampton, who sits on Carlin's board of appeals, shares that view."

This was all news to Margo, and apparently Amberly had been caught flat-footed also. "I never heard that Silas thought that way," he countered feebly.

"I assure you that Mr. Rampton's views are widely shared." Niell's voice was friendly and mellow. "No one who realized the historical value of Lattimer House would want it razed and made into common land." Evan Amberly muttered something. Niell said with even more cordialness, "I intend to make the zoning commission aware of this, naturally."

His eyes met the portly man's, and under that steady gray gaze Amberly looked away. He mumbled something about his not having any objections as long as the place didn't look like such an eyesore.

Margo thought it time for her to speak up. "I agree with you there," she said heartily. "The sooner the estate is cleared up and I can plan renovations, the better I'll like it."

Shortly thereafter, they watched Amberly trudge down the driveway. "That's that," Niell concluded. "I'll phone the head of the planning board tomorrow and request a meeting."

Zach pushed his baseball cap back over his forehead. "I don't understand why you waste time sweet-talking that fool," he rasped.

"It's in my client's best interests to have neighbors who aren't hostile." Niell nodded complacently after Amberly's departing figure. "My educated guess is that Amberly will pull in his horns and convince the other neighbors to withdraw their objections to Margo's staying on."

"That makes a lot of sense," Margo said. Then she added somberly, "But even if you're right about Amberly, we still have the zoning commission to face."

"Don't worry, I won't let anything happen to you. Trust me."

When he smiled at her like that, Margo felt an almost unbearable ache building up inside her. Even with Zach standing there, she wanted to walk forward into Niell's arms. She longed for him to kiss her.

With an effort she turned around and walked back to the wallpaper. *Trust me,* he'd said, and she did.

It was herself she didn't trust.

# Chapter Four

"Unbelievable," Margo commented as she and Niell walked down the town hall steps. "I mean, really incredible. I can't believe that those people in there actually *welcomed* me to Carlin."

In her well-fitting beige slacks and silky ivory blouse, Margo looked earnest and professional and good enough to eat with a spoon. Niell watched an errant spring breeze ripple through her hair and found himself wondering how it would feel to run his fingers through that gleaming silk.

Aloud he said, "The town fathers are smarter than you give them credit for. They just had to be shown the light."

"They'd never have seen it without you."

Niell had presented his facts with just the right combination of force, friendliness, and overall competence, and the selectmen had been so impressed that they'd gone belly-up with a smile. No doubt he used different tactics with his important, cooperative clients, but having observed Niell in operation, Margo was sure that he always got results.

*When I want something, I go after it.* She shook the thought away. Right now she had more important things to consider.

"How much time do I really have to clean up my place?" she asked him. "It was never specified. 'Reasonable time' seems pretty ambiguous to me."

"I purposely kept the time frame vague. That way, you can take all the time you need." Niell tossed his briefcase into the backseat of his late-model BMW. "I told you I'd take care of you."

"You're a man of your word." Margo grinned suddenly. "Know what? I feel like letting rip with a couple of wild rebel yells, West Virginia-style."

"Let 'er rip. These stodgy yankees could do with some shaking up."

Margo followed Niell's gaze and saw that her neighbor, Mrs. Sheridan, was marching up the town hall steps. The president of the Carlin Women's Club was dressed impeccably and groomed to within an inch of her life, and the haughty look she sent Margo was irresistible.

*"Eee*-haa!" Margo hollered. "Hooray for the home team!"

Niell broke up as Mrs. Sheridan, her patrician nose quivering with outrage, hurried into the building. "This calls for a celebration," Margo went on. "We are going to party the night away."

"*Are* we?"

The look in his gray eyes caught her unawares, spun her around, and caused her center of gravity to go askew. "I mean, I'll call Naomi and Zach and set up a celebration," she amended hastily.

What else could she have meant? Niell gave his wandering libido a shake and said heartily, "Good idea. They'll be anxious to hear what happened."

"I'll phone them right away and set up a date when all of us can get together. Then I'll cook dinner. Of course," Margo added thoughtfully, "getting those two to sit down to dinner together will be the neatest trick in the book. They don't even eat the same things."

Niell grinned.

"No, I really mean that. Zach's a vegetarian. Naomi likes T-bone steaks cooked rare. One time Zach said that meat-eaters polluted their bodies, and Naomi told him that if she'd been meant to eat grass, she'd have been born with two stomachs."

"Sounds about par for those two." Niell opened the car door for her as he spoke, and his hand brushed Margo's arm. It was like touching sun-warmed silk. He had to fight a need to clear his throat as he asked, "When do you plan to hold this event?"

"It depends on your schedule this week." Margo steeled herself to ignore the sensations that had been evoked by Niell's stroking fingers and added brightly, "So, are you flying off to some exotic place that I'd give my eyeteeth to visit?"

Niell was scheduled to leave for London next Monday. Armed with this information, Margo phoned her friends, but settling on a mutually agreeable day was harder than finding hen's teeth. Naomi's mother was scheduled for minor surgery early in the week, Zach had a rush job that would keep him busy until Wednesday, and when she phoned Niell later, she discovered that his plans had changed.

"I have to take the seven-thirty flight to London on Friday morning," he informed her.

Which meant he naturally didn't want to drive six hours back and forth to Carlin on Thursday evening. Flying around the world was what the man did, Margo reminded herself, so there was no call for feeling disappointed. "No problem, Niell," she said. "We'll postpone the grand celebration till you get back."

From London he was scheduled to fly to Monaco, to confer with a titled client, and then on to Paris. He had a meeting set for Thursday at four, and he was to have a business dinner with his partners in the evening. Common sense decreed that he bow out of Margo's invitation gracefully, but Niell found himself reluctant to hang up the phone.

"Don't do that," he told Margo. "I can still

make Thursday dinner. I wouldn't miss watching the Naomi-Zach fights for anything."

Planning a meal for her three friends was a nerve-wracking ordeal. Margo eventually settled on an asparagus soufflé, a pasta dish with penne and five kinds of cheese, homemade crusty Italian bread, and a spring salad.

She spent much of Thursday chopping and mixing. Her table linen was still packed, but she found a pretty white paper tablecloth and set the table for four with her best china and the silver candlesticks that Grandma Beth had given her when she left Taylor, Virginia.

Margo was putting twelve-inch tapers in the candlesticks when the phone rang. It was Zach. "Yo, Margo," he rasped, "afraid I can't come tonight. Had to get rid of the plumber who was working with me on this here job."

Zach sounded grim. "What happened?" Margo asked.

"Man took too many shortcuts—didn't do the job right. Told him he had to do the job my way, and he walked."

It was a familiar scenario. Zach was a perfectionist who demanded one hundred percent commitment from his team. He had high standards and expected his workers and contractors to live up to them.

If he'd only lighten up . . . Margo bit back advice she knew Zach wouldn't take as he went on gloomily, "Now I have to stay here and run down someone else, or we'll be late with the job. Might take a while. Hope you aren't too mad at me about zilching out on you, Margo."

Once she had assured Zach that she understood and had put the phone down, Traffy pounced in through the open kitchen window and commenced sniffing the soufflé. Margo picked the young cat up in her arms.

"I've been looking for you, kiddo. Naomi's coming, so I have to shut you up upstairs." Trafalgar looked mournful. "Don't give me that. You'll have your dolphin-safe tuna and your toys. You're the most spoiled cat in the world and you know it."

But as it turned out, Naomi could not make it to the dinner, either. She called later that afternoon to say she had to work late. "The boss came down with stomach flu, and I have to take care of one of his accounts personally. It's a *really* important account, so I couldn't say no. Will you hate me if I don't come?"

Margo sighed. "Of course not. Zach can't make it, either."

"No fooling." Naomi sounded hopeful as she asked, "So it's just you and Niell?"

Margo ignored the insinuating note in her friend's voice. "I'd better get him on his car phone and cancel. He's flying to England tomorrow early, so he'll probably be relieved."

"Don't be so certain. He sure didn't have to

represent Sanders and Company. And I don't have to remind you that's hardly the kind of client he chooses to work for." Naomi's voice grew earnest. "He's one incredibly attractive man. In case you haven't noticed, he's built, he's brilliant. Capital Bs, Margery Ann. Not to mention that he's on a career track that doesn't quit."

Margo groaned. "Will you give it a rest? I have to hang up now and call him."

"Don't let your fingers do the walking. Douse yourself with perfume instead. Oh, and wear something besides jeans and an old ratty shirt. Do you have candles on the table and a bottle of wine handy?"

"You're way off base, Nao," Margo protested. "We don't even look at life the same way."

"There's only one way to look at life . . ." Naomi retorted. "It's short, so it might as well be sweet."

She then gave a low wolf whistle and hung up. After staring wrathfully at the receiver for a moment, Margo began to laugh.

Naomi was right about one thing: Niell Kier was on a career track that wouldn't quit. But Nao was dead wrong about everything else.

Niell had taken her on as a client because he'd believed in what she could eventually accomplish. She was grateful for his vote of confidence, but to read anything else into his willingness to give her legal advice was cobwebs and moonshine. Their viewpoints—their *worlds*—were incredibly different. Niell was flying off to London and Monaco and Paris, and she, Margo, would remain grounded in her house.

Margo looked around at her home and experienced a thrill of pride. Though little had been done to the upstairs, the first floor was now definitely livable.

She'd stripped the paint from the wood panels in the living room. The hardwood floors had been repaired and they gleamed with wax and polish. The stone fireplace now showed handsome blue slate instead of a soot-blackened mess. The walls in the dining room had been repapered with grasscloth, and Grandma Beth's candlesticks stood proudly on a prettily-set table ringed by chairs that had been sanded and stained and buffed until they glowed like dark silk.

The house was a dream coming true—her dream, not Niell's or anyone else's. And somehow she knew Miss Lattimer would approve, too.

Determinedly squelching a twinge of regret, Margo dialed the number of Neill's car phone to tell him she was postponing her party.

He wasn't in his car, and there was no one in his Boston office. At a loss, Margo decided to leave two table settings—just in case. She then set the as yet uncooked soufflé on the counter and left the pasta in the freezer. She'd save it for another time. Then she changed into clean jeans and topped them with a simple amber cotton blouse.

"Okay," she told her reflection in the mirror, "we're ready for the celebration—if it ever begins."

Niell was nearly an hour late, but just as Margo was sure he wasn't going to show, he appeared at the door. He was dressed in a business suit minus jacket and tie and he carried a bottle of burgundy.

"I meant to phone you to tell you that I was late getting out of a meeting," he apologized, "but my car phone has something wrong with it." He took a deep breath and added, "Something smells delicious."

"I hope," Margo said. In spite of what she'd told Naomi, she found she couldn't quit smiling.

Her smile reminded Niell of spring sunshine. When the meeting had run longer than he'd anticipated, he had almost been on the point of canceling out on this evening's festivities. There'd been some last-minute changes in the Herris-Pruitt contract that needed careful study. But even knowing all this, he still hadn't wanted to make the phone call to Carlin canceling the dinner.

Margo looked scrubbed and wholesome. Her jeans hugged her softly rounded hips and slim legs, and the simple cotton blouse delineated the fluid curve of her breasts and small waist. Her hair shone, her cheeks glowed with health. Her eyes were brimful of pleasure that he was there.

Niell felt an anticipatory thrill before he recalled that he wasn't Margo's only guest. "Where is everyone?" he wondered.

Margo explained. "So there's just us chickens—and the cats. Or one cat, to be more specific. Lady Hamilton's hiding upstairs. She doesn't dare venture too far without Lord Nelson, and the old curmudgeon is out stalking a bear someplace. But Traffy has been eyeing the soufflé and making a pest of himself."

Trafalgar had padded out from behind the woodbox and was purring and rubbing against Niell's legs. "Want to see what I've been doing to the house all week, or would you like a drink first?" Margo asked. "I didn't dare put the soufflé in the oven till I saw the whites of your eyes. It'll take an hour for it to rise."

"Let's have the cook's tour." Niell walked into the dining room and looked around him. "You've really been busy."

He walked through the downstairs rooms, and Margo followed happily as he admired the changes she'd made. "The wallpaper went up really easily after we stripped the walls," she said. "Isn't the floor terrific? I waxed it this morning."

She bent down to run her fingers over the shiny surface, a lithe movement that Niell found indisputably provocative. The soufflé wasn't the only thing that seemed to be on the rise, he discovered wryly.

"Maybe I'll have that drink after all," he said aloud.

There was beer and his wine. Niell opted for a beer and sat down on one of the old overstuffed chairs. "Considering that it's May, it's still pretty cool in here," Margo remarked. "I guess these old houses don't warm up so easily."

Body warmth was the best kind. . . . Niell checked his wandering mind and hauled it back out of the danger zone. This was a celebration dinner and not a date, he reminded himself.

"What happened to our friendly enemies?" he queried. "Why couldn't they make it?"

"Work. Nao had to see one of her boss's clients, and Zach got shorthanded. One of his contractors didn't measure up to his standards—which are pretty difficult to live up to, as you know yourself. Zach's a perfectionist."

"Maybe he should be more flexible," Niell suggested. "I don't mean to criticize the guy, but from what I observed while we worked together on the house, he wants everything done his way. Is he a good businessman?"

"Hardly. One time while I was working for him, he asked me to help him balance his checkbook. I couldn't believe the mess it was in. Seems he balances his accounts only once a month—and not very accurately at that."

"Doesn't he have an accountant?"

Margo shook her head. "He did, but they parted ways. The accountant suggested some deductions that Zach didn't think were honest, and he said he didn't want a crook working for him."

Niell winced. "I'm amazed he stays in business."

"Well, one reason is that Zach's *good* at what he does, and he knows how to do plenty. He's an expert at fencing and putting down brick patios or putting up stone walls. And, of course, carpentry. When he starts a job, it gets done right."

Margo's eyes glowed with enthusiasm as she continued to praise her friend. "One time, a client wanted a pool edged with marble from different parts of the country. It was a tall order, but Zach found that marble and made that pool so beautiful that everyone was amazed! And he's a master craftsman who can see other people's ideas and add to them."

Though he admired Margo's loyalty, Niell wasn't sure he agreed with her assessment of Zach. Because he hadn't known the first thing about landscaping or design, he'd trusted her judgment about Alloway's work. But at the same time he'd also seen firsthand that Zach wasn't the sort of person who could adjust his plans or roll with the punches. And his brusque, take-it-or-leave-it attitude would hardly endear him to his clients.

"How is Zach going to fit into Sanders and Company?" he wondered aloud.

"He'll be my contractor and have a share in the firm's profits. Unfortunately, we had to let his as-

sistant go because of our financial situation."
Margo saw the skepticism in Niell's expression
and spoke defensively. "Zach's a fine landscaper,
and he's my friend."

Business and friendship seldom mixed well.
The old saying touched Niell's mind as he asked,
"He used to be your boss. Doesn't he resent
working for you?"

It was a point that she and Zach had discussed. "I don't think it'll be a problem. We respect and like each other, Niell. And even if Zach
and I have had our differences, we agree on the
important things."

Niell nodded. "But what about his ability to
deal with people? You say yourself he has impos-
sibly high standards."

"Zach can be hard-nosed, sure, but he has a
soft heart." Margo's voice was troubled as she
added, "People who know him understand that,
under his bark, he's a marshmallow."

She hadn't really answered his question. "Since
taking Sanders and Company on, I've been doing
some research into area landscapers," Niell persisted. "I have to tell you that I'm concerned at
what I found. While several of the local firms
have shown a marked growth over the years, Alloway's business has been losing money."

Margo felt even more troubled. If a man was
defined by his accomplishments, she had to agree
that her friend had little to show for years of
work.

By Niell's standards, Zach was a loser. The thought made Margo feel defensive. "Look, we're all different. You and Zach are . . . well, we're talking apples and oranges here."

She saw his eyebrows rise, questioning her, and went on, "You said yourself that your goal is to win, that the most important thing for you is to succeed."

"And Alloway doesn't believe in success?"

"What's important to him is the work itself." Margo wished she had Niell's ease with words as she tried to articulate her feelings. "Zach has the ability—no, the *need* to make something beautiful. He's like an artist except that his tools are rocks and plants and trees. If he'd had the chance, he'd have been a landscape designer himself, but he didn't have the money for a lot of formal schooling."

She paused to look at Niell. However, his expression was unreadable. "Helping to create beautiful gardens and landscapes is what's important to him. The fact that he makes a living from what he loves to do is a bonus. He's no fool, Niell, really. And as for dealing with people, he only asks that they're up-front and honest with him. I understand Zach," Margo added earnestly, "because I feel that way myself. That's why I know we'll make a good team."

From years of experience with negotiations, Niell knew it was time to back off. He pulled a packet from his pocket, asking, "Feel like looking at a couple of photographs? I finally remembered to pick up the pictures I took at the Villa d'Este."

Immediately sidetracked, Margo sank cross-legged onto the floor. She spread Niell's photographs out before her, delighted with what she saw.

Niell hunkered down beside her, and for the first few moments Margo was conscious of him at her shoulder as he explained the various shots he'd taken at the Italian villa east of Rome. Then her concentration shifted, and totally absorbed, she pored over the vistas of fountains and magnificent trees.

"These cypresses were planted by the Cardinal d'Este nearly three hundred years ago," she murmured. "How incredibly beautiful. How pure their form is."

Her form was beautiful, too, but Niell wasn't sure how pure his thoughts were. They were so close to each other that her slightest movement wafted her blossom scent closer to him.

"I meant to bring you flowers tonight," he told her. "I wish I had."

Margo didn't even hear him. "Here's the palazzo," she went on in a rapt voice. "Ez used to have a book on Renaissance gardens at home, and I think the entire section on the Villa d'Este is imprinted in my memory banks." She pointed to another photograph. "Look, here's the central staircase that leads from the palazzo to the Fountain of Dragons. In the old days the water used to shoot out of these guys with such energy that it sounded like cannon fire."

She shifted her position, and their shoulders bumped softly. Her silken hair grazed his cheek. Niell found that he'd clamped his hand tightly around his beer can.

It was either lighten up or pull her into his arms. "The cardinal played pretty rough with his water," Niell said. "There are 'surprises' all along the villa. Fountains turn on suddenly and give you a shower when you're not expecting it. I got caught a couple of times."

"People of that era used to like to play tricks on each other with water." A sudden picture of Niell caught in a silver shower of water came into Margo's mind. His dark hair would be slicked back from his eyes, and his clothes would cling to him, delineating every hard muscle of his body.

And right now that body was very near hers. In her eagerness to view the photos, she realized that she was sitting so close to Niell that her knee nudged his. Margo looked up and saw that he wasn't looking at the photographs at all.

He was looking at *her*. His smoke-gray eyes held an expression that she'd seen there before. Margo felt everything within herself go very still.

The oven buzzer went off at that moment. Saved by the proverbial bell! But it took an effort to get to her feet and head for the kitchen. Only then was Margo able to think clearly again.

Her heart was knocking against her ribs as if she'd run a mile, and the trembling in her hands was definitely unacceptable. Margo reminded herself of what she'd told Naomi. The fact that being near Niell brought on a sensation that could only be described as warm flashes must not interfere with reality. *Different worlds,* she reminded herself sternly.

"Time to bring the soufflé out," she called over her shoulder. "Will you light the candles, Niell, and pour the wine? We have to eat the darn thing before it falls."

"Sure thing." He'd have to get a grip on himself, or he'd start behaving like a hormone-crazed adolescent. Niell glanced at his watch and decided that he'd stay only until after coffee. Maybe he could get to the Herris papers tonight after all.

There was a thudding sound followed by a cry of dismay from Margo. "Oh, no," she yelped.

"What is it? What's wrong?" Niell rushed into the kitchen and saw that the oven door had fallen off its hinges and was lying on the floor.

"The darn thing just snapped off when I opened it," Margo exclaimed. "It just snapped off in my hand."

"Shut off the oven." Niell grabbed potholders, hefted the oven door, and carried it toward the kitchen door. The latter stuck as usual, and Margo had to shake and wrench it to get it open. "How did the soufflé make out?"

94

"Amazingly enough, it hasn't fallen—yet," Margo said. She was breathing heavily, and her hands were shaking, and Niell saw that she was struggling to control herself.

He put a steadying arm around her shoulders. "It's all right," he told her, "no damage was done. That oven was so old, it was almost prehistoric. You would have needed to get another one soon, anyway."

She cast an apprehensive look at the doorless oven, wondered how in the world she was ever going to afford a new one, then brushed away that troublesome thought as she carried the soufflé toward the dining room. "This thing's starting to collapse. We'd better eat it before—"

Margo stopped dead in the doorway to the dining room, causing Niell to bump into her. Simultaneously there was a flare of light and a frenzied meow as Trafalgar leaped off the table and raced up the stairs.

"Damn that cat!" Margo shrieked. "He's upset a candle!"

Niell saw over her head that one of the candles had fallen and ignited the paper tablecloth. He strode past Margo and looked around for something with which to stifle the flames. He saw nothing but his jacket. As he beat the fire out with it, one of the glasses of wine overturned and burgundy dripped down into the blaze. The fire sizzled and expired.

Margo stared in horror at the ruins of her

table. The bread was drowned, the salad, plates, and tablecloth were swimming in blood-red wine, and more wine was dripping to the floor. As she looked from the mess to the slowly deflating soufflé in her hands, Margo felt close to tears. Then her sense of humor surfaced.

Was she going to cry? Niell looked at her apprehensively and saw that she was laughing. "I should have had chicken flambé," she giggled.

"Or cherries jubilee," he agreed, deadpan.

She put the collapsed soufflé down on the ruined table and sank into a chair. He leaned against the back of another for support while they both roared with laughter.

"Your face when you saw what happened . . ."

"The way you whacked the fire with your jacket . . ."

They both whooped so loudly that Trafalgar, who had returned to the scene of the crime and taken refuge under the woodbox, stared at them with big blue eyes.

"Oh, come out of there, you dodo," Margo wheezed, "I'm not going to yell at you. I'm sorry about this, Niell. This dinner's not very eatable. And your jacket — is it scorched to bits?"

There was a huge burned spot on the back of the garment. "I'm *so* sorry," Margo moaned. "I'll replace it, of course."

"Don't you dare touch this jacket. It's proof that I once was a firefighter." Niell tossed the charred garment aside as he added, "Look, I'll help you clean this mess up later. Right now, something tells me we both need a drink, so let's make tracks for a local restaurant."

Margo wiped her streaming eyes. "I have a better idea. The soufflé's dead and the pasta's frozen, but I did bake two loaves of bread, so we have that plus beer and cheese and fruit. We'll have a picnic."

"In the middle of the night?"

From the way he stared at her, he clearly thought that she was demented.

"It's not the middle of the night. It's seven-thirty and there's a full moon."

"Not that I'd noticed . . ." But Margo had already taken down a big basket from the top of the refrigerator and was lining it with a clean tea towel.

"Here's the bread," she said.

Shaking his head, Niell took the loaf she handed him. "What am I supposed to do with this?"

"Put it into the hamper, of course. And here's a banana and some apples and a tangerine. Do you like grapes?"

"Yes. I mean, look, Margo, this is May. It doesn't really warm up till August here in the Berkshires."

"Potato chips," Margo continued, ignoring him. "And mayo—No, I don't have any mayo, so you'll have to do without. And—Oh, damn! The cheese has mold on it."

He looked over her shoulder to study the cheese doubtfully. "Looks like the stuff penicillin's made of."

Ignoring this, Margo cut off the moldy sections and handed over the cheese. "And we need—"

She broke off as she turned and ran squarely into Niell. His hard body was pressed against hers, and she felt the imprint of his chest against her breasts. She moved back swiftly, but not quickly enough. She felt as if she'd been surrounded and invaded.

And her treacherous body was welcoming the invasion. Slow tendrils of warmth were curling through her veins, and her heart had recommenced its heavy thumping.

"What else do we need?" she forced herself to ask.

He knew what *he* needed. That was the trouble. Niell felt his entire body ache with wanting Margo.

With an effort he pulled himself back to sanity. Even if he believed in casual encounters—which he hadn't indulged in since his teenage years—the timing was wrong. He looked at the gaping oven, the remains of the soufflé, and felt Traffy brushing his leg in apology. This was definitely not the time or the place for romance.

"Napkins," Margo said almost desperately. Her brain wouldn't function. "Napkins and, ah, salt. Definitely, salt."

Wasn't there some Middle Eastern custom about taking bread and salt with the enemy as a pledge against treachery? The problem, Margo thought, was that she was her own worst enemy.

She had to remove herself from contact with Niell—and fast. "I'll go get a blanket for us to sit on," Margo exclaimed.

As she practically fled from the kitchen, Niell glared at Traffy. "See what you've started?" he demanded. The cat closed his eyes and rubbed up against Niell's leg. "Think you're pretty cute, don't you? Watch it, buster. Cats have been turned into guitar strings for less."

Margo returned with a blanket at this point. "Are you ready?"

"Ready and waiting. Why are you taking the radio?"

"For music, of course. You can't have a picnic without music." Margo felt proud of herself and in control again. "Don't worry about a thing. I'm an old hand at this. My grandparents—"

"No doubt they had picnics all year long and danced under the May moon." Niell sounded resigned as he picked up the basket and followed Margo, who walked down the steps to the back porch and nearly tripped on the oven door. "Careful. And where, may I ask, are we heading? I can hardly see my hand in front of my—"

He broke off as the full moon floated slowly out from behind the clouds. The transformation was immediate and complete. The silvered grounds became a mysterious, magical place.

"I told you there was a moon," Margo said in an awed voice. "Isn't it incredible?"

Incredible wasn't the word, Niell thought. The bare grounds looked incandescent, the bushes shimmered. The fountain, its mold hidden by the darkness, looked ready to cascade into life at any second. Even the as yet unplanted flower beds held the promise of beauty.

Margo led the way in back to where the sundial rested. "The rose garden is already my favorite spot. See? Miss Lattimer's roses are blooming."

Their scent lay gently on the cool May night. Niell snagged his shirt on a thorn and extricated himself to help Margo unfold the blanket and spread it out. "The place does have atmosphere," he admitted.

"All we need now is good music." Margo turned on the radio to an oldies station, and a Beatles song wafted softly through the garden. "There. Now, is this a picnic or what?"

She busied herself spreading out bread and cheese and fruit. Niell popped cans of beer. "You're right," he admitted. "It was an inspired idea. Here's to Lattimer House."

They clinked cans and swallowed some beer, and then started to work on the food. Niell hadn't realized that he was hungry until he tasted the simple food.

"It's the fresh air," Margo told him. "Eating

outdoors always gave me an appetite. My grandparents' house is on a little hill looking over a valley of pines and rhodies, and around this time of year the hillside is covered with color. Ez says that nature is a poor man's art gallery." Her voice was tinged with wistfulness.

"Why did you leave West Virginia?" he asked her curiously.

"You mean because I miss my grandparents? They raised me, as I told you, and they're my only real family." Margo wrapped her hands around her knees and leaned back, her thoughtful face tilted to the moonlight. "The thing was that I wanted to get my degree in landscape design from the Rhode Island School of Design, and I wanted to work in New England. There's a sense of history here that really is inspiring."

The scent of roses wafted around them like a gently perfumed cloud. "I'm glad Miss Lattimer planted so many roses," Margo went on. "When I smell them, I feel as if I'm back in West Virginia."

"The sent of the sea affects me that way," Niell confessed.

"Did you grow up near the ocean?"

"No, but I used to summer with my grandfather Kier in Harwich." A reminiscent smile tugged his lips. "I spent my days on the beach exploring the rocks. I remember that the neighborhood kids used to be territorial about those boulders until I put a stop to the 'rock wars.' "

"How did you do that?" she inquired, intrigued.

"I got the idea of drawing up an agreement with the others showing just which rocks belonged to whom. Grandfather helped me with the language of the agreement. He was amused—and pleased."

"I should think he would be," Margo approved. "You used reason instead of violence."

"It wasn't the violence so much that I minded," Niell explained. "You see, I had a special rock, a favorite, and I wanted it for myself."

Margo didn't have to ask him if he'd got the rock he wanted. She knew he had. "So," she said, "you won the rock wars."

Niell started to nod, but when he turned to look at her, he forgot what he'd been going to say. All he could think of was how beautiful Margo looked in the moonlight.

The oldies station was now playing a sentimental melody, which added to the general confusion he was experiencing. Niell felt something tighten within his heart. He had to do something—anything—to break the spell that this place, the music, and the moonlight were weaving.

He moved backward and was immediately surrounded by a prickly soft waterfall of roses. Hardly thinking what he did, he plucked the flower closest to him.

"What's that for?" Margo wondered as Niell reached over and tucked the rose behind her ear.

"I didn't bring you any flowers tonight," he reminded her.

His voice sounded odd, husky. Margo looked into Niell's face and saw something there that made her catch her breath. *Get a grip, woman,* she lectured herself.

"You're right about New England weather," she said aloud. "It's time to break up the picnic. Especially since you have to drive all the way back to Boston."

"I suppose so," Niell agreed.

But neither of them moved. The moon slid behind a cloud leaving fragrant darkness. In that darkness Margo felt Niell's hand touch her cheek.

The wordless gesture sent her over the brink. As if it were the most natural thing in the world, Margo leaned forward into Niell's arms and raised her lips to his.

## Chapter Five

It was the lightest of kisses lasting only a second. In that heartbeat of time Margo learned everything about Niell—his scent, the tough-tender texture of his cheek, the taste of his firm lips.

Above the fragrance of the roses, Margo could distinguish Niell's subtle cologne. It wreaked havoc on her reasoning processes, and against that insidious assault, logic didn't stand a chance. She closed her eyes and waited for him to kiss her again.

There wasn't anything light about this next kiss. The force of it shook Margo free of time and place so that all the known boundaries of her world seemed to disappear. Sensations akin to soft implosions were setting up shock waves within her as their tongue-tips touched, their breath mingled.

Dimly Margo knew that kissing Niell was what she'd wanted to do all evening. There was no use even trying for logic now. Being in his arms was as inevitable as plants unfurling their leaves in spring.

Niell felt Margo's lithe body nestle closer. She fitted into his arms as if she'd been made to do just that. Against his cheek her skin was like warm silk, and her mouth . . . He'd fantasized about how her mouth would taste. Now he knew how much sweeter the reality was.

Niell drew her closer against him. His mouth teased hers, his tongue explored the periphery of her lips. The inner satin of her mouth tasted of apples.

She'd been kissed before, but never like this. Nothing she'd experienced in her life had prepared Margo for the sensitivity and the bold assurance of this kiss. His lips and tongue cajoled, invited her to indulge in delights that she hadn't dreamed existed. It was as though even now Niell knew exactly what he wanted and was out to win it.

The thought slid through her mind. She tried to push it aside, but it persisted. The mindless pleasure of the moment slipped a little, and instinctively she tried to get it back by tightening her arms around him.

"Margo." He murmured her name against her mouth so that she half heard, half felt the caress of it. He was stroking her hair, tracing the smooth curve of her neck and throat.

When his fingertips reached the V neckline of her blouse, the effect was so intensely erotic that Margo shivered.

"Are you cold?" He drew away from her a little, and she could see how the moonlight silvered Niell's eyes, threw the hard planes of his face into relief.

But she wasn't cold. Every single one of her nerve endings seemed to be on fire. Margo clasped her arms around Niell's neck and drew his lips down to hers.

This time their kiss invaded every space in Margo's consciousness. She felt as if she were floating in zero gravity. She didn't know anymore where he ended and where she began, but breathed with the air of his lungs while his hands slid up over her face, stroking her cheek and neck and down her shoulders to her arms. Incredibly sensual, his fingertips grazed her fingers, stroking them, caressing her sensitive palms.

Her veins seemed to bubble with heated wine as he kissed her neck, then bent to press his mouth to her cleavage, just where it was revealed by her blouse. Margo shivered as Niell bent lower, his lips grazing the peaks of her clothed breasts.

Now his lips found hers again, and his hands were roving the path that his mouth had taken. Very softly, so that it was almost no touch at all, they glanced downward across her breasts. The tips of their tongues touched, and Margo arched her back in his arms, trying to get closer to his featherlight caresses.

Once more his palm brushed one of her breasts. And again. She moaned deep in her throat. She wanted his touch. She wanted . . . him.

Had she said those words, or were they simply echoes thrown out by the firestorm that was raging inside her? Margo had no way of knowing, but Niell seemed to hear her, anyway. Still kissing her, he slid the hem of her cotton blouse from her jeans. He cradled her against him while sensitive fingertips courted, stroking upward over the bare skin of her back.

"You're soft and you taste sweet," he whispered against her lips. "Like velvet and honey."

Cool fingers against heated skin. She shivered with desire. Kissing her all the while, he lowered her until she was lying on the blanket. Now his lips left hers to follow the direction of his hands, and she felt the rasp of his cheek against her stomach, then his lips caressing the inner curve of her still-clothed breasts. Kisses, hot against her bare skin, teased those tender curves.

The sounds she was making were driving him out of what senses he still possessed. Niell had never wanted anything more in his life than to strip off Margo's clothes and make love to this woman. He wanted to love her here, now, under the ragged moonlight. He wanted to make love to her all through the night and into the morning. . . .

Morning.

The word had a warning sound. Niell didn't care for it. He tried to will it away, and once again he let his mouth worship Margo's satin skin. He wanted to be with her all night until the morning.

The thought nudged another, buried now under layers of desire. Something, Niell remembered dimly, was happening tomorrow morning. Something important.

He had to catch a plane in the morning.

Though he tried to suppress it, the knowledge surfaced inexorably in Niell's mind. It was at least a three-hour drive to Boston. And if he made love with Margo, he wouldn't want to leave.

Margo could feel Niell pulling away from her, and her body protested. But now reason and logic were making a comeback and asking her if she were out of her mind.

The Amberlys' back porch faced her rose garden. If they came out and looked this way . . . The thought galvanized Margo into action. Hastily rolling away from Niell, she pulled her blouse into place.

The skittish moon had chosen to retreat behind the clouds at this point, so she couldn't see his face. A good thing, since her own cheeks were burning — making out in the moonlight like a teenaged kid in the backseat of a car. The crazy thing was that she was ready to do it again. Her body was like a guitar string that thrummed uncontrollably, and she was still aching for Niell's lovemaking. Margo could hear his heavy breathing in the rose-scented dark, and the sound was like a magnet drawing her to him again. She had to say something — anything — to break the spell, but no words came.

"Are you okay?" Niell asked. His voice sounded ragged, like his breathing. "That damned flight," he groaned.

Margo swallowed hard. "I know. Look, it's fine. I guess it's true what they say about moonlight and roses."

The slight quaver in her voice was endearing. It made him want to pull her back into his arms and kiss the tremor away from her lips. In the depths of his soul, Niell damned the Herris Company and the negotiations that took him to London.

But he couldn't miss his plane. Millions of dollars were riding on the outcome of this trip.

He hadn't realized he'd spoken the words until Margo said, "I didn't realize it was getting so late." She turned off the radio and, getting to her knees, began to repack the picnic basket. "You'd better get going, Niell."

She was trying to sound brisk and cheerful, but her voice had a troubled undertone. *Never apologize, never explain:* the motto that had been his father's and grandfather's before him asserted itself in Niell's mind as he watched Margo in the moonlight.

He said, "I'd honestly rather stay here with you."

He meant it and his voice reactivated the madness in her veins. Margo didn't answer. She didn't dare.

If he stayed here any longer, he wouldn't want to leave. Niell tore himself away from temptation by pushing himself to his feet. Margo watched that lithe, easy movement and envied it. She herself felt as though all her bones had turned to oatmeal.

"I wish," he added, "I didn't have to go."

*Don't go,* she longed to say. Foolishness, when the man was already reaching down to help her to her feet.

His handclasp was strong, tender. It reminded her of the caressing touch of his mouth, and the memory did unspeakable things to Margo's shaky self-control. She still felt the liquid heat of recent desire, and her heart had begun once more to beat like a wild thing.

"I imagine that your trip to London is terribly important," she managed to say.

Continuing to hold her hand, he nodded. It was a relief to talk about work. "In more ways than one. The merger of the Herris Company and the Pruitt Brothers will create a great number of jobs both in Manchester, England, and also here in our northeast region."

"That sounds good, so far."

"The problem is that Alexander Herris — the founder and president of the London-based firm — has been taken ill, and we've had to conduct negotiations with his younger brother, the vice president. The man's not sure of himself, which makes him difficult to deal with."

From the sound of Niell's voice, his mind was already far away. Though he still held her hand, Margo didn't feel connected to him any longer. When she withdrew her fingers from his clasp, he didn't seem to notice.

"We could do with more jobs in this area," she said. "I hope you succeed."

"I mean to."

He took the picnic basket from her as he spoke, and in the moonlight Margo saw that his face was resolute. Then he added, "I'll try to call you from London, but I may be in conference at all hours, and there's the time change, too. If I can't get through to you, I'll be in touch when I get back in a couple of weeks."

"I'm sure everything here will be fine," she replied. "The selectmen won't go back on their word, and the neighbors have pulled in their horns, even though the Amberlys and Mrs. Sheridan are still snarling a bit."

That wasn't what he'd meant, but in a way Niell was glad that Margo had steered their conversation to a safer subject.

He helped her carry the remains of the picnic back into the house and offered to give her a hand cleaning up the mess. But it was late, and he was obviously anxious to be on his way, so she told him that she could deal with it. When Niell drove off in his BMW, Margo switched the radio back on and went briskly into the dining room where she stripped the soggy paper cloth off the table and began to carry the plates and silverware into the kitchen.

She couldn't quite figure out whether she was glad or sorry that the evening had come to an end in this way. She wasn't sure *how* she had wanted it to end. The trouble, Margo knew, was that she didn't have any answers that made sense anymore.

She knew how things *would* have ended if Niell hadn't had that early-morning flight. In his arms tonight her resistance had been zero.

Niell had that effect on her. And if they'd made love . . .

The oldies station was singing to her about an enchanted evening. Tonight had been as close to an enchanted evening as Margo had ever known, and it would have ended in making love. They were both adults, weren't they? They'd have gone into this relationship with their eyes open—whatever that meant. If they'd made love, it would have been magic. Incredible. A firestorm of desire. Margo drew a deep, long, yearning breath.

But then the morning would have come. "The morning after," Margo mused aloud, and Lady Hamilton, who had ventured down the stairs, rubbed shyly against her ankles. Margo hunkered down and stroked the cat's ears. "You and Lord Nelson are as different as they come, yet you're happy together. You're lucky, do you know that?"

Because cats didn't have to deal with things like differences that spelled a conflict in priorities and goals. Margo remembered Niell's assessment of Zach's ability as a businessman. The problem was that Niell saw only a small facet of Zach. He didn't—or couldn't—see the whole picture, as she did.

No matter how much she and Niell were drawn to each other, they were poles apart in their thinking. Margo knew that she might as well face facts. As Ez often said, sunshine and thunder didn't go together.

Suppressing a sigh, Margo stood up and began stacking the dishes in the sink. Enough of this nonsense, she told herself. It was late, she was tired, and though her work mightn't be as grand as Niell's, it'd be there waiting for her in the morning.

Coreopsis, gaillardia, marigolds . . . Margo murmured their names as she lugged yet another cardboard carton of seedlings out of her pickup. She felt like a triumphant general returning from the wars because she'd just cut a deal with old Theo Renfrew, who owned a nursery on the outskirts of Carlin.

She'd driven out there this morning and explained that she was a landscape designer, that she'd recently begun the restoration of Lattimer House, which would be a showpiece one day, and that Sanders and Company would undoubtedly be getting a great number of contracts in the area.

"In return for dealer rates on plants and supplies, I'd come to you for all my supplies," she'd concluded.

Theo Renfrew had sucked on his inner cheek. "Heard about you," he then said. "Heard you inherited that old eyesore. That don't mean you'll be getting contracts to work on folks' places hereabouts."

They went back and forth for a while, with the old fellow dickering like a pro, but Margo had held her own. In the end, she'd agreed to design a pond surrounded by a rock garden in front of his nursery and in return got Renfrew's promise to give her wholesale prices with a lot of extras thrown in.

As she carried the last of her annuals up the driveway of her house, she took a long look around her. She'd been hard at work all week, and now the front of Lattimer House had begun to take shape. The trees had been pruned, the undergrowth cut back or rooted out, the fountain scrubbed clean, and the area around it reseeded with grass. Now it was time to plant the annual garden that would lead up the driveway to the house.

Niell would have been proud of her. No, scratch that, Margo told herself firmly. *She* was proud of herself.

She'd been thinking altogether too much of Mr. Kier lately, partly because Nao had called to tell her she'd seen Niell's photograph in the business section of the *Boston Globe* together with a long article on how the Pruitt-Herris merger was going to prove a boon to industry in the northeast region.

Margo had bought the paper to read the article and then stared at the grainy photograph, trying to convince herself that it didn't affect her in any way.

Her thoughts were interrupted as an authoritative voice called her name. When she turned, she saw that Mrs. Sheridan was marching up the driveway. The woman's face was set in lines of deep disapproval.

So what else was new? Since the selectmen had given their verdict, Mrs. Sheridan had either ignored Margo or given her nasty looks.

"Ms. Sanders, I'd like a moment of your time." The president of the Carlin Women's Club made the request sound like a command performance. "Please come with me."

Margo was getting fed up with Mrs. Sheridan. "I'm rather busy at the moment," she protested, but her neighbor was already halfway down the driveway. Sighing inwardly, Margo set down her last flat of annuals and followed.

She'd never seen the Sheridan place up close and now noted that the garden was like an extension of its owner. The bushes had been pruned to within an inch of their lives, and the grass looked as if it had been manicured by hand. Someone had also been lopping unwanted branches off the trees, for Margo spied a hatchet propped against the front steps leading to the house.

"My problem," Mrs. Sheridan began without

116

preamble, "is these rhododendrons by the steps. They get buds but don't bloom. Since I hear that you are a landscape designer, I thought you would know why."

She should have guessed that Mrs. Sheridan wanted free advice. "Perhaps the problem is that the trees are too close to the foundation of the house," Margo said. "Try a general-purpose fertilizer and some chelated iron. That usually works."

She'd turned to go back to her own yard when Mrs. Sheridan stopped her. "And then there is this dogwood. It will *not* flower."

Count to ten, Margo reminded herself. Grandma Beth had often said that neighbors were something like family—if you wanted peace, you had to coexist with them. "Perhaps," she said aloud, "it's because you're using the wrong fertilizer. Super phosphate in July and August might do the trick for you."

"I *have* done all of that." Mrs. Sheridan's tone implied, *Is that all you can suggest?* "I have been gardening for a few years, Ms. Sanders, and I know when to and when not to use fertilizer." She paused to add coldly, "I am *very* displeased. This tree was an *extremely* costly specimen."

Margo looked at the tall dogwood. She looked at the hatchet by the steps. "In that case," she replied, "there's only one thing to do."

Mrs. Sheridan started as Margo went over to the hatchet, hoisted it, and advanced on the dogwood. "What *are* you doing?" she exclaimed.

Without answering, Margo marked a spot on the dogwood about eighteen inches from the ground and then whacked the tree sharply there with the blunt end of the hatchet

Mrs. Sheridan gave a hoarse shriek. Margo whacked the tree again.

"That should do it," she said cheerfully. "Sometimes a tree needs to be shocked into going about its business. It doesn't hurt the tree, and it gets results. It's a technique that works well with stubborn specimens."

She smiled at her stunned neighbor, replaced the hatchet, and then strolled back to her own property. She hadn't felt so good since she'd moved to Carlin.

Margo had been hard at work for an hour when she was again interrupted—this time by Emma Amberly. "What does *she* want?" Margo muttered under her breath as the familiar angular figure came stalking through the boxwood hedge that divided their properties.

Mrs. Amberly was dressed in denim overalls that made her look as if she were posing for *American Gothic,* and her angular face was

118

shaded by a yellow visor. She was staring critically at Margo's annuals, her brow furrowed.

"I suppose you got these flats from Theo Renfrew down on Hanlin Street?" she demanded.

Margo nodded. "Sure did."

"It must have been expensive as sin," Emma Amberly exclaimed. "His prices are outrageous. I've told him that unless he changes his ways, I'm taking my business elsewhere." She sniffed loudly before asking, "What do you know about hillside plantings?"

This must be the day for seeking free advice. "What do you have in mind?" Margo inquired cautiously.

"There's a hill at the back of our house. I started to make a hillside garden there, but it didn't come out right," Emma explained. "The plantings—I used impatiens and caladiums—didn't give me the effect I wanted. It's become such an eyesore that Evan is angry with me." She paused and added, "If you have a minute, perhaps you could give me your opinion."

Once more Margo put down her seedlings and followed her neighbor toward the fabled Amberly House. When she saw the grounds, Margo could understand why the Amberlys had been so upset that Miss Lattimer hadn't cared for her property.

Unlike Mrs. Sheridan's prim and proper establishment, Emma Amberly had planted a "white garden," which was truly delightful. There were many varieties of white roses, exquisitely arranged, and banks of white peonies beginning to bud. Beyond these were marguerites, astilbe, and the spires of white hybrid lilies in bud.

"It's lovely," Margo enthused.

Emma just sniffed. Margo wasn't sure whether she was expressing disapproval or had a sinus condition. "I should hope so. I spend half my life weeding and pruning," she replied. Then she added, "The problem slope is over here."

Behind the immaculately maintained, impressive split-level house rose a sloping, narrow hillside, and Margo immediately knew what Emma Amberly had meant. The hillside garden just didn't make it in its gracious surroundings.

"The trouble is that Evan was against my starting the hillside garden," Emma continued. She gave another of her sniffs. "He says that it'll serve me right if the Carlin Garden Club laughs itself sick at me."

Intrigued by the problem, Margo walked around the slope. Though narrow, it wasn't very steep and was half in shadow. Beyond it lay a copse of birches and junipers, and further on rose the imposing outline of Mount Graylock.

What would look right here? Margo squatted to feel the earth, then looked up, squinting at the outline of the woods and mountain. She recalled a spring day back in Taylor, West Virginia, when she and Ez had taken a walk over a shady hill sprinkled with wildflowers.

"Why not a wildflower garden?" she suggested. "If you have some paper and a pencil, I can show you what I mean."

When Emma had fetched these items, Margo swiftly sketched out what she'd envisioned. "You could use the woods for a boundary and form a bark path here. The plantings — here and here — would be Solomon's seal, violets, columbines, and iris for color. *Iris verna,* I think."

Emma Amberly had been listening closely. "What about wild ginger for ground cover?"

"Sounds good to me. I'd use trillium, too, though of course you know that trilliums don't like to be transplanted, so you'd have to be careful."

"I like it." Margo looked up in surprise and found her neighbor eyeing her with new respect. "It's so simple I should've thought of it myself." She took the sketch from Margo and nodded. "I'll phone Theo and see if he can get me these plants and the bark."

The Amberlys, Margo reflected ruefully, could go to a store and order anything they needed. They didn't have to look for bargains. She went back to her own yard and the work that awaited her and was finishing the last of her planting when Emma Amberly came hurrying back through the boxwood fence.

"I thought you'd like to know," she called, "that Theo says that he can deliver all the plants I need. He says that you two have a working arrangement because of your landscape design company." Mrs. Amberly stopped in front of her. "Do you have any contracts yet?"

"No, not yet. I'm tied up with the property right now, and—"

"Because, if you're free," Emma interrupted, "I'd like to hire you to help me with the wildflower garden." She gave a monumental sniff and added, "Evan is sure to look down his nose at my plans, the old poop. When the horticultural society goes into raptures over what I've done, he's not going to get one whit of credit."

Margo was speechless. Her mind had focused on one word. If Mrs. Amberly wanted to hire her, that meant—

"Of course, I owe you for this morning's consultation," the older woman continued. She held out a slip of paper—a check. "I believe that one hundred dollars should be sufficient?"

"It's not necessary," Margo protested. "We're neighbors."

For the first time Margo saw a smile soften Emma Amberly's thin face. "Nonsense. You're a businesswoman, and your advice is valuable. You shouldn't give your services away for free, Margo." Her smile widened into a grin. "I heard what Clara Sheridan tried to put over you. That woman is the bossiest creature around, and no one in the Women's Club can stand her. I'm tickled that you settled her hash!"

Margo made arrangements to draw up a detailed plan and an estimate for her services and then carried her check back to the house. Traffy and Lady Hamilton were fast asleep on the kitchen table, but Traffy opened his eyes as Margo propped the check against a vase on the table, sat down, and gazed at it. She'd never earned one hundred dollars so easily.

A surge of confidence made the aches in her arms and back disappear. "We're going to take off," she exulted, and Trafalgar meowed sleepily. "Lady Luck's on the move, kiddo. Sanders and Company is going for the big time. I'd better get a hold of Zach right away."

Lady Luck had apparently only just started with her. Two days later, when Margo was at Renfrew's picking up some plants for Emma Amberly's hillside garden, a deep voice spoke behind her.

"Busy, Ms. Sanders?"

Niell . . . Margo felt as though the ground had dropped away from under her and that she was falling from a very high place. It was as if all the air in her lungs had been squeezed out. But when she managed to turn her head, a middle-aged man dressed nattily in tweeds was standing there.

"I'm Mr. Portfax," he announced. "I saw the sketch you made for Emma Amberly's hillside, and I'm impressed. I want to add a fountain to my lily pond. Do you handle that sort of thing?"

Margo made an appointment to have an initial interview with Mr. Portfax the next morning. She then drove back to Emma's, where Zach and his helper were spreading bark. "And that's not all," she told Zach. "While I was at Renfrew's, a woman wanted to talk to me about a rock garden. I have a feeling that Sanders and Company is going to get pretty busy." She showed him her crossed fingers. "I hope."

Her words proved prophetic. While Zach and his assistants were putting in the fountain for Mr. Portfax a few days later, Margo successfully negotiated the deal for the rock garden. By the end of the week there were two more contracts—one from a retired gentleman who had always wanted a butterfly garden complete with a Black Knight butterfly bush to attract the delicate creatures, and another from a woman named Mrs. Sita Parsad, who wanted to have a "meditation retreat" designed for her in her family's yard.

"I think the jobs will level off," Margo said to Zach late one night when they sat in her kitchen after a long day's work. "We may need to hire some more workers. And we should consider finding a foreman to oversee jobs when you're in Boston or on other job sites."

"You know it's hard to get good help." Zach tugged at his mustache in a thoughtful way. "Listen, Margo, we have to slow it down. Right now it looks as if we'll be big fish in a small pond, so I vote that from now on we start picking and choosing our jobs." He paused to let this sink in before adding, "And I think we should quit taking on jobs in Boston. Hate to mess it up by spreading ourselves too thin."

"Right now I don't like to refuse jobs," Margo argued. "We're not established in Carlin—not yet, anyway. And the place is small. We could handle a few clients from the Boston area if we hired a reliable foreman—"

She broke off as there was a loud thump at the door. Margo went to the door and yanked it open, and Lord Nelson, his tail swollen to nearly three times its normal size, stalked in.

His ear was torn and bleeding, his eyes swollen shut.

"Good grief," Zach exclaimed, impressed. "That feline looks like he's tangled with a mountain cat."

"I wouldn't doubt it," Margo began but was interrupted by a horrible yowling. Lady Hamilton had entered the kitchen and was apparently registering distress at her consort's condition. "Hush," Margo commanded the Siamese. "I'll take care of your sweetheart."

She reached for Lord Nelson, who streaked into the living room and wedged himself under the woodbox, from whence he uttered growls of defiance. Lady Hamilton began pacing about, waving her tail and howling mournfully. Margo got down on her hands and knees and tried to coax Lord Nelson out. "Come here, good pussycat. I have to try to clean that ear. Good —"

Lord Nelson's paw, talons extended, slashed out from under the woodbox and nearly took her hand with it. Zach, who'd been standing back watching, whistled. "That's one mean dude," he remarked. "If he was mine, I'd drown him. Want me to hang around and help out?"

"No, I'll manage. You have a long drive home ahead of you." Margo saw Zach out and then got back down on her knees and resumed her cajoling. "I'll probably have to take him to the vet, anyway. Come on out, Lord Nelson. Go-od kitty!"

Lord Nelson let fly with the other paw. Margo swore, reached out and grasping the cat by the scruff of his neck, managed to haul him out. "Listen, you dim-witted beast," she snapped, "I'm trying to help you. Do you want to die of gangrene?"

Lord Nelson hissed, spat, and then suddenly subsided, glaring at her with one blue-green eye. "Okay," Margo panted, "now calm down. I won't do anything to hurt you. I just want to get you to the vet."

The phone rang. She ignored it, and the message taker clicked on. "You have reached Sanders and Company, professional landscapers. We specialize in servicing distinguished homes, industrial parks, and complexes in the Berkshires as well as the greater Boston area. Please leave your name and number, and we'll return your call as soon as possible."

"Hello, Margo," Niell's voice said.

Dropping Lord Nelson, who promptly disappeared under the woodbox again, Margo lunged for the phone. "Where are you?" she cried.

"In Paris," Niell answered. "I've been meaning to call you, but it never seemed to work out. How are things in Carlin?"

"Great. The grounds have a totally different look now that I've planted the annuals. And you? You've had a busy time, according to the media. The Pruitt-Herris merger made the business section of the *Globe* twice, and some Harvard economist talked about it on one of the TV news shows."

He seemed to take such publicity as a matter of course. "I've promised myself a few days off when I get back to Boston this week. I'd like to drive up and see you—What's *that?*"

Lady Hamilton had raised her voice in a long, lugubrious howl. Margo explained and then added, "Sanders and Company's been busy, too. Zach and I are swamped with business."

"So soon? Good for you, Margo." He listened as she detailed the various contracts she was working on and then asked casually, "How's Zach holding up under pressure?"

Margo thought of what Zach had just said about being big fish in a small pond. "Oh, just fine. Actually, we were talking about subcontracting this evening."

"I'd say that was a wise move. As I told you, the timing's good. You can't lose, Margo."

Lord Nelson was slowly emerging from the woodbox, and she winced at the look of his ear. "This mean old cat went out to win, but he didn't."

"You haven't seen the other cat, have you?" Niell quipped when Margo had explained Lord Nelson's latest escapade. Then he added, "It'll be good to see you again."

One minute they'd been talking business, and the next—Margo felt herself invaded by sensations that left her mouth feeling dry and her heart pounding against her rib cage.

And if this kind of thing could happen to her while they were talking on the phone—long distance, yet—there was no way she was going to be responsible for what happened when they *did* get together.

It was definitely time to take hold of herself. "I'll be glad to see you, too," she told him in the heartiest voice she could manage. "Sanders and Company needs you."

When she hung up, Margo took a deep, steadying breath. It didn't help. Sanders and Company wasn't the only thing that needed Niell, she knew, because she'd missed him something fierce. Because, as she stood in the kitchen here and now, she could remember the scent of his cologne and the cool brilliance of moonlight. Because all she had to do was close her eyes and she could feel Niell's arms around her and the taste of his lips.

The trouble was that this was illusion. Foolishness. As Margo scanned the shelves in the bathroom medicine cabinet and selected the iodine bottle, she reminded herself that nothing had changed. The relationship between Margo Sanders, up-and-coming landscape designer, and Niell Kier, international corporate attorney, was unequal at best. To take Zach's analogy one step further, Niell was a powerful marlin swimming confidently in the open seas while she paddled about in a safe little pond.

Margo let out her breath in what was almost a sigh. Niell was sexy and unconsionably attractive, two very good reasons she was going to make sure that their dealings henceforth revolved around business.

As she went looking for Lord Nelson again, Margo told herself that while Niell might have his motto for success, she'd start with a pinch of Ez's down-home wisdom: when in doubt, don't get involved.

# Chapter Six

The living room was silent except for the shuffle of papers. Outside golden finches swooped down to snatch thistleseed from newly erected bird feeders, and the roses were in full bloom, but Margo paid them scant attention. She was concentrating on Niell, who was going through Sanders and Company's contracts to date.

A beam of morning sun was slanting through the newly repaired living-room windows and had gilded his dark hair. The sunbeam also scattered gold dust on his long eyelashes and emphasized how they curled at the tips.

A man didn't have any right to own eyelashes like that. . . . With an effort, Margo bore down on the business at hand. "So," she said briskly, "what do you think?"

"You've signed five contracts this month. Two jobs are finished, and you're working on a third. Several estimates are out and you've put in a respectable bid to design the grounds of the new bank that's going up on Main Street. And besides all this, you've completed two jobs in the greater Boston area." Niell tapped the papers with his long fingers. "I'm impressed."

Margo beamed. She hadn't realized how much Niell's approval meant to her.

But of course the approval of a man like Niell should carry weight. In his cotton open-necked sport shirt and light summer slacks, he looked like a man on vacation, but that was a disguise. Margo didn't need Nao to remind her that Niell was one of the most sought-after attorneys around and yet he'd given the affairs of Sanders and Company the same time and absorbed study that he must offer his important international clients.

"It hasn't all been gravy," she confessed. "The costs of starting a new business were greater than I'd anticipated, and I've made a couple of boneheaded mistakes, too. The blue delphiniums I planted for Mr. Daniels's butterfly garden all died—every one of them—and replacing them cut into our profit margin. And then I badly underestimated the costs of putting in a perennial patio garden, and we took a financial bath."

She shook her head at her own folly as she added, "Zach warned me about the patio garden. I should've listened to him, but I didn't."

"It's not easy being at the top," Niell sympathized. "By the way, I note you did hire that foreman. How did you convince Zach to go that route?"

"It wasn't easy," she admitted.

As Niell gathered the papers together, Margo recalled the extraordinary sensitivity of his hands as well as their strength. *Good grief, woman, get a grip,* she told herself.

"Actually, Zach was the one who recommended Gerry Weiss," she went on. "Gerry is a very good man and a fine worker. Zach's right in that we have to have the best people working for us so that we can build up a good reputation."

"He's right about that." Niell tossed down the last of the papers. "So far, so good, Ms. Sanders. Not only have the Amberlys surrendered without a shot being fired, but half the town of Carlin seems crazy about you."

"I've been incredibly lucky."

She smiled sunnily, and Niell felt something in his deepest self respond.

He hadn't expected to have such a reaction. During his travels he'd put his mental house in order, convinced himself that the last evening he'd spent with Margo had been a delightful aberration, something rather like the Mad Hatter's tea party and as far removed from his normal life and routine as possible. Moonlit picnics,

133

oven doors that fell off in the user's hand, and cats who set fire to tablecloths were hardly his style. He'd almost made himself believe that the whole incident had amused him.

When he'd called her from Paris, it hadn't been because he was pining for her but because it was his custom to personally keep tabs on his new clients. Besides, he liked Margo and respected her spunk and creativity. Then he'd heard her voice over the transatlantic wires and realized how much he'd missed her.

But he wasn't sure how she felt. When he'd first seen Margo this morning, her eyes hadn't been able to conceal her happiness at seeing him. But she'd then proceeded to offer him her hand instead of a kiss, and her spoken greeting had been friendly but businesslike. How was London? How was the drive out to Carlin? Was he sure he didn't want some coffee before looking over the company's papers?

She was being professional. Niell stifled a sigh and reminded himself that perhaps it was for the best.

He leaned back in his chair and locked his hands behind his head. "I'd like to make a suggestion as your legal adviser. It's time to expand."

His movements caused the muscles of his chest and bare arms to ripple like steel under silk. Margo blinked hard to dispel her sense of imbalance. "We're already expanding."

"Have you heard about the mall that they're going to build between Carlin and Lenox?"

Traffy had jumped onto his lap and was rubbing against him. Watching that sleek head nuzzling at Niell's chest did crazy things to Margo's insides. She turned to look out the window to where Lady Hamilton was snoozing in the herb garden. Lord Nelson, at her side, was watching the feathered visitors fluttering about the bird feeder and licking his chops.

"There was a story in the local paper about the Mall at Mountain View," Margo admitted. "I hear it's going to be pretty exclusive."

"Its owners want the mall to be unique and charming, a cut above the competition. They're looking for a landscape designer with a sense of style—someone who can be both subtle and daring."

"How do you know all this?"

"I had lunch with Fred Troner, one of the owners of the mall." Niell put Traffy down, got up, and strolled over to lean on the open windowsill beside Margo. "I told him that I knew someone who'd be right for the job."

Margo realized her jaw had dropped. "Wh-what did he say?"

"He wants to see what you can do. My advice would be to send your card along with a note to Fred and tell him that we've talked and that

135

you'd like to discuss your ideas with him and the other owners."

As Niell shifted his position, his elbow brushed hers. That small contact sent warm shivers up and down her arms. Margo furrowed her brows in an effort to concentrate.

"Before I can make any kind of presentation, I have to formulate some ideas," she said. "I'd need to do a plan-view over the architect's blueprints."

Niell reached for his briefcase and withdrew several blueprints. "Fred gave me these copies."

Margo took the blueprints and pored over them. "It's an interesting concept," she commented after a few moments. "I think I can see what could be done, but I still need to see the site of the mall."

"Want to go over there now? It's a great day for a ride." *Or a picnic.* The thought was so strong in Niell's mind that he was almost sure he'd spoken the words. He glanced quickly at Margo and saw that she was still studying the blueprints.

"Something the matter?" he wondered.

"I'm thinking that this is a big undertaking," she replied slowly. "I don't know what Zach will think of bidding for it."

Margo was so absorbed in her own thoughts that she missed the speculative look Niell gave her. "Why not check the place out first?" he suggested. "You may not even want to try for the job."

That made sense. But when they reached the mall site, a single tour of the birchwood-studded acreage told Margo that she did want the chance. Built against the background of the proud Berkshires, the mall would be architecturally delightful. And she could see just how to incorporate the birch trees into the architect's plan.

Niell watched Margo pull her sketchbook from her shoulder bag and begin pottering about the proposed site. There was a sense of happy absorption about her, as though she didn't see acres of brush- and tree-covered land but a vision all her own. He leaned against his car and waited patiently until she was finished.

"What have you come up with?" he asked at last when she walked back over to him.

"Several ideas." Margo showed him her sketchbook, explaining, "I'd use the birch trees as a theme. There'd be birches outside and in the atrium, tying the whole together. And I'd also use water inside and outside the mall. The combined effect of the water and trees will convey a sense of tranquility."

There was a scant few inches between him and the glossy fall of Margo's hair. The need to feel its texture against his skin overcame him. Niell wasn't conscious that he'd reached out to

137

stroke it until he felt the silk curl about his fingers.

His touch shattered the absorption that had gripped her till now. His hand on her hair evoked images and sensations that should have been censored. Looking up at him was a mistake, Margo knew, but she could no more ignore the small caress than stop breathing.

Niell's eyes were a soft, smoky gray, and the curve of his mouth was tender. Margo knew that for the sake of all her carefully thought out resolutions she should put distance between them. The trouble was that she didn't want to.

"Tell me more about the effect of the, ah, water." Niell didn't give a damn about the water, but the effect that Margo had on him was almost frightening in its intensity, and he needed to back off. He drew his hand away from her hair—casually, he hoped.

Grateful to avoid his eyes, she looked down again at the sketchbook in her hand and pointed the highlights out to him. "I'd put a large oblong pool here, and another here, on the grounds. Groups of birches—here, and here—would shade the way from the parking lot to the mall entrance. The pools would be edged with weathered stone. And there'd be a fountain."

All the while she was talking, she was conscious of his closeness. Knowing that her bare arm would brush his if she shifted even slightly caused the fine hairs of her arms to quiver erect as though stroked by electricity. In the warm mid-May sunlight, the clean, subtle scents of his cologne penetrated her senses in an almost physical way.

It wasn't fair that *not* touching Niell was as provocative as touching him. Under her chambray shirt, Margo felt her breasts grow heavy, as though waiting for a caressing hand.

Almost desperately she continued, "I'd have carp in the pools. And water lilies. Water lilies of various colors and shapes. The flowers rising over the flat leaves will give a cool but sensuous look to the pool."

She was sensuous, all right, but there was nothing cool about her. Bright sunlight turned her eyes to warmest amber, her soft lips were flecked with sundust. They were waiting to be kissed. Niell felt slightly dizzy, as if he were affected by sunstroke.

Pulling out his handkerchief, he mopped his forehead. "It's getting hot," he said. "I'll spring for a cold drink at that tavern we passed on the way out here."

A tavern had people in it. It was a neutral, safe place in which to talk. "You're on," Margo agreed gratefully, "except that I'm buying. I still owe you a dinner after that disaster the other night."

"I wouldn't have called it a disaster."

The look he gave her could have liquefied an iceberg. Margo's glands were shooting so much adrenaline into her that she felt lightheaded. As she climbed into Niell's car, she wracked her brain for a safe subject.

"Did you have a chance to sightsee when you were in London?" she asked him as he got into the BMW beside her.

"It's beautiful at this time of year. I took a walk in Kew Gardens one day when the sun actually came out. The roses were beautiful. They reminded me of you."

He hadn't meant to say that. She knew it from the surprised look in his eyes. A wave of happiness—foolish in the light of the resolve she'd made to keep things on a business-only footing—filled her.

"I mean," Niell amended, "it reminded me of what you told me about roses." *And about you,* he thought. Hastily he added, "I'm learning about plants and garden design, thanks to you."

Margo realized that her hands had started to shake. She folded them tightly across her sketch pad. "I think the Dandelion Café is around the loop in the road," she said in what she hoped was a brisk tone. "We could—Oh, look, there's Zach's pickup."

"How are the battling duo?" Niell inquired.

"Actually, they've been reasonably peaceful

140

lately." Margo sent up a prayer of thanksgiving for the first really safe subject of the day. "Nao and Zach haven't seen too much of each other since we got so busy, but last weekend when we were working, Naomi brought us lunch. We actually had a pleasant time. No accusations or name-calling. Nao even agreed with Zach a couple of times. I was in shock."

As they went into the tavern, Zach hailed them from a booth across the room. "So you two finally finished going over the legal stuff," he said as they joined him. "Impressed at how Sanders and Company looks on paper, Kier?"

As usual when talking to Niell, Zach's voice had undertones of both suspicion and respect. Niell waited for Margo to seat herself across from Zach and then slid in next to her. "I'm so impressed that I've suggested you put in a bid to design the atrium and grounds of the Mall at Mountain View."

While Margo elaborated, Zach pulled his mustache thoughtfully. "It's a big job, Margo," he cautioned at last. "Something like that gets complicated because we'd have to do a lot of subcontracting. A good mason'd be essential, and we'd also have to have carpenters to make the forms, as well as a plumber." He sipped his cup of coffee for a moment and then repeated, "Hardest of all, we'd have to make sure that all these people coordinated their schedules without a hitch. You remember what happened when we did that job down in Canton."

Margo winced as she recalled that nightmare. Murphy's law had prevailed from the start. The schedule had been tight, the plumber hadn't arrived in time to put in the pipes, the mason had thrown out his back at the last minute and had to be replaced, and Zach had miscalculated the monies needed.

"Everyone ended up mad at each other," she mused. "But that needn't happen here. We'd be careful to be on top of things."

Zach pushed back his baseball cap and leaned back in his seat. "We've got other jobs waiting. Way I see it, Margo, I don't like us to bite off more than we can chew."

*If the heat's too strong, get out of the kitchen*—Niell bit back the words that rose to his lips and said instead, "A new company has to be aggressive in order to get itself known."

Zach scowled. "A *small* new company's got to build itself up first," he retorted. "In a year or two, working on that mall might be right for us. . . ." He shrugged away the rest of the sentence.

"But in a year or two, the job won't be there," Niell pointed out.

Margo's heart sank as an obstinate expression settled on Zach's lantern-jawed countenance. "That kind of talk is okay if you've got a lot of money and a lot of muscle behind you," he said bluntly. "No offense, Kier, but we're not one of your billion-dollar corporations. What you do and what we do are different breeds of cat. Big business is light-years away from us poor folks at the bottom of the trickle-down theory."

She could see Zach's point, but Niell was right, as well. Zach was being careful, and Niell wanted to take a chance. Margo weighed both sides of the question before she spoke. "I hear you, Zach. Still, I feel we should at least test the waters. I doubt if my bid will be accepted, but I'd like to meet with Mr. Troner to see what he says."

"You're the boss." Abruptly Zach put down his coffee and got up. "Well, back to the salt mines. See you over at the work site, Margo."

"You know that ultimately it's your decision, don't you?" Niell asked as Zach stalked off.

She nodded. "When I was working for Zach, I used to think that it was so easy to make the right decision. I used to get after Zach sometimes because of the things he did. Now I know that it isn't easy being in charge." Margo sighed. "I really want to do that mall, Niell, but at the same time I'm not sure it's wise to get stretched out beyond our abilities."

She meant beyond Alloway's abilities, Niell thought. No matter how good a craftsman the landscaper was, right now he was holding

Margo back professionally. Designing this mall for Troner could well be the break Sanders and Company needed.

Still, as he'd just told her, she'd have to make up her own mind. Niell leaned back in the booth and smiled at Margo. "There's going to be a party this Saturday," he said.

The change of focus caught Margo by surprise. From the somber expression on his face, she'd been sure Niell had been thinking about business.

"What kind of party?" she asked.

"A cocktail party-dance that's held each year for charity. My partners are going, and I'll have to put in an appearance." He paused. "Would you go with me?"

Her heart gave a swift jolt she suppressed at once. "Thanks, but I—"

"Don't tell me you have nothing to wear," Niell interrupted. He had a sudden vision of Margo wearing nothing but a smile and a rose in her hair and added hastily, "It may be interesting for you—in a business sense, I mean. Fred Troner mentioned that he'd be there."

So the invitation had been commercial, not personal. Mentally naming herself a fool, Margo focused on the implications of what Niell was saying. Perhaps Zach was right, she thought. Perhaps Sanders and Company wasn't ready for the big time.

"I'm going to fly back to London early Sunday morning to meet with our client there," Niell was saying. "I'd truly like to see you again before I go."

Margo looked up into Niell's eyes, and what she saw there made her catch her breath. He *wanted* her to go. Not for any business advantage that might accrue for Sanders and Company, but because he wanted to see her again. Joy, so strong that it flowed through her like a sweet-scented wave, caught her and flung her up high above caution, above logic, over the moon.

"Yes. Yes. Thank you, I'd love to go."


It was vaguely intimidating, Margo realized, to be in a room filled with people who regularly made the Who's Who column in the society pages.

There had to be three hundred people here. Everywhere she looked, men in black tie and women in designer outfits were standing about talking and laughing, and she caught snatches of conversation about cruises and vacation homes in Bermuda and on the Vineyard.

And the setting matched the elegance of the guests. The grand ballroom of Holton House was draped with pale peach and cream satin curtains that glowed in the light pouring down from many chandeliers.

Margo admired the masses of flowers arranged tastefully near the door, the French windows, and the bandstand. The furniture looked to be vintage Louis XVI; the enormous, gilt-edged paintings on the wall had an air of noblesse oblige. Even the carpet on which they stood appeared costly.

"And me a girl from Taylor, West Virginia," she exclaimed.

Niell grinned at the whimsical expression in her eyes. He snared two glasses of champagne from one of the white-gloved waiters circulating among the guests with trays of drinks and hors d'oeuvres.

"Let's drink to Taylor," he suggested.

The serving staff were better dressed than she was, for Pete's sake. Margo looked down at the dress she was wearing. It was made of polyester masquerading as silk, cut so simply that it could be called plain. Only the color—a deep, rich gold—made it acceptable.

Margo wasn't much of a follower of fashion, but she knew elegance when she saw it. There were dresses that had to have come from the finest shops in New York or Newbury Street in Boston or even from Paris, dresses that were breathtaking in their simplicity or stunning because of their daring. There was also a sprinkling of glitz.

But glitzy was one thing Holton House was

not. Margo had been impressed at first sight of the elegant melding of glass and steel that towered over the waterfront. She'd been fascinated by the layout of its lobby with the atrium that shot ceilingward forty stories. Above the tall trees in the hall, a spiral of modern lights had been hung like a showerfall of stars.

Niell, in his impeccable evening clothes, seemed perfectly at home in this milieu. He also looked incredibly handsome. Margo had noted the many female eyes that had followed Niell's progress through the ballroom.

"All this luxury," Margo commented. "Maybe Nao was right. When she heard I was coming to Holton House, she went on and on about it being *the* new, ritzy hotel patronized by the most exclusive people in Boston."

Niell wondered if Margo would believe him if he told her she was the loveliest woman there. Her dress brought out the color of her eyes and draped over her gently rounded curves, displaying them to perfection. Her glossy hair framed a face that was vivid and animated.

Other women might need jewels and pricey clothes as props, but Margo needed simply to be herself. Niell suddenly found himself wishing that he hadn't brought her to this boring event but that they were alone somewhere where—

"Niell! Niell Kier!" A stout man was coming forward, hand outstretched. "I've been trying to track you down all evening," he exclaimed.

Niell looked surprised but pleased. "And I've been trying to reach *you*. Don't you ever return calls? I thought you'd already left for California, Barry."

"Day after tomorrow." The stout man turned to Margo, adding, "I've been trying for years to get myself and Bruno out of this horrible climate."

"Bruno! Then you own that lovely golden retriever," Margo cried. "Has he been getting his ice cream lately?"

The stout man's face lit up like a sunrise, and Niell broke in hastily, "Before you pooch lovers get into a conversation that'll last all evening, let me introduce you. Margo, this is Barry Field. We went to law school together."

Barry Field shook Margo's hand enthusiastically. He had a round face, reddish hair, and bright blue eyes, which were shrewd but friendly. "Now I know who you are," he declared. "You're the gorgeous redhead Bruno and Niell met at the arboretum. I was on the west coast negotiating with a law firm there that wanted me to come on board, and now, we're heading out there. I've rented a house with a big backyard. Bruno'll love it, and so will I."

Liking him instinctively, Margo returned his smile. "Because of the climate?"

Barry nodded solemnly. "New England

weather keeps you unsettled, you know? In the morning it's warm, and then it snows by afternoon. In May, no less. Niell, you should have taken that offer form Masters and Reeve. You don't turn down carte blance to join the best law firm in Sacramento."

Someone hailed Barry at that moment. As the stout man excused himself and trotted away, Niell explained, "Barry keeps hinting that I should make a career change. Masters and Reeve is an excellent firm specializing in international law, but so far I've been too busy to be tempted." A worried note crept into his voice. "I hope Barry knows what he's doing."

"About relocating to California? He sounded pretty sure to me," Margo said. "Why are you concerned?"

"I'm not so sure about the new law firm he's joined. It's a decent enough firm, but it's what you'd call small town. Not up to Barry's potential."

He paused, looking around. "I suppose it's time to circulate. I don't see Fred Troner anywhere. Maybe we should see if we can find him."

But Margo's attention had drifted. "That's an incredible arrangement of succulents and orchids over there. I'll just take a quick look at it and catch up to you."

The orchids were elegant and strikingly dis-

149

played, and the succulents had been chosen with originality and a sense of color. Margo first walked around the arrangement, then stepped back to admire the effect.

"They are elegant, no?" a pleasant female voice asked.

Margo turned quickly and saw that a lady was sitting in a gilt chair nearby. In contrast to most of the other guests, she wore a black dress unrelieved except for a strand of pearls.

Yet the simplicity was deceiving, Margo sensed. The dress was exquisitely cut, the pearls luminous, and the woman's fine-boned face, framed by softly waved gray-blond hair, was undeniably patrician.

"I have observe' your interest in the flowers," the lady remarked in a friendly tone. She patted the chair next to her. "Will you not sit down 'ere with me?"

She spoke with a slight accent. French? Intrigued, Margo perched on the chair next to the lady in black.

"I introduce myself. I am the Contessa Alicia Delfiori. And you?" When Margo responded, the woman exclaimed warmly, "Ah, Miss Sanders, I am delight' to make your acquaintance."

The Contessa Delfiori had a firm handshake and a smile that lit up her eyes. But how did one address a countess? As Your

Grace? Your Ladyship?

"Thank you, ma'am," Margo temporized.

"I sense in you a spirit kindred," the contessa confided. "I confess that I prefer a garden to this crowded place. I would rather be walking in the—'ow you call it—the Arnold Arboretum."

"Would you really?" Margo asked wistfully. "So would I."

The contessa nodded approvingly. "I perceive you are a woman of sense. *Va bene*—that is good. Gardens are my grand passion. And you? Do you feel the same?"

When Margo explained that she was a landscape designer, the contessa's face lit up in another of her smiles. "I 'ad not 'oped to meet a kindred spirit in this squash of people." She added drily, "These assemblies, they are exhausting, no? Talk, talk, eat, eat, and afterward, the dancing, which is for me boring these days. Me, I would rather talk of a garden of roses."

"Do you have a rose garden?"

"*Certo*—of course! There are many flowers and trees at the Villa Delfiori, including an island of roses in the middle of my reflecting pool. My Roberto, the late conte, designed the pool for me many years ago. 'E wanted the roses to cascade into the pool but unfortunately, this does not 'appen. The roses, they are 'opeless."

"You mean that they don't cascade?" Margo

pulled her chair closer to the contessa's. "What varieties have you planted?"

The contessa named several shrub roses. "My gardener, 'e is an old man and 'e is stubborn. What 'e does does not satisfy me. I require the grand fall of roses and I get only a small trickle. Per'aps you can advise me?"

"Not offhand, but I'll try to think of something," Margo promised. "Please, tell me more about the Villa Delfiori. It's been my dream to go to see the Italian gardens someday."

The contessa's eyes gleamed as she launched into an animated description of her estate, which, she said, was near Florence. But before she could get past the palazzo, which had been built in the late sixteenth century, there was a stir nearby and the orchestra commenced playing.

"So this is where you are."

Niell was walking across the room to them and, with old-fashioned courtesy, bent over the hand the contessa extended to him. "I haven't had the pleasure of seeing you for a long time, madama. How have you been?"

Astonished, Margo watched the contessa and Niell smile at each other like old friends.

"*Cosi, cosi,* so and so," the contessa said cheerfully, "now that I 'ave found this young lady who shares with me a passion for 'orticulture. But I am convince' you 'ave come to steal

152

'er from me, Niell Kier, now that the dancing begins."

The sounds of the waltz filled the air. "Not at all. I've come to ask if you'll honor me, contessa?"

But Niell couldn't help glancing at Margo as he spoke, and perceiving this, the contessa chuckled.

"*Grazie. Lei é molto gentile.* You are very kind, but I will not let you suffer for your gallantry. I dance the waltz terrible and stamp upon my partner's feet. However, the young lady and you will make a fine couple."

The contessa made a shooing motion that was irresistible. "Ms. Sanders?" Niell asked, deadpan.

As he guided her toward the crowded ballroom, Niell remarked, "I wonder how the contessa guessed I wanted to ask you to dance?"

But "dance" was hardly the word since they were immediately mashed into the crowd where moving, let alone waltzing, was impossible.

Someone jostled them and pressed Margo closer to Niell. The sensation of his hard body against hers sent warm prickles through her and brought memories that hovered tantalizingly in her mind.

"Watch it!" she exclaimed.

Determination and quick footwork saved them from colliding with a large lady dancing with an equally large man. "This is an obstacle course," Niell groaned.

He suddenly stopped, detoured, and whisked them out of French windows and onto a balcony beyond. There, gratefully, they collapsed against the stone railings.

"Talk about taking your life in your hands." Margo gasped for breath. "Now I know how sardines feel."

She leaned against the balcony, drawing in the soft, warm air and looking at the glittering curve of the Charles River winding below them. "It's so beautiful out here," she murmured.

"Beautiful," Niell agreed, but he wasn't watching the river.

Margo's face was alive, glowing in the reflected lights from inside the hall. There was starlight in her eyes. Nerve endings Niell hadn't known he had were making themselves felt, and he wanted—needed—to kiss her. The effort he had to make to prevent himself from doing so made him feel as if there was a knot in his throat.

"I couldn't find Fred Troner, unfortunately," he told her around that knot, "but one of his associates is here and would like to meet you."

Something was wrong with Niell's voice, and when she looked up at him, she caught her breath at his expression. The sound of laughter and talk and the music from the crowded ballroom faded. All she could hear above the hammer of her own heart was his voice.

"Margo," he whispered. "Oh, Margo."

There was no contest. She didn't have a chance. Without thought or even volition, she walked forward into his arms.

Their lips found each other as if they'd been searching for a long, long time. Held so tightly she couldn't breathe, Margo heard him murmur words against her mouth. "I've wanted to do this ever since I came back from London."

It was what she'd wanted, too. Useless to try to deny that, Margo knew. She'd missed his arms around her and his mouth on hers and the scent and texture and taste of him. She couldn't get enough of his kisses. She wanted to be absorbed into him.

"I want to keep on kissing you." His words formed against her cheek, her temples, the corner of her mouth as he rained small kisses over her face. Margo felt as if fiery butterflies were dancing against her skin. "Lord, I wish I didn't have to leave tomorrow. I'll miss you the entire time I'm away."

"I'll miss you, too." Insane as it seemed, she was already missing him. As Niell bent to press his lips against her throat, Margo felt her entire being quiver with that coming loneliness.

The warm silk of her skin brought back the memory of roses and moonlight. He'd had to leave her that night, but not this time. "Stay with me tonight," Niell said.

He kissed her again before she could reply, his tongue tracing the periphery of her mouth, claiming admittance. The stroking of his tongue, the firm, sweet pressure of his lips were taking away any reasoning power she might have retained. Some inner voice was twittering objections, but she didn't pay attention to what that coward in her mind was saying. Margo only wanted this kiss to go on and on. She wanted . . . him.

"My town house isn't far form here," Niell was telling her. "Let's get out of this place and be alone. I want to make love with you."

The words shimmered between them. They weren't new to her, Margo realized. She'd said them, heard them in her heart since the night of that moonlit picnic.

"I want that, too."

She said it simply, as though wanting him was as natural as breathing or the beat of her heart. An ache of tenderness filled Niell, enhancing and enriching his desire. Holding her even more closely, he showered her with small, swift kisses.

Their lips came together again and stayed that way until a lack of oxygen drove them apart. "Ready to leave?" Niell whispered.

She nodded, then paused. "Oh, darn it," she groaned. "I forgot about the cats!"

The orchestra had begun a spirited disco number. Niell had to raise his voice to be heard. "What about the cats?"

"I had no idea I was going to—I thought I'd be going home tonight and so I didn't leave them any food. And Lord Nelson is out someplace prowling. The wounds he got in his last catfight have just healed, Niell. I can't let him stay out all night."

It was on the tip of his tongue to tell her that cats usually took care of themselves, but Niell checked himself.

He wasn't going to coerce Margo into doing anything she might regret. She loved those cats and was committed to them and would blame herself if anything befell them. And there was another thing, too. The thought touched Niell's mind that Margo would surely be just as committed to every relationship in her life.

Niell knew he was standing on shaky ground. Margo was beautiful and exciting and moved him more deeply than any other woman had, but he wasn't ready for that kind of commitment. Omitting for a moment the heavy emotional aspect of things, starting a relationship right now wasn't really practical. He was leaving to go overseas in the morning, after all.

He saw that she was watching him apprehensively and managed a smile. "I understand," he assured her.

157

Margo was badly shaken. For a second back there she had come near the edge of a precipice. If it weren't for the cats, she'd have walked happily off the edge.

"I think it's time I got back to Carlin," she told Niell. "We both have a full day ahead of us."

He didn't try to dissuade her. Margo said her goodbyes to the contessa, then spoke briefly to Fred Troner's associate and arranged an interview with the owners of the Mall at Mountain View. Then it was time to go.

Niell had picked her up earlier that evening at Naomi's, where she'd changed into her party clothes before driving with him to Holton House. They were silent as Niell drove her back to the apartment. Since Naomi was out for the evening, Niell insisted on waiting until Margo had changed back into shirt and dungarees for her trip to Carlin.

"It's a three-hour ride at least to Carlin," Niell reminded her as he walked her to her Chevy. "I should have picked you up instead of having you meet me in town. Are you sure you'll be all right?"

"Hey, we Taylorites are pretty tough. I once drove from Taylor, Virginia, to Florida in a snowstorm." Margo felt in full control, and when Niell bent to kiss her good-night, turned slightly so that the light kiss settled

158

on her cheek.

"Good night," she said. "Thank you for asking me to come. I really enjoyed myself."

"Thank you for coming."

Their polite words sounded inane after the emotions that had buffeted them both. Niell found himself wishing that there was some way he could keep Margo with him. And yet at the same time his newfound logic told him that it was for the best.

Best to let her leave now and go to London and the challenges of a world he knew and enjoyed. It was time to let reason take over the raw feelings that were coursing through his blood. "Drive safely," he counselled.

"Have a safe trip to London, Niell. Say 'hey' to Picadilly Circus for me."

She waved. He waved. *Time for the getaway,* Margo thought as she got into her pickup.

She turned the key in the ignition. Nothing happened. She turned it again.

Nothing. Neither the pickup nor she was going anywhere, Margo realized. The engine was as dead as yesterday's news.

# Chapter Seven

Niell stuck his head in the window. "Is the battery dead?"

She tried to start the vehicle again and groaned at the whining noises. "It sounds that way."

"Put the hood up and I'll give you a jump," Niell offered. But when the cables were in place, nothing happened.

"It's not the battery, obviously." Niell peered into the engine, adding darkly, "It could be your alternator."

Margo didn't like the sound of that. She couldn't afford expensive repairs at this stage of the game. "I'll ask Zach to take a look at it right now," she said. "He doesn't live too far from here, and he's pretty good with engines."

"You may need to replace the alternator *and* the battery." Niell slammed down the hood and wiped his hands on his handkerchief. "That happened to me once when I was in grad school. But don't borrow trouble," he added quickly as he saw Margo's expression. "It could be nothing serious."

There was a phone in the parking garage. Margo dialed Zach's number, then groaned as she heard his gravelly voice intoning, "You've reached Zach Alloway Landscapers. If you want to talk business, leave your name and number. If you want to sell me something, forget—"

There was a click as Niell broke the connection. "Don't worry him by leaving a message. I'll drive you home."

"But your flight—"

"Leaves at seven-thirty tomorrow morning," Niell replied. "Three and a half hours up, three hours back on account of there being no traffic in the wee hours. I'll catch the plane with time to spare."

"You'll also be beat. I'll stay in town with Naomi—No, I can't." Margo frowned as she recalled her cats. "I'll try Zach again in a while."

The thought of Zach's battered old pickup negotiating the dark roads with Margo as passenger made Niell grateful that the man wasn't home. To his mind, Alloway's pickup was in even worse shape than Margo's.

"Forget it. I'm taking you home," he insisted. "It'll be all right. Trust me," he continued as Margo hesitated. "I don't mind driving. I find it relaxing."

161

There wasn't anything to do but give in. As Margo locked up her pickup and followed Niell to his BMW, however, she was wondering how she was going to rescue her pickup in the morning. Possibly she could ride into Boston with Zach after their workday.

"I'm sorry about this," she said.

"Don't give it another thought," Niell replied. He'd realized that he actually felt happy at the prospect of driving seven hours just to take Margo home. He hadn't wanted the evening to end by Margo getting into her pickup and driving away. He hadn't wanted to say goodbye that way. "As I told you, I'm not one for big affairs."

No doubt he preferred more intimate occasions. . . . As she tried to clear her brain of such insidious thoughts, Niell went on, "Anyway, this will work out fine. On the way back to Boston, I'll have time to go over my London schedule."

Margo didn't ask if the schedule was important. Niell's business dealings always were. And he'd known so many people at the glamorous party they'd just left, including the Contessa Delfiori.

"I enjoyed meeting the contessa," she said. "You mentioned she was a client of yours?"

"Actually, her husband was our client. Conte Roberto Delfiori had shares in various corporations and needed our help with one of his firms, which has a branch office here in Boston. I'd just come on board the firm then and accompanied Leo Simons to Rome. Later I went back alone, and the Delfioris and I became friends."

He paused. "The contessa comes to the States every year to visit her husband's company and see how things are with his employees."

"So the conte was a businessman? That surprises me. From what she said about the fountain he created for her, I thought he was a gentleman farmer."

"Conte Roberto was a renaissance man—a hardheaded man of business with the soul of a poet. He actually helped design his villa, which is quite beautiful. You'd love it."

Niell had a sudden vision of Margo wearing some kind of diaphanous gown and walking through the rose gardens. The image did dangerous things to his self-control and made him wonder if it was bad timing that took him to London in the morning or a blessing in disguise. Once again he had the inkling that making love to Margo wouldn't be as uncomplicated as an act of mutual pleasure.

He glanced at Margo's profile and saw the curve of her cheek and the shadow of her mouth. In the instant that his glance touched her, she half turned to look at him, and their

163

eyes locked in a contact that was as physical as an embrace.

The effect of that one fleeting look almost sent the BMW off the side of the road, and Niell had to concentrate hard to pull himself back on track. He'd been right, he thought, bemused. Any relationship involving Margo would be far from simple. He was damned if he knew whether he was glad or sorry that he wasn't going to find out this time.

There had to be something wrong with her when mere eye contact affected her like this. Margo berated herself for being a double-dyed ninny, sat up straight in her car seat, and with eyes staring straight ahead tried to regain her train of thought. "The contessa was telling me about a problem she had with her roses," she said. "I didn't have any answers right at the moment, but I told her I'd try to come up with some suggestions."

"*Va bene,* as the contessa would say." Niell paused, then added thoughtfully, "Alicia Delfiori's not only a lovely lady, but she can also help Sanders and Company in ways you can't imagine."

Margo was taken aback. She'd been thinking of the contessa as a charming woman she'd have enjoyed getting to know better. Niell thought of her as a possible business connection.

"I hope your meeting with Troner and the

others goes well," Niell went on. "It's a shame you couldn't meet Troner himself. It would have given you an edge."

Silence closed around them again, and Margo reasoned that Niell's mind had drifted to his international clients. She was glad of a chance to regain her mental balance. Niell excited her as no one had ever done before, and if she didn't watch her step, she'd be drawn to his fire like a moth to flame. And once having dipped her wings in that fire, she wasn't sure whether she could ever fly away.

The trouble was that those few moments on the balcony hadn't changed anything. She and Niell saw the world from diametrically opposed perspectives. Niell's natural habitat was the kind of gala event she'd just left, while she herself was—

"A small fish in a little pond," she muttered, then glanced quickly at Niell to see if he'd heard her. But he was sliding a CD into the car's compact disc player. Soon mellow notes filled the BMW, and Margo took refuge in pretended sleep.

She must have drifted off, for in almost no time at all she heard Niell say, "Here's the exit for Carlin. We've made good time."

It had also turned so misty that she could hardly see the exit sign. She glanced at her watch and saw that it was a quarter to one. If

165

Niell was lucky, he'd be back in Boston by 4 A.M., "Will you quit worrying so much?" he added as though reading her mind. "I'll sleep on the plane."

Mist haloed the streetlamps as they drove down Main Street, and when they turned onto Peachtree Lane, visibility went down to almost zero. "I hope it's not going to be foggy on the way back to Boston," Margo fretted.

Niell pulled his car into the Lattimer driveway, shut off the engine, and swung out of the car. "Come on, I'll see you inside."

"It's not necessary," she protested, but he paid no attention.

They traversed the short distance to the door in silence. Even though he didn't touch her, Margo was very conscious of him walking near her. The knowledge that she could reach out and take his hand made her skin tingle. She tried to counteract her need to do just that by concentrating on the cats. Lady Hamilton would no doubt be asleep on the bed with Traffy. And perhaps Lord Nelson had hopped through the half-open window in the basement and come home.

Naturally the kitchen door wouldn't open. She gave it a shove, but it stayed shut. "Let me," Niell offered.

They brushed against each other as he tried the door. That one meager touch made her shiver with longing, and Margo was disgusted at herself. She was thankful that it was too dark for Niell to see her confusion. "Someday I have to get that door fixed," she said.

Niell was grateful for the cranky old kitchen door. Struggling with it gave him something physical to do, an outlet for his out-of-control adrenaline. If just brushing up against Margo could affect him this way, his brain was turning to mush—

The door swung open so suddenly that Niell stumbled into the kitchen where he barked his shins against a chair. "Are you all right?" Margo asked, worriedly.

For answer, a fiendish howl reverberated through the house. "What in hell?" Niell exclaimed.

As Margo switched on the kitchen light, Lady Hamilton came careering around the kitchen door. She raised another awful yowl and darted back into the interior of the house.

"Something's happened." Margo hurried to follow the cat into the living room. Lady Hamilton ran toward the woodbox by the fireplace. "Oh, my Lord," Margo gasped.

Lord Nelson was lying in front of the woodbox. He saw her and started to get up but couldn't make it.

"What's the matter with him?" Niell had followed her into the living room. He hunkered

167

down beside the cat, who hissed weakly and then went suddenly rigid. "He's having some kind of a seizure!"

"I don't know what it is," Margo replied distractedly. "I've got to call the vet."

She got Dr. Molinski's answering machine. It instructed Margo to phone again at eight on Monday morning. "I forgot, it's the weekend," she groaned. "I think there's a vet in Wolfboro. I'll try to get him."

But this call, too, resulted in a recorded message instructing her to phone in the morning. "Where does this Molinski live?" Niell asked.

"On Main Street. I took the cats to him when I first came to Carlin, and I took Lord Nelson to him the night he got into a fight—" Margo broke off as Lord Nelson went into another paroxysm. Lady Hamilton yowled her concern, and Traffy began to race up and down the room in an agitated way.

"Bundle up the cat," Niell decided. "I'll drive you to the vet and wake him up."

On the way to the car, Lord Nelson threw up. In spite of Margo's efforts, he threw up again inside the BMW. Niell tried to comfort him, "It's not far now, buddy. Hang on."

Margo was grateful for Niell's attitude. If a cat had vomited in *her* expensive car, she wasn't sure if she could have managed that sympathetic tone. "The vet lives around that corner," she directed. "His clinic is next door to his house."

The Molinski clinic looked dark and silent, and so did the house. "Right," Niell said, and left her cradling the cat to go and ring the doorbell. When nothing happened, he hammered on the door.

Maybe the vet was away for the weekend. But just as that thought formed in Margo's mind, the door opened a crack and a man peered out. He was in his bathrobe and pajamas and looked anything but pleased to find Niell standing there. His expression didn't change when the situation was explained, and he said something that Margo didn't catch. Probably he was telling Niell that he didn't see patients in the dead of night and that they should try the animal hospital in the third town over.

Then Niell began to speak. Margo couldn't hear him, but in a few seconds Dr. Molinski nodded and said, "All right. Bring the cat around to the clinic door, and I'll meet you there."

"How did you convince him?" Margo wondered as Niell came back to the car.

"He remembered his oath to heal all creatures great and small." Niell didn't add that a hefty bribe worked wonders, even with well-heeled vets in places like Carlin. "Here, let me carry the cat for you."

Lord Nelson was too sick to attack Niell, but

he still let out a barely audible snarl. "Shut up," Niell said amicably. "We're doing this for your own good, you scruffy barbarian."

"Don't call him names—he may be dying." Margo hurried after Niell, who was striding toward the clinic.

She was sure that Dr. Molinski's change of heart hadn't come from innate goodness and decency. From the way he'd looked down his nose at Lord Nelson when she'd taken him in for his shots, she'd deduced that Molinski was the quintessential society vet with a plush office, pampered pets for patients, and a penchant for dropping names. More than likely Niell had dropped a few himself, she thought, but she wasn't about to complain. Whatever he'd done had worked.

Dr. Molinski examined Lord Nelson and then announced, "This cat's been poisoned. I'd guess it was rat poison, or possibly weed killer."

Her neighbors had plenty of weed killer. "W-will he be all right?" Margo stammered, but the vet said he didn't know.

"I'll pump his stomach and then we'll see," he said. "You can leave him here and check back in the morning."

Margo looked at Lord Nelson. Even though he was half dead, his blue-green eyes blazed with fight. The old cuss was definitely not going to go gently.

She didn't want to leave him to die with only a stranger nearby, but she couldn't possibly ask Niell to hang around and await the outcome, and she had no transportation. Well, she mused, it wouldn't be the first or last time she'd had to rely on her feet.

"I'd like to stay until he's out of danger," she told Molinski.

The vet shrugged as if to say, Suit yourself. "You can wait in the waiting room," he said.

Niell ushered her out into the plush waiting room. "Are you really going to stay?" She nodded. "So will I, then," he said. "I kind of admire that roughneck in there."

He sat down on one of the padded chairs. Margo said forcefully, "Oh, no, you don't. Niell Kier, you have a plane to catch. I can take care of this myself."

"Did anyone tell you you worry too much?" Niell patted the chair next to him. "Take a load off your feet, and let me deal with my plane. *You*'ve got more important concerns—such as how to keep your cat from poisoning himself."

Her brows furrowed in thought. "You'd think people in Carlin would be more careful, especially with so many pets running loose. I'll go up and down the street and talk to everyone and hope they'll listen."

"They had better. Next time it could be a child who accidentally gets poisoned." Niell's voice held a grim note as he added, "If you have any problems convincing your neighbors, let me know. Meanwhile, you've done everything possible."

"I wish I'd come home sooner. Niell, if we—if I'd stayed in Boston, that poor cat would have died without anyone to help him."

He put an arm around her shoulders and gave her a comforting little shake. There was caring in his touch. His shoulder was strong, his arm incredibly reassuring as he said, "Give it a rest, Margo. Tying yourself into knots won't help the cat."

He started to talk to her again about the people at the party, notably the Contessa Delfiori. As Niell described his visits to the Villa Delfiori, Margo was distracted in spite of herself. But her attention was still tuned to the closed door behind her, and when Dr. Molinski opened the door to the waiting room, she jumped to her feet.

"How is he?" she cried.

"Through the worst of it and still very much alive," was the weary answer. "That animal has the constitution of a buffalo. I still want to monitor him closely for the next twenty-four hours, so you can give me a call tomorrow night. I don't usually take calls on the weekend, but since this is an emergency—"

The vet paused significantly and looked at

Niell, who said, "I appreciate what you've done, Doctor."

And judging from Molinski's smug expression, he would send a vastly padded bill. Niell didn't care. Margo looked as if Mount Washington had rolled off her shoulders.

Then she looked at her wristwatch and yelped. "Niell, it's three-thirty. You'll just make it into Boston to—Niell, *hurry.*"

She practically dragged him to the car and back at Lattimer House protested vigorously as he walked her to the door. "Look, will you *please* get going? I can't tell you how grateful I am. Now, scat."

But though her voice was brisk, there was something in her eyes that disturbed Niell. Her initial relief had been replaced by an odd, vulnerable look. Niell said, "Give me that key and let me open the door for you. I want to make sure you don't have to battle this crazy door half the night."

"It'll be okay. I—" Margo inserted the key but before she could turn it, the door swung open. "I guess I didn't lock it."

"You should always lock your door." Niell switched on the light and looked around. "Seems okay," he told her, "but I think I should look through the house, just in case."

He strode through the kitchen and Margo followed, protesting. "Niell, it's not necessary.

173

Nothing's wrong."

Her voice broke on the spar of a shiver. She was feeling cold, Margo realized, but that was to be expected. Though Boston had been warm, the Berkshires were at least fifteen degrees cooler. Besides, the old house held a distinct chill. Margo wrapped her arms around herself for warmth as she continued to follow Niell through the house.

"I tell you, everything's fine. There's no intruder lurking around in here."

Not in the living room, not in the dining room, not in the downstairs bathroom. Niell started up the stairs with Margo trotting at his heels. "Look, no burglars," she proclaimed as she threw open the bathroom door. The second bedroom was a morass of planks, boards, tools, electrical wire, and dust. "No ax-murderers in there, either. This is Carlin, not Boston."

Two pairs of bright-blue eyes glowed at them out of the darkness in the second bedroom. Niell switched on the light, and the two Siameses cats in the center of the bed blinked at him. Traffy got up and, tail waving, advanced to be patted. Lady Hamilton took a look at Margo's face and gave a doleful howl.

"Don't worry, baby, he's going to be okay." Margo sat down on the bed and gathered Lady Hamilton up in her arms and held her tight. After the night she'd had, she needed to hold *something* close. She shivered again, as the cold seemed to settle deep down into her bones, and Lady Hamilton protested and jumped out of her arms.

"I'd better be going," Niell said. Then he added, "Are you sure it's okay to leave you?"

He felt even more troubled. The odd, vulnerable look in Margo's eyes had intensified, and she looked suddenly so *alone*. Sitting on the big bed, bereft even of her cats, she didn't seem her usual competent self. She looked scared and young and rather fragile.

"Would you listen to yourself?" She attempted to say it brightly, but her teeth had developed a chatter. "Will you please make tracks?"

She held out her hand to him. "Thank you for everything you did for—"

"My God," he interrupted. "You're freezing." He took her other hand and rubbed both in his. "Look, are you sure you feel okay?"

Her teeth-chattering smile didn't inspire any confidence. "You need a hot shower and bed," he said, really concerned now.

"I wish. The wa-water heater's busted," Margo replied. "I'm okay. I th-think I g-got chilled at the vet's."

Niell knew better. Margo had had a scare, and her body was going into a kind of delayed-reaction shock. And it wasn't just Lord Nelson's poisoning. Margo had been pushing herself with work, with her house, until she was going on sheer nerves. In spite of her resilience, Niell thought, something had to give eventually.

He yanked the cover from the bed and wrapped it around her. Stifling her protests, he put a blanket that was lying on the bed around her, too. "Stay there," he commanded. "I'm going to get you some hot tea."

Margo wanted to object, but her mind felt dull and her head had suddenly begun to ache. And she was suddenly bone-deep tired. If she lay down for a minute and drank the hot tea, she'd be all right, she told herself. But when she curled up on her bed, jumbled images filled her mind: Lord Nelson spasming uncontrollably, Lady Hamilton keening her grief and fear.

Margo felt scared and helpless as the nightmare images took hold of her mind. She heard someone give a frightened whimper and realized it was herself. *Stop it,* she ordered herself, but though she tried to pull herself together, she couldn't.

"It's okay," Niell said in her ear. "I'm here, Margo, and you're going to be fine."

He'd sat down on the bed next to her. She tried to speak to him, but all she could manage was another whimper. He muttered something under his breath, kicked off his shoes, then lay down next to her on the bed and took her into his arms.

Margo felt strong arms enfold her. Here was warmth and security. Here was sanctuary. The tormenting fears let go of her mind and left her feeling as exhausted as if she'd run fifty miles. She tried to tell Niell she was all right now, but her lips couldn't form anything more than a single word.

Niell watched Margo's soft lips soundlessly shape his name. He could feel her whole being slacken, and when he tested her cheek with his lips, it felt warm. Her eyelids had trembled shut, and her breathing was even. She was asleep.

He hadn't realized how worried he'd been until he began to relax. Margo would be all right now, and by morning she no doubt would be her old self. He could safely leave her, he knew, but he didn't want to quite yet. He could no more drive away and leave her in trouble than he could fly.

*Fly.* Niell reminded himself that he had a flight to catch within a few hours. He started to get up, then stopped as Margo instinctively nestled closer. What the hell. He still had a little time. Niell settled Margo more securely against him and gently kissed the tip of her now warm ear.

"Don't worry," he told her softly. "Go to sleep, Margo. I'm here to take care of you."

\* \* \*

Niell wakened to the soft light of dawn brightening the walls of an unfamiliar bedroom. For a moment he felt disoriented, and then he realized that he was holding Margo in his arms.

Somewhere during the short darkness she'd discarded blanket and bedcover, and now she lay curled up against him as if he were the only warmth that she needed. Her shining hair lay across the pillow, and her lips were inches from his. Niell drew in a deep lungful of her sunlight-and-flowers scent at the moment he realized that it wasn't dark anymore.

Without disturbing Margo, he propped himself up on his elbow and stared at his wristwatch. It was half-past six. His first thought was that he'd missed his plane to London. His second thought was that he didn't care.

He sank back down on the creaking bed and pondered the second thought. There were other flights, other planes. He could probably catch an interconnecting one from nearby Pittsfield Airport to Boston and save time that way. Then Margo murmured something in her sleep, and Niell forgot about flight schedules.

He gathered her firm, gently rounded body close to him. When he stroked her back and felt its silkiness under her rumpled shirt, the tenderness he'd felt for her last night warred with an almost painful desire. He wanted her, wanted her now — but she was fast asleep.

Her slight smile told him she was aware of him on some level and that if he continued to caress her, she'd awaken. Niell was sure that she would turn to him eagerly, that her sleep-warm body would welcome his. Lovemaking between them would be delicious, incredible for both of them. And yet he hesitated. Margo looked so peaceful asleep, but there were delicate violet circles under the fanned dark lashes.

Working too hard had contributed to her reaction last night. Niell frowned. He'd always felt that Margo was wasted on the rock gardens and backyard plantings that kept her so busy. Sanders and Company needed some project of scope and significance, something that would establish her firmly in her field.

Margo was stirring in her sleep. If he stayed there, she'd awaken, and she definitely needed the rest. Carefully, regretfully, Niell got out of bed.

Two cats, their eyes round and unwinking in the morning sunlight, watched him from a chair near the bed as he padded in his stockinged feet to the bathroom. As he splashed ice-cold water on his face, Niell wondered at himself. He'd never missed a plane or an appointment with a client in all his working years.

"There's always a first time," he told himself.

179

Time later to think of work. Right now, his mind kept returning to Margo.

She was as wholesome as sunshine, and she was exceptionally talented. He'd said he'd advise her, and she trusted him. His heart tightened with caring, with affection—

Niell stopped himself right there. Caring and affection were about as far as he wanted to go right now. Restlessly he went downstairs, where he made three phone calls. Two were to the airlines. The third was to his mechanic's answering machine. Then he turned on the percolator and looked around the sunny kitchen at the white roses growing just outside the window. On impulse, Niell opened the window and picked a spray of the large creamy blooms.

When he went upstairs again, Margo was still asleep. He was wondering if he should wake her when she stirred, stretched, and opened her eyes.

In that first moment of waking she wasn't surprised to see Niell standing by her bedside. She'd been dreaming that she was walking in a garden with him. Then he'd taken her into his arms and kissed her and drawn her down among the flowers to make love.

"Good morning, there," Niell said.

Margo blinked and then came wide awake. The scent of flowers came from the fragrant white roses that were lying on the pillow next to her. And Niell— "Wh-what are you doing here?" she stammered, then sat bolt upright, gasping, "Oh, good grief, you didn't miss your plane?"

"Relax, I'm taking a later plane," he reassured her. "I guess we were both so tired we fell asleep." He sat down beside her bed, holding out a mug of tea. "I made you some tea last night—or, this morning, I should say—but when I brought it up here, you were out like a light. Here's some fresh."

Had she dreamed the fact that she'd felt so lost and hopeless until he'd lain down beside her and taken her in his arms? Margo couldn't be sure. Niell's hair was rumpled, there was a stubble of beard on his cheeks, and his clothes looked as if he'd slept in them.

The thought made warm shivers invade her. "You're not getting chilled again?" he asked anxiously.

So it hadn't been a dream. She and Niell had slept together—in a manner of speaking—all night. And then this morning he'd brought her roses. Hastily Margo began to sip the scalding tea.

"I'm sorry about your having to miss your plane," she told him, "but I'm glad you were here. Lord Nelson might have died if you hadn't convinced Molinski to work on him."

He grinned at that. "Don't underestimate that

rascal. He's got more than nine lives tucked away in a Swiss bank account." He paused to add, "I hate to break up the party, but I've arranged to catch a plane at Pittsfield Airport that'll take me right to Boston."

Of course he had to go. There was no reason for the sudden ache in her heart. "I'm really sorry to have messed up your schedule. Can I at least fix you breakfast before you go?"

"No, I'm not hungry." At least, Niell amended silently, not for food. Aloud he added, "Don't worry about your pickup, by the way. I've left a message on my mechanic's answering machine and instructed him to tow it to his shop on Beacon Street and have it repaired. Meanwhile, if you'll drive me to the airport, you can have my car."

"Your mechanic!" Margo's eyes narrowed as she shook her head. "Oh, no, you don't. I won't have you paying anyone to fix *my* pickup. I pay my way or I don't travel. And I couldn't possibly drive your bimmer."

"Sounds like another one of your grandfather's sayings," he retorted. "You're going to call the contessa, aren't you?"

The sudden shift in the conversation made her frown. "After everything that happened last night, I don't even remember where she's staying. Besides, I haven't decided how to solve her problem with her roses."

"She's staying at the Copley Plaza. She always does."

He sat down on the edge of the bed and began to pull on his shoes. "Mind you" he added mildly, "I'm just talking as Sanders and Company's legal adviser. If the contessa likes your ideas, she may commission you to do some work for her. She's an influential person among her set, Margo. Please her, and scads of wealthy Italians will want your services."

It was a dream, but a good dream. Margo leaned back against the headboard and smiled mistily.

"Hey, don't laugh," Niell said, "it really could happen. You have talent and I have the background in business. All you need is the right exposure."

"And a lot of luck."

"Good luck just means being in the right place at the right time—"

"And taking advantage of your opportunities. I know, I know." Margo picked up the roses from her pillow and ruffled their cool, fragrant petals. "All right, I'll phone her. But, Niell, about my pickup. I insist on paying whatever your mechanic charges. I really mean it."

She looked so earnest that he couldn't help bending over and kissing her ever so lightly on the lips. The sweetness he found there caused a tightness to form in his chest.

"I promise I'll send you his bill," he told her. "Meanwhile, I want you to be driving a safe vehicle. I care very much what happens to you, Margo. Remember that while I'm gone, please?"

His eyes were earnest. Almost tender. The touch of his lips lingered gently on her mouth. In the stillness of her sun-dappled room, Margo felt as though her heart was unfurling like the creamy-white roses in her hand.

"I'll remember," she promised.

# Chapter Eight

On the Tuesday after the party at Holton House, Margo kept her appointment with Fred Troner and the other owners of the Mall at Mountain View. The appointment was in downtown Boston, so she stopped at Naomi's office afterward.

"Sounds as if it really went well," Naomi commented when Margo had given her an account of her presentation. "Now you see what I mean about knowing people with clout. Stick with Niell—he has the contacts."

"Nothing says Troner will hire Sanders and Company," Margo pointed out. She'd been trying to downplay her own excitement all morning, but small prickles of anticipation kept shooting through her, like emotional pins and needles. "Anyway, contacts can get you in the door, Nao, but you stand or fall by your own abilities."

Naomi wrinkled her small nose. "Do I recognize an Ezra Sanders quotation? Don't worry, Margery Ann—you're a shoo-in."

"From your lips to God's ears. I wish Zach shared your confidence," Margo added pensively. "He feels we're not ready to take on a big job like this."

"He's got bats in his belfry," Naomi said stoutly. "You hold on a second, and you can buy me lunch while I convince you how wrong that big lug is."

But Margo shook her head. "Rain check, Nao. I already have a lunch date with a contessa."

Naomi was full of questions at the end of which she said, "Are you dressed right? Your suit's okay for a business meeting but for a lunch with aristocracy . . . This contessa's probably dripping with jewels."

But when Margo met Alicia Delfiori in the lobby of the Copley Plaza Hotel, that lady was dressed as simply as she had been the night of the cocktail party. Garbed in a plain black suit and a white scarf set with one lustrous black pearl, the contessa still exuded wealth and noblesse oblige. Margo noted how the maître d' fluttered about as he seated them at "Madama's usual table."

The contessa waited until they had ordered a lunch that, to Margo's thinking, was sinfully expensive. Then she smiled at Margo and said,

"*Va bene, cara* Miss Sanders. You 'ave truly found a solution for my roses?"

Margo had brought some sketches. "It's simple enough, ma'am. I suggest that the roses be planted in three tiers, with shrub roses at the base — perhaps Polyantha roses, which are tough and compact and flower almost constantly. The second tier could be cabbage roses, or Gallica roses."

"And the third?" The contessa's dark eyes were watching Margo with unnerving attention.

"The third tier would be composed of English roses, which are large and showy and can grow as tall as six feet."

Margo paused, somewhat breathless, and waited for the contessa's reaction. That lady was silent for a moment and then shook her head as if in wonder.

"So simple . . . but so right. And all these roses you speak of can be found in shades of my favorite color, yellow? *Mi piace molto* — I like this very much." She smiled happily down at the sketches. "Margo — you permit I call you Margo? — you are a genius. Now my roses will not go plop into the fountains but will cascade with grace, with elegance."

The contessa's questions about the roses kept them busy until well into the main course. But when their table had been cleared, she sat forward and fixed her dark eyes on Margo again.

"*Adesso*—and now, you must forgive that I ask—it is a delicate matter, but important, no? I should like to know your fee for this kind advice."

But Margo was already shaking her head. "No fee, contessa. No, please," she added firmly, "It didn't take me long to think of the solution, and besides you've already given me this lovely lunch. Perhaps you will send me a photograph of the roses when they bloom."

"*Va bene.*" The contessa looked pleased and suggested coffee. "And perhaps a *gelato?* Ice creams are my greatest craving," she confessed. "I 'ave, alas, the tooth sweet."

She smiled. "And now that you know my darkest secret, *cara,* tell me about you. Your grandfather was also a designer of gardens, you told me?"

Over two cups of coffee Margo told Alicia Delfiori a great deal about her childhood in West Virginia. At the end of these reminiscences, the elder woman said, "So, the grandfather creates the gardens and the *nonna* makes the quilts. It is in your blood, this love for beautiful things. Tell me, *cara,* is your company very busy just now?"

Surprised at the switch in topics, Margo nodded. "Yes, I'm glad to say that we are."

"I ask because I would ask a great favor. I wonder if you could come to Firenze."

"To *Florence,* ma'am?"

"Call me Alicia. Margo, I am flying back to Italia tomorrow, but since you 'ave suggest' the idea of the roses, I would like you to supervise the acquiring and planting of them."

The contessa paused. "You are concerned about your work. *Va bene,* this I understand. But per'aps you can leave the business in the 'ands of an associate? If you consent, you need only name the day, and I will 'ave my secretary make the arrangements with the airlines. My chauffeur will meet you at the airport at Roma and bring you to Delfiori."

Swallowing hard, Margo managed to speak around the lump in her throat. "It's a very generous offer, ma'am — I — I mean, Alicia. I'd like very much to come to Italy. I've dreamed of it. But I need to discuss this with my associate before giving you an answer."

The contessa beamed at her. *"Excellente!* But this time I will not allow you to work for nothing. Do not argue," she added almost sternly as Margo protested that an all-expenses-paid trip to Italy was worth a great deal more than her expertise. "We will arrive at a sum." She paused and added casually, " 'Ave I told you that the gardens at Delfiori were designed by Carlo Monchatto?"

Monchatto was one of the most respected landscape architects in the world. Niell had been right, Margo thought dreamily as the contessa began to describe her villa. Alicia Delfiori had just opened an entirely new and wonderful world to her.

She was sure that Zach could handle the work at hand for the week to ten days she would be gone, but she hadn't reckoned with the owners of the Mall at Mountain View. That evening when she returned to Carlin, there was a message from Troner on her answering machine. He and his associates had talked things over, he said, and had decided to hire Sanders and Company. They only needed to set up a time frame and go over a few details.

Predictably, Zach had mixed emotions about this windfall. "We need to talk this over, Margo," he told her when she telephoned him with the news. "How about we grab a bite together in Boston after your meeting with Troner?"

Because she needed another viewpoint, Margo also invited Naomi to the dinner meeting, which was held at a Hub restaurant that Zach recommended. The Greenery specialized in vegetarian dishes. Zach ate heartily, but Naomi moved her falafel burger around her plate as she listened to Margo detail the proposed agreement between Sanders and the mall owners.

"Shouldn't you have Niell take a look at the contract before you sign it?" she asked.

"I'm going to fax his London hotel a copy of the contract as soon as it's drawn up," Margo replied. "I'll ask him to send me a fax via Carlin Business Supplies. Now, apart from the legalities, what do you guys think of Sanders and Company taking on this job?"

"Glad Troner likes your ideas," Zach said promptly, "but I'm still concerned about the tight time frame. After the mall's foundations are poured next month, it's going to get pretty darn hectic."

"So what's a little pressure?" Naomi sniffed. "Zach, this is big business, and you have to learn to play hardball. Anything else would keep Margo down."

"I'm not trying to keep her down." Zach's mustache was beginning to bristle, and Margo hastily made a time-out gesture.

"I need both your points of view, so stay cool and help me out. Zach, if you're really not comfortable with what Troner wants us to do, I'll tell him we can't do the job."

Zach hesitated.

Naomi cried, "Of course you can do it. From what you say, it's just a matter of organizing and coordinating. Get the best people for the job and you won't have problems."

"Now you're an expert contractor, no less," Zach rasped. "There's no such thing as no problems on a job this size, Naomi." He frowned at his dish of vegetable ravioli as he added, "Still, like you say, it's a shame to turn this Troner down. What about money, Margo?"

"Troner will give us a purchase and sales agreement for the materials we'll need," Margo answered. "He specified that he wants a certain kind of tile for the fountain, which should be no problem for you, Zach." Zach nodded. "What do you think of using Roger Duxe for the plumber? He's worked well with us before." Zach nodded again. "Janette Fier is a super carpenter." Again, a nod. "And what do you think about George Evans for a mason?"

Once again, Zach inclined his head. "Okay, it could work. I'll talk to them and set up a timetable."

They threw ideas back and forth, and Margo was relieved to see that Zach grew steadily more enthusiastic as he saw how the job could successfully be done. From experience she knew that once Zach set his mind to do something, he saw it through. By the time the kiwi-lime yogurt was served, he was telling her where he'd find the right tiles to line the pool at the base of the fountain and arguing with her about the types of trees that would do well in the atrium.

"So that's settled." Naomi said. She tasted the yogurt suspiciously and made a face. "I hope your lunch with the contessa was better than this, Margo. How did it go?"

"So well that she asked me to go to Italy for a couple of weeks and do some work for her." Margo grinned at the expression on her friends' faces. "Of course I'm not going. I wouldn't leave you high and dry at a time like this, Zach. But can you believe that the grounds of the Villa Delfiori were designed by Carlo Monchatto?"

Even with her excitement over the mall contract, she couldn't help but feel a twinge of regret. With what had to be built-in radar, Naomi honed right in on it.

"I don't see why you'd have to refuse the contessa's invitation," she protested. "From what you both say, nothing much is going to happen for a month until the foundation for the mall is poured. Getting the subcontractors together is Zach's job. And going to Italy's always been your dream."

"Naomi's right."

Margo swiveled around and stared at Zach. "Will wonders never cease! Are you *agreeing* with Nao?"

"I could take care of things. I mean, you've done your part, and now it's up to your contractor to do his—er, I mean mine." Zach jutted his jaw at a combative angle. "Unless you think I can't take care of things?"

"Of course you can. I just don't think it's fair for me to go off and leave you when—"

"Go on and have some fun for a change, Margo," Zach interrupted. "All-expenses-paid working holidays don't happen every day. Don't worry about the felines, either. I'm in Carlin every day, so I'll feed them and watch out for them. Even that Lord Nelson character's been pretty mellow since he got his stomach pumped." A thought occurred to him. "Could even bunk out in the second bedroom while you're gone. That way, I could get some work done on the house in my spare time."

They both smiled at her in rare accord.

Naomi said, "And I'll watch the books for you while you're gone."

"You'll do *what?*" Zach demanded. All traces of glasnost disappeared as he snapped, "I don't need any help. I can handle the books myself."

"Sure, and you can also balance the national budget." Naomi rolled her eyes. "Don't worry about a thing, Margo, I'll make sure you don't come back to a royal mess."

"I won't come back to a mess because I'm not going anyplace," Margo declared, whereupon her friends changed tactics and spent the next half hour convincing her that if she missed this opportunity, they would never speak to her again.

"I'll think about it," she finally conceded, "but I first need to talk to the subcontractors personally. And . . . and, Zach, if I go—and I'm not saying I'm going—please let Nao help us out. She's a terrific bookkeeper, and I *need* you to be on top of things in the field. Promise me that you'll try to get along."

Zach growled under his breath but agreed. "I guess it'll be okay," he said grudgingly.

"Of course it'll be fine." Airily Naomi waved Margo's fears aside and then added with genuine anxiety, "Margery Ann, do you have anything decent to *wear?* I mean, you're going to be rubbing elbows with all kinds of big wheels out there. We can't let those highbrow Italians think Americans don't have any class."


Margo flew to Rome several days later on an Alitalia flight arranged by the contessa's secretary. Margo had little to do besides stretch out in her business-class seat and dream over the glossy book on Italian gardens that Naomi and Zach had given her as a going-away present.

At the airport she was met by a white-haired personage who pronounced himself the contessa's chauffeur and conducted Margo to a vintage Rolls. The vehicle glided smoothly through the most incredible traffic into the Italian countryside, where Margo found herself composing mental postcards.

*Dear Ez and Beth, you've never seen anything like a blue sky over Rome. Zach, the umbrella pines here are something else. I wish we could use them in the mall atrium! Nao, I actually just passed a shepherd leading a flock of real sheep. And oh, Niell, I wish you were here with me—*

Margo's thoughts broke off sharply as she realized that of all the people she knew, Niell was the one with whom she most wanted to share this moment.

She had sent him a fax of the Troner contract. He'd sent the document back almost immediately with a few additions, questions, and deletions. His accompanying note added congratulations and said that he'd tried to telephone her, but they hadn't connected.

He'd left a message on her answering machine; she had called the number he'd given her in London but had just missed him. Finally Margo had simply left word with Niell's secretary that she could be reached at the Villa Delfiori in case he needed to talk to her.

As the Rolls crested a gentle hill and for a moment poised itself over a valley, Margo caught her breath at the panorama that unfolded before her: trees and green rolling acres that embraced a stately villa.

"How lovely," she exclaimed.

The chauffeur's patrician face creased in a smile. *"Eccola, signorina,"* he declaimed dramatically. "Behold—the Villa Delfiori."

In a short while the Rolls was gliding up to a great stone gate flanked by sleepy-looking marble lions. A liveried man hastened to swing open the iron gate and doffed his hat to Margo as the car surged past.

For a while they traversed a road flanked by perfectly formed umbrella pines. Then this pathway opened into a clearing, and the contessa's palazzo came into view.

It was built in the Grecian style with sweeping marble columns and a generous terrazzo that overlooked both the gardens and a wide, rectangular pool of water. On either side of the pool jets of water arched over an island composed entirely of yellow roses. Clearly, these were the roses that were giving the contessa so much trouble. Margo craned her neck for a better look and saw that the roses did not cascade at all.

Before she could form any further impressions, the car drew up in front of wide marble stairs, and the chauffeur hurried to open Margo's door. In such a setting she half expected to hear trumpets announcing her arrival. Instead, a brisk voice exclaimed, "Welcome! You 'ave arrived at last, *cara.*"

The contessa, dressed in slacks and a sweater and wearing a shapeless garden hat, was crossing the green lawn toward her. She drew off gardening gloves to shake hands, adding cordially, "I 'ave been awaiting your arrival impatiently, Margo. The plane was comfortable? *Excellente.* When you 'ave refreshed yourself, I will show you the gardens."

"From what I saw as we drove up, they look wonderful," Margo said as the contessa slipped an arm through hers. "But then, I couldn't expect anything less from Carlo Monchatto."

The contessa nodded placidly. "Carlo is a friend of the family."

Margo wondered how it felt to be able to call Carlo Monchatto "a friend of the family." Many years ago designated as "the maestro," Monchatto had designed only a handful of gardens throughout his career, but each one had been a masterpiece. Margo had seen photographs of a country estate he had created for an English duchess and a Zen garden he'd made for a master of the tea ceremony in Japan.

"I can't wait to see the villa grounds," she told the contessa happily.

Arm in arm they climbed the steps and entered a hall of white and black marble. A bronze lion, rampant over crushed bronze flowers, stood guard over ebony columns inlaid with marble.

"The lion and the flower are of the crest Delfiori," the contessa explained rather diffidently. "It is an old title. When we were first married, the palazzo was full of the most 'orrible weapons and suits of armor such as English ghosts wear when they 'aunt castles. Roberto banished them all to the cellar, where they no doubt continue to frighten the spiders."

She pushed open the door of a room as she spoke and ushered Margo inside, and stepping through the tall door, Margo felt as though she were embraced by gold. Amber taffeta curtains hung over the windows, and the printed fabrics that covered the chairs and sofa were a melange of gold tints. Shafts of sunlight piercing the tall windows touched the gold and black of an ornate Chinese writing desk and an oval table made of gilded bronze. On this table photographs were arranged among masses of fragrant yellow tea roses.

The photographs were all of the same man — first as a young man playing polo and then as an aristocratic, gray-haired gentleman who smiled from a plain gold frame.

The contessa touched her fingertips to this frame and spoke softly. *"Ciao, caro."* Then she added, "Margo, this is my Roberto, the master of the villa. I 'ave told 'im of your coming to 'elp with the roses, and 'e approves. Roberto always enjoyed looking at a pretty young woman."

She spoke humorously, but Margo saw the expression in the contessa's eyes. The underlying loneliness there was so poignant that Margo felt as if she'd inadvertently spied on a personal moment.

"My 'usband loved roses and the growing of roses," the contessa went on. She gestured to a wing chair, herself relaxing into an apricot-covered sofa by the gilt bronze table. "These yellow rose were 'is creation. They are named *Contessina,* or little countess, after me. 'E said they were not only the most beautiful roses 'e ever grew but 'ad the sweetest perfume."

A servant now entered bearing a silver service and delicate Sevres cups. As the contessa poured espresso into the cups, she added, "It is Roberto's birthday that I remember next week. The guests I invite to honor 'is memory on that day are old friends. You will enjoy them, I know. One of them is Claudio Barini, who painted that portrait of me when I was young, and I 'ave also asked Monchatto to come. 'E is old, now, and almost a recluse, but I 'ope to see 'im again."

Perhaps she'd actually *meet* the maestro. Margo felt as though she were operating in mist. In order to counteract this dreamlike state, she got up to examine the portrait of the young Alicia Delfiori.

"That was me thirty years ago. I 'ave changed much over the years," the contessa remarked calmly. "That is as it should be. I 'ave no patience with my friends who demand a face-lift every few years. These wrinkles and lines 'ave all been earned with laughter and tears. They are the medals of life."

She paused. "And you, too 'ave the face of a woman 'oo gives love with all the 'eart. A blessing and a curse, *cara*. The sweetest roses only bloom for a season—one short season—and then they die."

Margo spoke impulsively. "You must have

loved him very much."

"So much that I cannot bear that 'e died before me," the contessa replied frankly. "I believe that every woman since Eve 'as prayed to die before the man she loves."

For a moment she appeared somber. Then she shook off her mood and smiled. "We were speaking of the party I give to honor Roberto's memory. On that occasion, I really wish the roses to flow into the reflecting pool. I do not wish those so-stiff roses to disgrace the memory of my 'usband."

She looked questioningly at Margo, who said, "I'll start transplanting full-grown plants as soon as I can find the ones I need. Is there a good nursery that you deal with regularly?"

"*Certo*. My gardener will be at your disposal, as will the chauffeur, and I myself will accompany you whenever possible." The contessa raised her Sevres cup in a toast. "*Salute*, Margo, we begin! And once you are rested, I will show you the gardens that my Roberto and Carlo designed together."

The Villa Delfiori was less a garden than a work of art that juxtaposed trees and flowers with water and harmonized the whole with the vista of the hills beyond. In order to achieve this effect in the inherently dry valley, Monchatto had actually diverted a mountain stream. Now the twenty acres of the villa were lush and green.

More than an hour was needed to walk about the villa grounds, with the contessa saving her favorite view for the last. This pièce de résistance was a small pond, where a rustic gazebo had been built to overlook the water. The gazebo, which seemed to blend naturally with its surroundings, was encircled by fragrant Contessina roses and shaded by delicately drooping willows.

"These willows my Roberto 'ad brought from Japan," the contessa told Margo. "The willows of Europe were not delicate enough for our favorite place together. Often, *cara,* we would come to drink a glass of wine or a cappuccino here in the twilight."

A white heron that had been feeding in the pond took wing and flew with a rustle of feathers. The contessa followed the bird's flight with her eyes. "When Niell Kier was 'ere last," she mused, " 'e said that Villa Delfiori is like a symphony of nature."

Margo wasn't prepared for the quick sharp twist of want evoked by Niell's name. She had a sudden, vivid impression of him standing in this same spot watching the willows and the water, and the mental image was so real that for a moment he really seemed to be there.

She had to blink hard to dispel the fantasy. "I didn't think Niell cared for gardens," she said aloud.

"A man of many surprises," the contessa observed. "The Kiers are a prominent old family with much money, but the privileged life did not make Niell weak. Instead, he boldly makes his way in the world. Where is 'e now, do you know?"

"In London," Margo answered. "He's negotiating a merger between the Herris Company and the Pruitt Brothers, an American firm."

"Ah, yes. I remember 'aving read in the newspapers about this. 'E will be successful, of course, as 'e will be successful in life. Niell 'as charm and money, and the world for an arena."

And *her* arena was the rose island. The next few days were spent in almost ceaseless activity, for Margo's daylight hours were taken up in searching for the right roses. This proved no easy task, since none of the area nurseries seemed to have Gallica roses in the exact shade of gold that the contessa wanted, and they had to be ordered from Bologna.

But the evenings more than made up for the frustrating delays as Margo and the contessa sat on the terrazzo overlooking the rose island and talked about gardens and art. Sometimes Alicia Delfiori would bring out photographs or rare books of gardens she had seen on her travels around the world. Other times she encouraged Margo to sketch ideas for a moss garden that she wanted to have built at Delfiori. One of these ideas — a pool surrounded with moss and shielded with trees in the style of the Saihoji Gardens in Japan — so impressed the contessa that she insisted Margo use colored markers and pencils to work it into a full rendering.

"You 'ave much talent," she said. "Of this I am convinced." She tapped the sketch thoughtfully for a moment and then added, "Margo, I 'ave invited Niell to come to the party."

There was no reason, Margo thought, for her pulse to quicken. The contessa and Niell were friends and it was perfectly natural that she ask him to a party honoring her late husband's memory.

"Really? Is he coming?"

"This I do not know. Niell is a busy man. But I did invite 'im to come to the party and to stay as my guest at Delfiori. Will you be glad to see 'im?" the contessa then asked innocently.

"Sure, I will. He's my company's legal adviser. If you really like that sketch, Alicia," Margo continued, "I'll do it in watercolors. It's something to do while we wait for the yellow Gallica to appear."

On the eve of the contessa's party, the golden roses were finally delivered. Margo spent the following morning on the rose island with the contessa's gardener and later helped him cut masses of flowers with which to decorate the house. Then it was time to dress.

Margo felt both excited and nervous. She was

pleased with the way the rose island looked now, but the prospect of rubbing elbows with people like Carlo Monchatto had brought on an attack of cold feet. In many ways the contessa's party reminded her of the affair at Holton House.

Suddenly the sounds and scents of Italy disappeared and in its place came a cool balcony overlooking the Charles. There was the sound of music and dancing and the starlight reflected on the river and Niell standing so close behind her that if she turned, she would be in his arms.

Slowly Margo turned and faced the mirror of her Louis XVI dressing table. She frowned at her own troubled reflection. *Oh, no, you don't,* Margo admonished herself.

She was not in love with Niell Kier. If she'd thought of him often lately, it was because the contessa had invited him to her party. And since he hadn't made an appearance or even telephoned, she had to assume he wasn't coming, which was just what she'd expected since the man led a busy life.

So what if she occasionally dreamed about him? She had an active subconscious. She dreamed about Lord Nelson on the prowl and attacking Zach; she dreamed about Grandma Beth and Ez; she'd even dreamed about Fred Troner once. And anyway, she'd been surrounded by roses lately, and roses reminded her of Niell. After all, he'd picked those cream-white roses and placed them on her pillow. . . .

Margo shook her head as if to physically clear away the insidious sensations that were stealing through her. This kind of thinking, she told herself sternly, didn't amount to a hill of beans because the reality was that Niell was merely Sanders and Company's legal adviser.

Her reflection in the mirror looked doubtful. "Okay, so we're also friends," Margo muttered aloud, "but that's it."

*I care about you, Margo.*

"Friends," Margo repeated sternly. "Friends care about each other. Anyway, why am I dithering here when Alicia needs me downstairs?"

Hastily she descended to the first floor where she found the contessa sitting on the terrazzo with a tall, lean man who had a face like a hawk. When he rose at her appearance, Margo's heart seemed to leap into her mouth. The maestro had come after all.

*"Cara,* come and meet my friend Carlo," the contessa called cheerfully. "I 'ave been telling 'im about you and your ideas."

The maestro bowed graciously, and Margo had to restrain herself from curtsying. "I've admired your work for years, sir," she managed to say.

He replied in almost unaccented English. "You are gracious. I, too, admire your work with the roses. And I am impressed with your sketches."

"M-my, ah, sketches?" Margo caught her

breath as she saw that several of her sketches were laid out on the table in front of the contessa.

"I asked Carlo to come early," the older woman explained serenely, "so that 'e could look upon your ideas. 'E agrees with me that you 'ave talent."

"I especially like the simplicity in your drawing of the contessa's proposed moss garden," Monchatto added gravely. The fierce old face did not soften, but his eyes were unexpectedly kind. "Your design has the same quality of stillness as the moss garden I once saw in Kyoto. Who was your first teacher in landscape design, signorina?"

"My grandfather, sir," Margo answered. Monchatto nodded encouragingly, and after that it was easy to talk about Ez and his work.

"So your grandfather often revitalized old gardens, and in doing so he did nothing to change their original character." Monchatto spoke courteously as though Ez were his equal. "That is the kind of artist I admire."

He was telling Margo and the contessa about a garden he had created for a favorite grandchild, when the other guests began arriving. Soon the terrazzo was filled with laughter and talk and praises for the cascading roses on Conte Roberto's island.

Margo had been mentally crossing her fingers, but now there was no need. As the conversation lapsed into excited Italian, she drew back a little to watch the contessa and her friends. Margo had actually talked to Monchatto, and the cascading roses had been a success. Nothing could be better than this, she thought. Everything else had to be anticlimactic.

The sun had begun to set, and the villa as well as the roses were banded with dusty gold. A flutist, hired by the contessa for the occasion, was playing just inside the house, and the dulcet tones filled Margo with emotions she couldn't quite analyze. In order to savor this moment to the fullest, she needed to be by herself for a while.

Margo slipped down the terrace steps and began to walk away from the crowd of guests. The path down which she was walking was edged with tall bamboo, which the conte had imported from Indochina, and the sharp leaves sighed in the wind. It was a lonely sound, and Margo felt a stir of sadness as she remembered that this was Roberto's birthday.

Well, the contessa had made the day truly memorable, and she for one would never forget it. Margo continued to walk down the path until she came to the gazebo and its surrounding willows, the couple's favorite retreat.

Parting the green curtain, Margo entered the gazebo and sat down on a comfortably cushioned bench. Only a few feet away the water lapped gently and the sweet scent of the Contessina roses kissed the air. The dying sun shimmered on the pools, and a bird called softly.

Perhaps it was the spirit of Roberto Delfiori seeking his Alicia. . . . Margo shook her head at such fanciful idiocy, but her feeling of loneliness intensified. "What on earth's the matter with me?" she wondered aloud.

"I'd say you're fine just the way you are."

Margo turned her head and saw Niell pushing back the living green curtain of the gazebo. For a moment surprise and pleasure took speech away, and then she cried, "You did come after all!"

"I wasn't sure I could make it until today." Niell let the willow branches fall behind him as he stepped into the gazebo to take her hands in both of his. "Glad to see me?"

His touch evoked memories that shivered through her like a sigh of wind. "Very glad."

"And you missed me?" He was smiling, but his gray eyes were serious, and Margo knew that whatever happened now was up to her.

All of her resolutions rushed to aid her, but before she could make a lighthearted response, the white heron that she'd seen here before rose from the water and flew up into the trees. The sky was filled with streams of coral cloud, and the air was tinged with the scent of roses and the ghosts of old love. How could she lie in a place like this?

"Yes, I missed you."

He'd forgotten how honest she was. Niell caught his breath as he saw the sunset reflected in her clear eyes. For the space of a heartbeat they looked at each other. Then he drew her into his arms.

Their kiss was like an earthquake. It cut through pretenses and mere words to something buried so deep within her as to be imprinted in her DNA. Margo simply put her arms around Niell, holding him close.

"I thought of you all the time," he muttered. "One day I nearly accosted a woman in a cab because I thought it was you."

Her chuckle died away as their lips met again. Amid a jumble of sensations, Margo remembered everything about the taste and texture of Niell's lips. Her mouth opened under his, welcoming the sweet invasion of his tongue. Their breaths mingled as Niell's tongue stroked her inner mouth.

She'd thought she remembered the way her body reacted to his kisses and to the way his hands traced sensual patterns down her back. Now she knew that memory had nothing on the real thing. Margo had the sense that being in Niell's arms again was almost like coming home.

Her knees had turned weak, and she held him even closer for support. The hard wall of his chest seemed imprinted against her breasts. She gave a little moan as his lips nuzzled her throat. Her stomach seemed fused against his lean belly, his powerful thighs cradled hers.

"I used to lie awake in the dark and want to hold you in my arms."

He'd formed the words against her mouth. Warm honey flooded through her veins as she felt his hands stroking her bare arms, scattering jewels of fire across her skin. They slipped down her back, stroking up over her hips and ribs to the proud mounds of her breasts before rising again to cup her face.

This kiss left Margo shivering with a desire that was almost primal. The world, the night, the contessa all drifted away on a spasm of longing. The earth seemed to stop rotating; the stars ceased to move across the heavens. The universe held its breath.

In the hush Margo heard the sounds of the flute again. It had changed, and the flutist was now playing a ballad in a minor key. The sweet, melancholy notes seemed to haunt the darkness. *Love now and be happy,* it seemed to say, *because life doesn't last for ever.*

*The sweetest roses only bloom for one season. . . .* As the contessa's words touched Margo's mind, Niell spoke. "Margo, nothing's changed since Holton House. I want to make love to you."

His voice was rough with need for her. And surely she didn't have to tell him that this was what she wanted, too? Margo pressed closer to Niell's caressing hands as the haunting flute music wound its tendrils around her, enfolding her.

Had it been this way for the contessa and her Roberto? Is that why he had built the gazebo here, so that they could listen to the sounds of the water as they made love?

But that was in the past. Roberto was gone and now his contessa was alone except for her guests—all of whom would soon be sitting down to dinner.

The thought touched Margo's mind lazily at first and then with greater intensity. The contessa would expect her and Niell to come to dinner.

"Niell," she murmured. "The contessa."

After a moment's pause Niell drew in a deep breath that was almost a groan. "The contessa."

His voice was tinged with rueful humor. His arms loosened until they held her gently. "It must be an atmosphere thing," he said. "I'm acting like one of the lecherous ancient Romans."

And she'd hardly been complaining. Margo felt a stir of regret as she rested her head against Niell's shoulder and looked out over the water. The sun had long set, and stars were shining white in the sky. Fireflies glinted as they dipped and darted over the sweet waters.

After a long moment Niell asked, "How much longer do you have to work for the contessa?"

"Actually, I'm almost finished here." Margo was proud of the way she managed to make her voice sound so normal. "I want to make sure that the roses are all right, and then I'd hoped to do some sightseeing first — to take in the Boboli Gardens in Florence before going home."

"Why not also see the Villa d'Este?"

"There isn't much time." Margo's tone was full of regret. "My flight's in three days."

"You're flying from Rome, aren't you?" When she nodded, Niell went on, "We can take in Florence in the morning, and then motor on to Tivoli." He met her astonished look with a smile. "I'd like to see the Villa d'Este again, this time with a personal guide."

She couldn't keep the surprise and pleasure from her voice. "You mean that you don't have to fly back to London right away?"

"The vice president at Herris has asked for some time to consider certain points in the contract with Pruitt, so there are no meetings planned for a week."

Usually he'd have stayed in London, but wanting to see Margo again, he'd rearranged his schedule. "I have to see a client in Monaco on Wednesday morning," Niell resumed, "but before I leave, we have a dinner date with a man called Cosimo Bartolomei. He's an old and valued client of mine, and he's invited us to dine on Tuesday."

"But why would he invite me?"

"He's recently bought the Villa d'Argento, an old property he'd like to restore. When I told

213

him I had a landscape designer for a client, he wanted to meet you." Niell's arms tightened around Margo as he asked, "So, Ms. Sanders, are you or aren't you going to guide me through paradise?"

The word was like a caress. It conjured up images that had to be incendiary. But before those images could take hold, Niell added, "I read in the guide book that the renaissance men called their gardens 'paradise.' "

Once again he was joking—and not joking. Margo was positive that Niell wasn't just requesting a guided tour around the gardens, and when she glanced up at him, the expression in his eyes made her catch her breath.

And with the wayward fire that had been rekindled in her came a sense of recklessness. *What will be will be,* Margo told herself.

"All right," she said aloud. "We'll see paradise together."

# Chapter Nine

If "paradise" meant a world of greenery and water, the gardens of the Villa d'Este perfectly fit that description.

Margo and Niell had left Delfiori early in the morning after breakfast with the contessa, who had given them directions, instructions, and advice. Alicia Delfiori had not only approved of Margo's plans to visit Tivoli—it had been one of Roberto's favorite places, she said—but had also insisted that she and Niell stay at her residence near Campagnano di Roma.

"Roberto and I had a house built there so that we could go to the eternal city often," she explained. "We called it the Farmhouse because Roberto designed it to resemble a genuine country farmhouse." The contessa then added that she would join her guests in a few days. "I must be present at a friend's daughter's wedding in

Rome on Wednesday. After the exhausting trip from Delfiori to Campagnano di Roma, it will be delightful to see friendly faces."

Italians looked upon a few hours' drive in the same way that Americans regarded a cross-country trek. Made of sterner stuff, Margo easily endured the trip to Tivoli and then spent the day happily walking around the gardens. Even though it was nearly sunset, she still felt fresh and full of energy.

"We've come to the fountain of dragons again," she exclaimed.

Strolling behind her with his hands in his pockets, Niell watched Margo run up to the rim of the stone fountain, kneel, and dip her hands in the cool water. Her hair was windblown; there was a touch of pink sunburn on her nose. In her pale peach cotton shirt and summer skirt and sandals, she looked like the quintessence of summer.

He'd come to these gardens for Margo's pleasure, but he, too, had been impressed with what the cardinal d'Este had created. Now he stood next to her on the stone lip of the fountain and watched the water arc almost as high as the Palazzo d'Este above them.

"I've dreamed about this place for a long time," Margo was saying happily. "Photographs and drawings don't do it justice." She drew a deep breath of pure pleasure. "A sense of grandeur and a feeling of antiquity. It's as if the old stones and the trees have secrets that they keep to themselves."

She looked about her into the branches of the tall cypress trees. "Three hundred years old—they're almost immortal by our standards. I wonder what they could tell us if they could talk?"

"Nothing that we don't already know." Niell remarked. "I don't think much has changed in a few centuries."

"Meaning that people back then used to eat and sleep and have children and go about their business just as we do."

As Margo spoke, the lights in the villa went on with the dusk. The water cascading over the rocks of the illuminated waterfalls seemed magical. Getting to her feet, Margo watched the transformation thoughtfully.

"Niell, what sort of man was the conte?" she wondered.

"Roberto Delfiori?" Niell's voice was tinged with surprise at the unexpected question. "He was a shrewd businessman who enjoyed the challenge of commerce. He worked hard and played hard and enjoyed life."

"And he loved his contessa passionately." When Niell nodded, Margo asked, "How did he die?"

"A stroke," Niell said. "He went almost in-

217

stantly, Alicia told me, which was the way he'd have wanted it."

Alicia's conte and so many more who had enjoyed these same lights on the fountains had lived and loved and gone, but this magnificent old place remained with all its memories and secrets.

She didn't know what made her look up at Niell, but what she read in his expression told her he'd intuited her mood and shared it. She didn't say anything—she didn't have to. All she had to do was walk into Niell's arms.

His arms closed around her, and he held her close. As Niell's lips grazed hers in a tantalizing half kiss, the world seemed to shiver into silence. The old trees, the stones, even the rushing water that surrounded them seemed to be waiting.

There was a burst of laughter and footsteps, and a group of tourists came walking down the oval tier of steps that led to the fountain. They were gesticulating and pointing to the fountain and talking in excited German.

Niell glared at the other tourists. "Shall we keep walking?" he asked.

Margo swallowed hard to rid herself of the lump in her throat. "I guess we've seen enough of the gardens. It's getting late. We should be heading toward the contessa's Farmhouse, shouldn't we?"

"According to the map, Campagnano di Roma isn't far." Niell didn't say anything else, but Margo understood what hadn't been said. The contessa wasn't in residence at the Farmhouse, so they'd be alone except for the servants. And though Margo was certain that Niell and she would be given separate bedrooms, it needn't follow that they'd stay alone through the night.

Margo wondered if he could hear her heart beating at twice its normal speed as she began to walk up the circular stairs. A day more and she'd be back in Carlin wrestling with normal, everyday problems — problems that didn't include whether or not to give into temptation. She glanced at Niell, who was following her up the stairs. The problem was that temptation never had looked so good.

What would be would be, Margo reminded herself.

Aloud she asked, "How far is the contessa's Farmhouse?"

"Not far." They'd reached their rental car, and he held the passenger door open for her as he inquired, "Do you have the directions she gave you?"

"Sure do." She drew a folded piece of paper from her purse. "We have to get to Campagnano di Roma first, then turn left on Via Garibaldi."

"I saw a sign for Campagnano di Roma back along the road." Niell started the Fiat and Margo leaned back against the car seat. She felt restless and full of adrenaline-fed nerves. It was almost as though she were holding her breath, waiting for a thunderstorm to break. Long ago Grandma Beth had told her that whenever she was overexcited, she should take three deep breaths. She gave it a try now.

"Damn," Niell exclaimed suddenly.

"What's the matter?"

"I made a wrong turn." He switched on the overhead lamp so Margo could study the map. "That sign said Marinella. I think we're going the wrong way."

"You're right. We'd better ask someone for directions."

As she spoke, a gas station came into view. Niell swung into the service station, rolled down his window, and called a question in Italian.

Two attendants approached. They conferred with each other and then, with broad gestures, began to talk to Niell. Margo, who couldn't follow any of the ensuing dialogue, could make out only a few words. *"Dritto. Va sempre dritto."*

"What are they saying?" she asked.

"Apparently we're on the right track. They say we have to go straight along this road." Niell took the map from Margo and frowned at it.

"I could've sworn we were going the wrong way."

"Gas station attendants usually know what they're talking about." Margo peered out the windows, trying to make out a sign—anything.

Ten minutes later Niell stopped to ask the way again, this time of a police officer who was directing traffic in a town square. The man considered, scratched his head, and spoke the by-now familiar word.

"Don't tell me," Margo said, when Niell started the engine again. "We're supposed to go straight again—right?"

*"Dritto, sempre dritto,"* Niell agreed. "Why am I getting a bad feeling about this?"

"Supposing we telephone the Farmhouse?" Margo suggested.

Niell muttered something that sounded like, "That's too easy," but the next time they passed a gas station, he went in to telephone. A few moments later he emerged to report, "Their telephone's not working, but I have directions again. We've been going around in a circle. Campagnano di Roma is three miles back the way we came. We only have to turn around—"

"And go *dritto, sempre dritto,"* Margo tried to say it deadpan, but she couldn't help it. For a moment they stared at each other. Then they erupted with laughter.

And to think this started out to be a romantic

evening, Niell thought dryly. "I wonder where we are?"

They had arrived at what appeared to be a small town. As Margo craned her neck to try to discover road or street signs, Niell exclaimed, "That looks like a trattoria up ahead. Hungry?"

"Very," Margo answered. "Ravenously. Bring on the pasta."

They were parking the car at the side of the road when a young man in jeans and a bright yellow polo shirt came hurrying out. He began a volley of Italian, and Niell translated, "He says that we should park the automobile in the back. He warns us against *i ladri*—thieves. He also informs us that the food in the Trattoria Bel Canto—seems the cook is his mother-in-law—is the best in the whole of Italy."

Inside, the trattoria definitely had atmosphere. Hams hung from the ceilings together with bottles of Chianti. Long wooden tables, covered with snowy cloths, lined the walls. Groups of people were seated at these tables, eating and laughing. Apparently the Bel Canto went in for communal dining.

The young man led them to a corner of a long table. "Sit, please," he said in English. "What you like to eat?"

The noise level rose as a group sitting nearby burst into loud song. Above the din Margo shouted, "Is there a menu?"

*"Certo,* I am menu," the young man announced. He rattled off a number of dishes and stood by expectantly.

Margo looked helplessly at Niell who again seemed to be struggling with laughter. "The chicken sounds good," she began.

The young man looked pained. "No, signorina, no. You can eat chicken anyplace. I bring you a nice lamb cooked wonderful by my mother-in-law. First, you should have *insalata,* and after the salad, a dish of beans. Very good for you. *Va bene?"*

Meekly Margo agreed that it was very good. Niell ordered *bistecca,* the beef that was the specialty of the house, and added, "And *vino.* I think we'll need a lot of vino."

*"Eccolo, signore."* An enormous bottle was plunked down on the table, glasses appeared. "No worry," the waiter said, correctly interpreting Margo's stunned expression. "You pay only for what you drink."

As he walked away, Margo asked, "Is he going to remember all our order?"

"What?" Niell yelled over the latest burst of song.

Before Margo could reply, a new group of diners — two men, two women, and a young girl — entered the restaurant, made their way over to Margo's and Niell's table, gave a friendly greeting, and sat down.

Introductions followed. The newcomers were from Padua, and had been in Rome visiting their relatives. When they saw that Margo couldn't understand Italian, they switched to a fractured English in which they described their adventures in the city. Then, learning that both their table companions were from the Untied States, they proposed a toast to *gli Stati Uniti*.

The Italians all sprang to their feet. The toast was drunk with verve and flair. Niell then suggested a counter toast to Italy. The health of Padua was then demanded—and toasts to each of the hills of Rome—all of which were drunk enthusiastically.

Talk began to flow freely. English or Italian, it didn't seem to matter. All the words were accompanied with dramatic gestures, and when the people at the next table began to sing again, Margo joined in, even though she had no idea what the words were.

This resulted in intertable toasts and compliments—and more singing. By the time their meal arrived, the enormous wine bottle was empty.

It was, Margo decided groggily, like being caught inside a Woody Allen flick. The food was delicious; the wine kept appearing as if by magic. By the time the group at their table had eaten and left—they had to depart early, they regretted, in order to continue their trip back to

Padua—Margo's head was whirling. She ordered espresso in order to steady herself, but the caffeine didn't prevent her eyelids from drooping.

Meanwhile, Niell was asking their waiter a question. "He says that we're near Santa Marinella," he explained. "That's at least thirty miles away from the contessa's place."

"Thirty miles!" The thought of driving all that way in the dark wasn't appealing. "What shall we do?"

"Our waiter says that his cousin operates a pensione that's charming and is *con bagne*—with bath. It's conveniently located at the corner of this street, so we can leave our car parked where it is. It's the height of the tourist season, so he's not sure if the cousin has accommodations, but he can try."

"It sounds good to me," Margo mumbled. Her eyelids were getting heavier by the minute. "All I want is to go to sleep. How bad can the pensione be?"

"It'll have a bed." A few hours ago those words would have had quite a different connotation. Now Niell's jaws cracked in an enormous yawn. "I don't know what they put into the vino, but I'm ready to drop."

The waiter returned, all smiles, to state that it went well. His cousin had a suite of rooms with a bath. Arrangements were made, the bill was paid, and to many choruses of *"Arrivederci, si-*

*gnore, signorina,"* Margo and Niell left the trattoria and walked down the street with their bags slung over their backs.

"We must be somewhere near the sea," Margo said as a soft night breeze brought the scent of salt. "I wonder if we'd have driven right into the drink if we'd kept on going straight?"

"Don't mention the word," Niell groaned. Then they both chorused, *"Dritto, sempre dritto."*

They were still chuckling when they reached the pensione, but here complications arose. The owner of the pensione, a dimpled little old lady called Signora Antonia, needed information from Niell as well as identification to honor his credit card.

"Go ahead to the room," he told Margo, "and I'll finish up with the red tape. I have to make a phone call, anyway."

Signora Antonia nodded maternally. "You look fatigued, signorina. *Stancha morta*—tired to death. My cousin says you have traveled far today. Come with me and I will place you in your suite."

She conducted Margo to a bedroom with narrow twin beds and a small adjoining bathroom. Margo tried to pay polite attention as Signora Antonia proudly displayed the claw-footed antique bathtub, an antique shower fixture, and even—the ultimate triumph—shower curtain.

Then that lady retreated, benignly hopeful that the signorina would have a good rest.

She was for sure going to try. By the time Niell got to the room, Margo had showered and changed into her nightgown. "Beware of the water," she warned. "It comes out fiercely hot or cold."

"We should be grateful it runs out at all." Niell eyed the narrow beds askance. "Are they as uncomfortable as they look?"

"Who cares?" Margo crawled into one of the beds, sure that the second her head hit the pillow she would be asleep. But there was an unruly spring that hit her squarely in the small of her back and, even worse, a light shining through the window and directly into her eyes.

She'd never get to sleep with that spotlight on her. Reluctantly Margo got up and padded to the window to draw the curtains. Then she paused, amazed. Their room overlooked a little garden, which was illumined by a huge golden moon.

Margo felt her weariness slip away under the beauty of the scene. As she leaned her elbows on the windowsill, a liquid sound, so sweet as to pierce the heart, rose from the moon-drenched garden, and a line from *Romeo and Juliet* she'd learned long ago in an English literature class touched her mind. Something about a nightingale.

" 'Nightly she sings on yond pomegranate tree. Believe me, love, it was the nightingale.' "

She hadn't heard Niell come out from the shower, but he was standing behind her. The vibrant note in his deep voice as he greeted her reached into her heart and seemed to squeeze hard. His hands on her shoulders banished any vestige of sleepiness.

Margo turned to look up at him. His hair was damp and sleek from the shower, and he'd wrapped one of the signora's skimpy towels around his lean hips. Moonlight softened the hard planes of his face and silvered his eyes.

"Margo," he whispered.

Then she was in his arms. It was where she belonged, after all—where she'd always belonged.

Niell's kisses tasted of wine and desire. His hands on her hair, her back, her arms were tender, as if he were playing her body like a delicate instrument. And as if keeping pace with the cadence of that music, slow ripples of desire began to course through her.

The perfume of honeysuckle and roses enveloped them as they held each other. Niell felt Margo's heart beating wildly under the flimsy fabric of her nightgown. He wanted to draw her into himself so that she could become a part of him. When he bent to kiss her, an emotion that was so strong as to be almost frightening enveloped him. He didn't just want to make love to Margo — he wanted to love her in every way.

Margo leaned back in Niell's arms and welcomed his kisses. The feelings that had swept her in the contessa's gardens had returned, and those primal, untamed feelings completely fitted this enchanted night. Pressed so close together, she didn't know where she ended and Niell began, and when the nightingale stopped singing, the only sound was their ragged breathing and the beating of their hearts.

"You know how much I care about you," Niell whispered. "I care so much."

The break in his husky voice told her more than the words. And words couldn't express what she felt, either, because what she felt for Niell was beyond caring. Though she couldn't get enough of the taste of him, or the feel of him, her need for him went beyond the merely physical. And if that wasn't loving someone, she didn't know what was.

Her hands moved over his damp skin, registering as she had so many times in her imagination the different textures of his body — the tickle-soft curl of his chest hair, the smooth muscles of his arms and back. When her hands dipped lower, the towel dropped away from his waist.

She shrugged out of her nightgown while he was still kissing her. Possessively, lovingly, his

229

hands caressed her, and his lips followed the pathway mapped by his hands. His mouth roved over her bare throat, then traced the mound of her breasts. When his lips brushed her erect nipples, sensations spiraled through her, sensations without name or form except incredible, aching desire.

And with the desire came an aching tenderness that filled her heart so deeply, so strongly, that it needed some release or it might shatter. Margo kissed Niell's throat, his shoulder, and gave a muffled chuckle. "You taste salty. Almost like a pretzel, but nicer. Where did I read that you need salt to keep up your stamina?"

She tasted him again, working her lips down to nibble on his flat nipples, and to deliver soft, tickling kisses against his chest and flat belly. Her hand stroked him, loving his power and his gentleness.

"Umm . . . need to savor you some more."

Niell's need for her increased, almost out of control, as Margo's lips and hands teased, touched, and nibbled, but he held himself in check, relishing the thread of humor that even now twined between them. Somehow their shared laughter raised the physical act of love to something incredibly dear and precious.

Still kissing and touching each other, they lay down on one of the beds, which didn't seem so narrow or uncomfortable anymore.

The coolness of the sheets contrasted with the warmth of Niell's body. His hands had slipped down Margo's ribs to her thighs, her hips, and once again his mouth followed that sensual pathway.

"I've wanted to make love to you for a long time," she heard him say. "I want you more than anything in the world. Margo . . ."

She opened her eyes and looked into his. Moonlight silver and tenderness and desire — and a question. She answered it by wrapping her arms around him and drawing him down to her. Into her.

She sighed his name as he entered her. For a moment they were joined, poised together in a world entirely their own, a universe created by them and only for them. Then, slowly, they began to move together in a rhythm older than time.

She wanted it to last, to be forever. She wanted to spin out the magic. But the need to get closer, to join more deeply, to become one drove them both, made them move faster and still faster, until they were gasping with the force of their need, until she was telling him that she loved him, that she would always love him, and then they were falling together into a release so deep it was like oblivion.

For a long moment they clung together, their breathing slowing, their fevered heat cooling into something gentle and shared. Margo wanted to hold this moment, which was as sweet as the loving, but her eyelids were closing. When she heard Niell murmur her name, she wanted to wake up and pay attention, but she couldn't.

And then she heard him say it. Against her cheek, his voice blurred with sleep, Niell muttered, "I love you, Margo. Love you . . ."

Margo fell asleep holding the words close to her heart.

Dawn woke her. With runnels of passion still undulating lazily through her blood, Margo opened her eyes. Niell was sleeping beside her, close but slightly apart. He lay on his back with one arm around her. The other pillowed his head.

Sometime during the night they'd awakened, pushed the beds together, and made love again. Now she studied his face and saw that, asleep, he looked younger, somehow gentler. There was a tenderness to his usually firm mouth, and with those smoky-gray eyes closed, he even looked vulnerable. Niell vulnerable—now, that was a new concept.

But she didn't want to start thinking, analyzing, at least for the moment. Margo nestled closer to him and closed her eyes again. That way she could hold onto the dream a little longer, before reality intruded.

But reality was already there. Sunlight had replaced the gentler moonlight, and a rooster was crowing in the back garden. The Villa d'Este was a memory, and tomorrow she would be leaving Italy.

She wasn't going to try to fool herself. Almost from the first time they'd met, she'd wanted to make love with Niell, and now they were lovers and would probably be so again. The thing to remember, Margo told herself, was that love hadn't changed either of them.

Yet, when she was with him like this, the boundaries of the differences that separated them seemed to blur. After all, in the short time she'd been in Italy she'd worked for a contessa and had met Carlo Monchatto, who'd been gracious enough to say he liked her work. When she was with Niell, she could almost believe that the world was her arena, too.

"Sanders and Company, International Landscape Architects." Margo mused.

"You can make it happen."

She opened her eyes and saw that Niell was watching her. His gray eyes were lazy and satisfied, and his mouth was curved in a smile. She kissed that smiling mouth before she said, "Are you into reading minds now? How did you know what I was thinking?"

"You said, 'Sanders and Company, International Landscape Architects.' You're starting to have big dreams, Margo. I like that."

"I like you," she told him.

He drew her closer. "Believe me, it's mutual. I also happen to like the effect you have on me."

His lips caressed her throat, dipped lower to nuzzle her breasts. "I like how you taste," Niell went on. "I care about you and everything about you."

Last night he'd said that he loved her. But then, night and day were poles apart. Something within Margo seemed to wither, but she immediately rallied.

Better to be open and frank about that, better to enjoy something that gave them so much pleasure without looking too far ahead, without looking for more. To ask for the moon would be like the fisherman in the story Grandma Beth had told her as a child.

"What's this about the fisherman and the fish?" She hadn't realized that she'd spoken aloud until Niell drew back a little and looked at her quizzically.

"It's an old fairy story about a fisherman who caught a magic fish," she explained.

Niell perceived that her mood had changed. The passion that had been igniting in her had been stilled into something like reflection. "Tell it to me. I like fish stories."

She leaned her cheek on his chest, and he

stroked her hair as she said, "It's not a fish story . . . well, not exactly. As I said, this fisherman caught a magical fish that offered to grant its captor's wishes in return for its freedom. The fisherman first wished for riches, then power, and then more power — and pretty soon the golden fish got fed up and took all its gifts away."

Though she had spoken lightly, Niell detected the serious note in Margo's voice.

"It's a bad analogy," he told her bracingly. "You have talent, Margo. Monchatto was impressed with your work. The contessa is ready to be your patron. *I* believe in you. The sky's the limit for Sanders and Company, International Landscape Architects."

He kissed the top of her head and, rolling over, sat up in bed. Golden sunlight washed over his powerful torso and turned the curly hairs at the nape of his neck to gold. Margo watched him stretch and thought that Niell couldn't read minds after all. He'd thought she was hesitating about her profession, while she'd been talking about feelings.

Apples and oranges . . . Margo sat up and watched Niell stride purposefully to the shower. "It's a beautiful day," he called over the running of the water. "A perfect day to go and see the Villa d'Argento."

Margo had almost forgotten about the villa

that Niell's client, Cosimo Bartolomei, had bought, but she was glad to turn her thoughts in a new direction. She asked questions about Bartolomei's villa as they dressed and later, over the basket of crusty rolls and coffee that constituted breakfast, listened with interest as Niell asked Signora Antonia if she knew where the Silver Villa was.

An animated discussion, half in Italian, half in English, followed. "According to the signora, we're not far from the villa," Niell explained to Margo. "It's in Casetta, a little town beside the sea. She says that the villa was beautiful in her grandmother's day but has since gone to seed. Still want to stop for a look?"

"I'd like to, yes. But won't we get lost again?"

The signora said that this was impossible. They only had to follow the sea road. "It is simple," she added. *Va dritto, sempre dritto.*"

"Now, why don't I have any faith in those directions?" Margo muttered as they went out into the dazzling sunshine. Then she exclaimed, "I *thought* I heard the sea last night before I slept!"

The road seemed to fall away from her into the bright ocean. Gulls danced across the water, and a ship moved slowly across the horizon. "The Tyrrhenian Sea," Niell said. "According to the signora, Casetta is northwest of us."

Casetta turned out to be a tiny town perched

on high ground above the sea. Margo was enchanted with colors: silver-gray olive trees, bright green fields accented with occasional flashes of wildflowers, dark green cypresses. But she looked doubtful as they drove up to a formidable metal gate flanked by marble pillars. The gate was locked, and nobody seemed to be around.

"Maybe we'd better not do this," she said hesitantly. "We could be shot for trespassing on private property."

"There's a side door." Niell left the car and swung open a humble wooden door some distance from the imposing main gate. "Don't worry, Bartolomei said it would be perfectly all right for us to look around."

The Villa d'Argento had definitely seen better days. The road was rutted, and the shaggy umbrella pines standing like sentinels on either side of the entrance to the road looked embarrassed to be in such a state. Beyond, overgrown holm oaks and unkempt laurels shaded statues that lined the road.

Margo felt a stab of homesickness. "This place reminds me of Lattimer House. I hope Zach is getting along with the cats."

"Don't worry about them," Niell replied. "Tell me, instead, what do you think of the place?"

Margo pushed aside a tangle of wild rose and laurel branches to admire a statue of Ceres. "I wonder who sculpted these wonderful statues? There's a feeling of . . . well, almost of wilderness here. And antiquity. I can almost imagine that Pan himself might live here."

They passed a bone-dry fountain presided over by a statue of the winged horse Pegasus, then climbed an oval staircase past a cascade of linked volutes carved in gray stone. Once this spiral-shaped cascade had been a runoff from another fountain at the top of the stairs.

"I can imagine the effect of that cascade with water from the fountain running down it. I wish I could see this place as it used to be," Margo sighed.

They strolled up the road to a spacious palazzo on top of the hill. Like the gate it was also locked and shuttered, but from any window facing west there would be an incredible view of the sea. From this vantage point, the Tyrrhenian glowed like a sunlit turquoise.

Margo sat down on a grassy bank just below the palazzo and looked dreamily over the landscape. She drew in a breath of salt-laced air sweetened by herbs and scented shrubs.

"You mentioned that your friend wants to have this place restored," Margo said.

"He and two others have formed a consortium. They mean to turn the Villa d'Argento into a hotel. They've hired a landscape architect called Fabio Luna." Niell sat down on the sunny hillside next to her and stretched out his long legs. "If *you* were Luna, how would you go about restoring it?"

Margo tilted her head to look up at the palazzo again. "I'd want to keep the feel of the place. It has what Monchatto called 'the sense of stillness.' "

"Can you be more specific?" Niell fished Margo's sketchbook out of her purse and handed it to her.

Then he watched her busy fingers and absorbed face and smiled to himself. Margo didn't realize how rare were her perception and talent. His respect for her artistry grew as the neglected villa gardens sprang to life under her pencil.

"It's very rough, of course," she was saying. "I'd have to study the place more and work up some finished sketches for you to get the idea." She paused and added dreamily, "But if I had the chance, I'd *really* go wild. It's something I've wanted to do all my life."

"You could very well have your chance," he replied.

Still half lost in her vision, she asked absently, "What's that?"

"Remember that we have a date with Cosimo Bartolomei?" She nodded. "The other two members of the consortium and Luna will be there as well."

Margo stopped sketching. She blinked several

239

times at him before realization dawned. "Niell, what's going on?"

"Luna's looking for a team to work with him on this project. Several talented landscape designers have already applied."

She realized that her mouth had fallen open. With an effort she closed it and stammered, "What m-makes you think that he'd consider me? I'm not even Italian. And I'm a complete unknown."

"Luna's team is open to international applicants. As to being unknown, Monchatto admires your work. If you ask the maestro, I'm convinced he'll put that in writing."

Margo tried to follow what Niell was saying, but her brains felt scrambled, like an unsolved jigsaw puzzle. "But . . . but wasn't our dinner with Bartolomei set for tomorrow night?"

"That was the original plan. But when I phoned him last night, he told me that he wanted to reschedule our dinner date for a meeting this afternoon. It's the only time he could get the consortium and Luna to meet with us."

"This after—" Margo couldn't even finish the word.

Niell took Margo's hands in his. "I know this is short notice, Margo. I realize that you haven't had time to complete your sketches or ready a formal presentation, and Bartolomei and the others will understand that. But I feel that it's important that they meet you, talk to you, recognize your talent."

He'd phoned Bartolomei from the pensione. The thought that he'd talked business before they'd made love made Margo feel odd. But that was Niell, she reminded herself. That was the way he was.

Margo's chest felt as if a metal bar had been clamped over it. Taking a deep breath didn't help, either. She closed her eyes and tried to think, but all she could do was imagine Ez sitting beside her on the grassy hillside, his blue eyes half hidden under bushy gray eyebrows. She recalled one of Ez's favorite sayings: If you say you can't do something, it usually means you don't want to do it.

"Why didn't you tell me all this before?" she demanded.

"I did tell you about Bartolomei, remember?" Niell asked. "It wasn't till last night that he suggested your also meeting Luna and the other members of the consortium. And I did mean to tell you last night, but we got, ah, sidetracked."

"But this morning? You could have told me this morning, for Pete's sake!"

"I wanted you to see the villa first. If you didn't care for it, that would have been that."

"I can't go to these people with just a few sketches." Margo looked down at herself in dismay. "And I sure can't go to any meeting looking like *this*."

"No problem. The contessa's farmhouse isn't far. If we leave now, we'll have time to drive there and change for the meeting before driving into Rome." Niell turned to rest his hands on her shoulders. "You have to go after what you want," he added softly.

As he repeated his credo, his hands on her shoulders conveyed warmth and confidence. Yet Margo wasn't certain. "How can I even think of getting involved in a project like this? I have work waiting for me at home. Troner's mall—"

"It'll take some time for Luna to pick his team. Then the consortium will have to decide on when to start work. Italians move slowly, so you could certainly finish your work in the States before you were needed over here." Niell slid his hands gently down her arms and took her hands. "The first time we met, you told me you'd like a chance at creating real beauty. Remember?"

Of course she remembered. Margo looked about her at the old garden and knew that to restore it to its former magnificence would be the dream of a lifetime.

Niell's hands on hers tightened. "You're a winner, Margo Sanders. I know that once you're on the right track, you'll go to the top."

The contessa believed in her. Carlo Monchatto

liked her ideas. Zach could deal with what was going on at home. And Niell . . .

"I know this has been pretty sudden," Niell was saying. "I'm sorry about the way things worked out, but that's how things happen sometimes. Still, if you feel this isn't right for you, there's no problem. I'll call Bartolomei and cancel if you want me to."

But if he did that, the opportunity might never come again. This was her chance to reach for the brass ring. Margo drew a breath full of sun-drenched fragrance and knew she couldn't let that chance pass her by.

"No, don't cancel," she told him resolutely. "Let's go for it!"

## Chapter Ten

"Signorina Sanders, will you now tell us about your plans for the Villa d'Argento?"

Margo rose to her feet. In spite of her outward air of assurance, her throat felt dry, as did her mouth. Her knees were shaking as if she'd been running for miles.

This wasn't the first presentation she'd made, for goodness' sake. She had to get hold of herself. Margo looked around the oval table at the four people she had to impress and wasn't reassured by what she saw. There was the man who'd requested her to speak, Bartolomei himself, silver-haired, impeccably groomed and attired, with the subdued luster of a diamond-and-gold tie pin in his designer neckwear. There were his partners in the consortium: Arturo Proli, heir at thirty to a fortune that had been made by his entrepreneur father; Beatrice del'Sarrano, the hardheaded businesswoman who'd married an ancient nobleman who'd left her a very wealthy widow.

Finally there was Fabio Luna. Thin, intense, and self-important, Luna had been barely polite when he greeted Margo. From the biographical profile that Niell had given her to read as they drove into Rome, Margo knew that Luna was a popular landscape architect much favored by stylish Romans. Luna apparently had style, verve, and ambition. There was something definitely predatory in the watchful black eyes behind rimless glasses.

Above Luna's head hung a massive oil by Tintoretto, and a Rubens and a Cézanne were also displayed in Bartolomei's luxurious conference room. A da Vinci sketch was almost casually exhibited in a bookcase lined with an assortment of books.

And she was supposed to impress these people. Margo realized how clammy her hands had become as she cleared her throat and began, "Unfortunately, as Mr. Kier has explained, lack of time didn't allow for anything more than rough sketches. However, these will give you some idea of how I'd proceed in restoring the Villa d'Argento."

Though she was trying to sound calm and professional, Niell could sense Margo's tension. Since entering Cosimo Bartolomei's office an hour ago, she'd been quivering with nerves, and he'd regretted subjecting her to such an ordeal. But when he once more suggested they abandon the idea, Margo had dug in her heels and stayed with it.

He hadn't been wrong about her quality, he thought proudly. She was a winner through and through.

"As I explained before, for unavoidable reasons this meeting was moved up," Niell said in a conversational tone. "Miss Sanders only had half an hour at the Villa d'Argento this morning, but even though her sketches are roughs, I think you'll agree that her concepts are unique."

He smiled at Margo as he spoke. *Courage.*

The warmth of Niell's smile connected them for a moment, and Margo stiffened her spine. Resisting an impulse to lick her lips, she began to outline her ideas. "In restoring an old estate like the villa, I feel that it's essential to retain the original mood of the place while allowing for the modern conveniences that a hotel would require. I hope I've been able to convey these ideas in my sketches."

As she continued to speak, Niell watched Margo's audience. Bartolomei nodded once or twice. The others looked unconvinced.

Arturo Proli reached out to pick up one of Margo's sketches. "A successful hotel must please its clients," he demurred. "Their perception of value may not agree with this concept of yours, signorina."

"True. The look just isn't right." With a flick

of jeweled fingers, Beatrice del'Sarrano dismissed Margo's efforts. Cynically she added, "Tourists want to see antiquity as they perceive it, not as it really is."

Margo pulled her sketchbook toward her. "I believe I understand what you mean," she replied. "Let me try a different direction, which will still preserve the *sense* of the place." Her hands moved swiftly. "Is this more to your liking, madama?"

Del'Sarrano glanced at the new sketch, then took a closer look. Her eyebrows arched in surprise. Proli pulled at his underlip. Bartolomei exclaimed, "You have changed the entire mood."

"And yet she's kept to her original ideas," Niell pointed out quietly.

Fabio Luna said something in Italian. Of them all, he alone had refused to speak in English, so Niell translated. "Signore Luna says that you've left most of the trees along the road up to the hotel intact. So many trees create a dark mood. The trees as well as much of the shrubbery must be pruned back."

Luna's tone had been dismissive, and Margo's nervousness increased.

"I agree that a lot of pruning is necessary," she said, "but it's my feeling that we must be careful when cutting down any trees. I'm sure you know that Monchatto, in his 'Essay on Ancient Gardens,' writes that before cutting down a tree he waits a year. His reasoning is that trees have different appearances during the various seasons."

For the first time Luna addressed Margo in very passable English. "I understand that you met Signore Monchatto?"

"I met the maestro at the Villa Delfiori."

Niell interjected, "You'll recall my saying that Miss Sanders has recently completed a commission for the Contessa Delfiori. Signore Monchatto saw her work and was impressed by what he feels is her considerable talent."

Luna pursed his lips. Cosimo Bartolomei gave Margo an urbane smile, then turned to the others. "I confess that I, too, am impressed. What are your thoughts, my friends?"

Beatrice del'Sarrano played with a diamond pendant the size of a hazelnut. "She has imagination and knows how to listen. Those are rare gifts. However, I reserve judgment until I have seen the final drawings and a formal proposal."

Margo felt her heart swell on a beat of hope, but Bartolomei then added, "It would not do to raise your hopes with false promises, signorina. We are interviewing several promising landscape designers. They—and you, we hope—will make a formal presentation of sketches, plan views, and written supporting statements to Signore Luna. His is the final decision. Is that agreeable to you?"

"It's very fair," Margo agreed. "I appreciate the

opportunity to compete and would like your permission to return to the villa for closer observation."

"As Miss Sanders is staying at the home of the Contessa Delfiori, she'll be conveniently close to the villa." Niell noted with satisfaction the startled look in Luna's eyes as he let *that* bit of information fall.


"How do you think it went?" Margo asked as they walked out of the plush office and into the afternoon sunlight.

Niell tucked his arm through hers. "You did a wonderful job under the circumstances. Bartolomei liked you, and you won Beatrice del'Sarrano's respect. Proli will swing with the others."

"I know I didn't impress Luna." Margo's brows were furrowed in a worried frown. "He and I aren't on the same wavelength, Niell. Cutting down all those trees will totally change the look of the place."

"The consortium will have the final word," Niell reminded her. "Don't worry about Luna, Margo. He's a snob—and a social climber. You saw how he acted when I mentioned that you were staying at the contessa's Farmhouse. Now that he feels you're the contessa's protégée, his manners toward you will improve." His voice held a trace of contempt as he added, "Luna's the sort of man who's awed by titles."

"I'd rather stand on my own merits," Margo protested.

He gave her a one-armed hug, and she was conscious of the lean, hard-muscled body pressed against her side. "You've got plenty of . . . merits. Want me to tell you about them?"

"Yes, please, but later. Right now I've got to focus. I'm going to give those other candidates a run for their money."

Niell watched Margo's eyes turn to gold as excitement overtook her. This was Margo as she should be, he thought, vibrant and alive with ideas and challenge. He'd been right. Once away from the penny-ante jobs that had held her captive in Carlin, she was finally ready to soar with eagles.

"I wish I didn't have to leave for Monaco tomorrow," he said. "On the whole, though, it may be a good thing. You'll have plenty of time to work — without interruption."

The implication in his deep voice brought images that spun her away out of time and place. The consortium, the afternoon's talk, her own plans, the traffic around them all drifted away, and she thought of moon-drenched flowers and pleasure so intense that she wanted to ignore the busy Roman street and walk into Niell's arms.

When she looked at him like that, Niell found it hard to concentrate. Her eyes expressed everything he wanted—and more. Her mouth was curved softly, inviting kisses. Niell was really tempted to forget about his client in Monaco and stay at the contessa's Roman villa with Margo.

But then, he reasoned, he would spend only a day—two at the outside—in Monaco. That would mean he could spend a few more days with Margo before returning to London. And they would still have tonight.

"We'll have dinner on the terrace overlooking the eternal city." With his mind on the night to come, he was surprised when she didn't respond. He looked at her, and her expression told him her mind was far away. "Why are you looking so serious suddenly?" Niell asked.

"I was thinking that now that I'm going to do a presentation for Luna, I'll have to call and tell Zach that I won't be home for another week."

Another week with Niell. Happiness chased away all other thought as they drove through the gathering twilight to the contessa's Farmhouse, a sturdy yet attractive stone house set into the side of a verdant hillside. Margo had loved its ageless look since she'd seen it this morning, and now the Farmhouse welcomed her like an old friend. So did the smiling maidservant who greeted them at the door and told Niell that a telephone call had come for the signore in his absence.

While Niell returned the call, Margo went upstairs to her room to wash and change out of the suit she'd worn for her presentation. It was a balmy evening, and from the window of her room, Margo watched as the sky began to darken over the city. The scent of honeysuckle rose from the garden below, and leaning on the windowsill, she drew in the sweet fragrance. The place reminded her of Taylor, she thought. It was hard to believe that she'd just made a presentation to a consortium worth billions of dollars.

She wondered how Zach would react to the news that she wanted to work on Luna's team. No doubt he'd be appalled. But then, Margo reasoned, Zach hadn't seen the Villa d'Argento. Her heart swelled at the memory of that beautiful place. Once Zach looked at her sketches and the photographs she was going to take tomorrow, he'd understand that the chance to reconstruct the villa was an opportunity no landscape designer could bear to pass up. And if he didn't . . .

"Darn it, I'll *make* him understand," she muttered.

There was a light knock and Niell's voice at the door. When Margo opened it, she found him looking grave. "That phone call was from my client in Monaco," he explained. "A problem's come up. Nothing serious, but I have to drive out there tonight."

Margo felt a sense of loss. "Really? Must you?"

He nodded and, putting his arms around her, held her closely for a moment. "I really wish this hadn't happened."

But some part of him was already gone, Margo knew intuitively. Though his arms held her, Niell's concentration had shifted to Monaco and to whatever challenges lay ahead. "I'm sorry, *amore*. I'll be back as soon as I can. I need to take the rental car, but the butler assures me that one of the contessa's automobiles will be at your disposal tomorrow."

He'd called her "love," but the word had been said lightly, and he was whistling as he went off to prepare for the journey. Margo reminded herself that she was living in reality, not in a fairy tale where a kiss was all that was necessary to transform a man's character.

Last night was last night. Tonight Niell would be on his way to Monaco. For a moment she felt a sharp twinge of regret, and then her heart lifted. Niell would be back soon . . . and meanwhile she had work to do.

After Niell had gone, she tried to reach Zach at Lattimer House. He wasn't in, so she left a message and then went to work. Her labor continued late into the night, but sunrise found her driving to the Villa d'Argento where she spent the day photographing various sites and sketching others. The maid had packed her a lunch, and

Margo blissfully munched crusty bread, cheese, and fruit as she prowled about the old villa, finding new delights: a lovely old fountain surrounded by laurel, holm oak trees screening caryatids, a garden of boxwood arranged in geometric patterns.

She'd taken several rolls of film and her sketchbook was bulging by the time she returned to the Farmhouse where the first thing she saw was the contessa's Rolls. Margo went in search of her hostess and found Alicia Delfiori on the terrazzo enjoying a cappuccino after her exhausting drive.

She welcomed Margo enthusiastically. "I learn from the servants that you 'ave been busy, *cara,*" she exclaimed. "I am exhaust' from this long trip, but you look 'appy and busy. *Va bene.* Tell me what you 'ave been doing."

The contessa was deeply interested in Margo's meeting with the consortium. She approved of Margo's drawings and sketches and called them a true balance between nature and art. "Carlo is right — you 'ave talent," she declared. "The consortium is sure to see that. It is, as you Americans say, a sure bet."

"Thank you. Let's hope Fabio Luna will feel the same way."

"We shall see. I am invited to a party at my friend the Princess Lancetta's tomorrow evening, and you will come with me. I will ask Marcella to invite Luna also so that he sees us together."

The contessa added shrewdly. "The man will have respect for you. He adores titles."

"So Niell told me," Margo murmured.

The contessa's dark eyes grew even more interested. "Tell me more about you and Niell and your adventures at the Villa d'Este. I 'ear that you became lost the first night. It was most romantic, I think?"

Moonlight and the scent of roses and a nightingale singing its heart out . . . Margo felt her cheeks grow warm under the contessa's worldly gaze. "Yes, it was."

"I'm not surprised. When you were together at Delfiore, there was *attrazione*—the attraction between you," the contessa said. "It is natural that you are drawn together."

Margo looked beyond the cheerful garden to where Rome had begun to sparkle with light. The moon hadn't yet risen, and the tiny splinters of electricity seemed suspended in space.

"I wonder. We're very different, Alicia. We don't always see things the same way."

"And for you that is a problem?"

"Yes, it is. At least, I think so." Margo sighed. "I'm really not sure what I think anymore."

"In every relationship there is a moment of truth, a point where one proceeds forward or backs away." With true Italian pragmatism, the contessa shrugged. "You will know what to do when that moment comes, *cara*. Till then, why not 'go with the flow,' as you Americans say?"

There was a footstep behind them, and the contessa's maid coughed apologetically. "There is a telephone call for the signorina," she said.

"Ah, 'e misses you already," the contessa observed. Then she added, "Remember what I say. Go always with the flow."

But when Margo went into the other room to take the call, she heard Zach bellow, "That you, Margo?"

Margo winced. Zach seemed to be under the impression that she couldn't hear him when they were talking long-distance, so he always shouted. "Yes," she told him. "Listen, I called earlier because—"

He interrupted her. "Sorry I didn't get back to you sooner. We've got problems, Margo. Troner wants to bring in his own mason, plumber, and carpenter to work on the mall. You know that means trouble."

Margo's heart sank. "Do you know any of the people he wants to bring in?"

"The plumber and carpenter seem okay, but the mason's a guy called John Gifford. I've worked with him before. Talks a good game but likes to cut corners."

Zach had other bad news. Troner had had second thoughts about the layout of the mall. "He wants to move the central staircase, and that means you'll have to redesign part of the atrium,"

Zach explained gloomily. "We'll probably have to get more tiles—which won't be easy on such short notice, not to mention the fact that the p. and s. that Troner gave us isn't going to cover the costs."

"Have you tried talking to Troner?" But Margo realized before she finished speaking that this wasn't Zach's job—it was hers. There was no way that she could take care of these problems from overseas. "I'll be home tomorrow," she said, and noted the intense relief in Zach's voice as he volunteered to pick her up at Logan Airport.

The contessa looked astonished when Margo explained why she needed to leave for America in the morning. "This man Alloway, is 'e not your representative in the United States? Why cannot 'e manage your affairs in your absence?" When Margo explained that it was her responsibility to talk to the owners of the Mall at Mountain View, the contessa added, "And the presentation you are to make to Luna?"

Margo realized she hadn't even been thinking of Luna or the Villa d'Argento. Watching the moon rise over Rome, she'd been thinking that she and Niell were to have watched it rise together. Now she would be leaving Italy without a chance to see him again.

"I've taken many photographs," she told the contessa. "They and my sketches are all I need to create finished drawings. I can send plan-views

257

and drawings to Luna—fax them, even."

"*Va bene*." The contessa put an arm around Margo's waist as she added, "I will be your advocate, *cara*. I will speak to this Luna tomorrow at Marcella's and will keep 'im—'ow you say it—on 'is toes while you attend to difficulties back at 'ome."

Huddled into her sweater, Margo stood on the curb just outside the international arrivals terminal at Logan Airport and looked around for Zach.

Where was the man? Her plane had landed forty-five minutes ago, and yet he was nowhere to be seen. Margo winced as a cab pulled up and sprayed her with water. She'd forgotten that in Boston June days were often dreary, rainy, and cold.

"Margo! Hey, Margo!" Zach was splashing through puddles as he jogged toward her. "Sorry I'm late," he exclaimed as he panted up. "There was an accident on the expressway. You know how that can hold you up for hours."

Talking nonstop, he caught her in a bear hug and reached for her luggage. "Logan has got to have the worst parking system in the world. The guys that designed the place had to be on something. Had to park at the other end of the world."

"How's Naomi? And how have the cats been?"

Margo managed to ask as Zach dodged a puddle the size of a small lake.

"Felines are fine. Been feeding them every day, like you asked me to. Lady Hamilton and Traffy are nice animals, but that Lord Nelson's got to be the meanest dude this side of the Mississippi." Zach loaded Margo's suitcase into his pickup as he said, "Naomi told me to tell you she was sorry not to be able to come to meet you. Her mom's in the hospital."

"Again? Is it serious? Why didn't anyone tell me?"

"Why would we worry you when you were too far away to do any good?" Zach demanded. "She's okay now, but it was pretty hairy for a while back there. Old lady got pneumonia, which isn't good for people her age. Naomi's worn herself out worrying—almost got herself sick, too. Watch out for the puddles," he added unnecessarily. "Been raining for a solid week, which is bad for business."

"Tell me what's happening with the mall," Margo asked as Zach began to turn his pickup toward Carlin.

"Like I told you, Troner's dead set on bringing in his people. Tried talking to him, but it didn't do any good." Zach's mustache quivered with insult as he continued, "These corporate types are all the same—all's they care about is making a buck."

Margo had a sudden image of Zach talking to Bartolomei and his consortium. "I'll set up a meeting with Troner as soon as possible,' she promised. "Now, about your problems with this mason, Gifford. You didn't get into a fight with him, did you?"

"Who, me?" Zach cried indignantly. "I'm the most flexible guy I know. But Gifford's not *right*. Troner or no Troner, I don't want him on my crew."

Zach's pickup had a faulty defogger, so they had to drive with the windows open. As if to accompany the rain that gusted in from the windows, Zach gave Margo the local news. Mrs. Sheridan down the street had been amazed when her rhodies actually bloomed this year. The Amberlys had been almost friendly since Emma's wildflower garden won an award from the Carlin Garden Club. And he'd read in the Carlin *Herald* that Rupert Brooke, attorney-at-law, was set to retire after practicing in Carlin for fifty years.

"But what about you?" he added. "What've you been up to in Italy, Margo? From your postcards it sounds like you had a blast."

A description of the Rose Island and the Villa d'Este kept Margo busy until they took the Carlin exit, but her spirits suffered a check when she saw how dreary her property appeared. Soaked by rain, Lattimer House fairly drooped, and the garden looked sodden. Once inside the house, however, she was welcomed by Lady Hamilton, who yowled with joy as she rubbed up against Margo's leg, and by Traffy, who leaped on her shoulder and purred in her ear.

"Where's Lord Nelson?" Margo wondered.

Zach looked grim. "Who knows and who cares? That feline gave me a big scratch the other day when I was feeding these guys." He ruffled the fur around Lady Hamilton's ear. "Left the basement window open a crack for him like you said, so he's probably out someplace raising Cain."

Margo went to the back door and shouted for Lord Nelson. When this didn't produce results, she rattled a cat-food can with a fork. "He shouldn't be out in the wet," she worried. "After what happened to him, I mean. I hope he's all right."

Zach muttered something about cats who were too dumb to know when to come in out of the rain. Then he added proudly, "Want you to see how we've been doing while you were gone. I'll get the books."

As she looked over Naomi's carefully entered ledgers, Margo's spirits rose considerably. "This is great," she exclaimed.

"Have to admit Naomi helped a lot while you were gone," Zach allowed. When Margo stared at him in surprise, he added with studied nonchalance, "Her politics are all messed up, but she's

261

not so bad as a bookkeeper."

A peremptory thump at the back door interrupted him. When Margo yanked the door open, Lord Nelson swaggered in. Ignoring Zach, he padded forward and, to Margo's astonishment, rubbed against her. When she bent to stroke his shaggy head, a thunderous sound erupted from him.

"He's *purring*," Margo gasped. "Will wonders never cease! Now I can believe that Luna will hire me after all."

"Luna?" Zach demanded. "Who's Luna? You haven't taken any other jobs for us, have you?"

His alarm seemed to grow as he listened to Margo's explanation. "I don't know about all this, Margo," he protested. "We have more than we can handle on our plates right now."

Well, she hadn't expected handstands, Margo reminded herself. Aloud she said, "I'm aware of that. But as Niell explained, the restoration of the Villa d'Argento isn't going to happen overnight. Italians like to take their time."

"I might've figured it was Kier's idea," Zach grumbled. "Anyway, first things first, Margo. When are you going to talk to Troner?"

She phoned that afternoon and set up an appointment for the next day at Troner's office. The interview wasn't a successful one. Troner was adamant about making the changes to his plans of the mall, and he was equally insistent about bringing in his own subcontractors.

Zach didn't seem surprised at the news. "Are we staying with it, or are we walking?" was all he asked.

Since she'd had time to think things through on the long, rainy drive back to Carlin, Margo had an answer ready. "We stay. We can't allow ourselves to be flapped by a shift in plans. You said that the carpenter and plumber are okay, so just keep an eye on Gifford."

"You're darn tooting I will," Zach growled.

Margo canceled a lunch date with Naomi and spent the rest of the afternoon reworking her design for the mall. She was still hard at it when the phone rang. "How are things over on that side of the world?" Niell inquired when she picked up the receiver.

He seemed so near that by closing her eyes, Margo could almost imagine him in the next room. "Fine," she replied.

"That's not what Alicia said. I wish I were there for you."

Every nerve and fiber in Margo echoed that wish. "Don't be silly and don't worry. It's not terminal. Troner just wants changes in the original design."

"I'll look over your contract with him, but at this stage of the game he's probably within his rights to make changes." Niell paused. "How is Zach taking the shift in plans? The contessa told me he was upset when he phoned you at the Farmhouse."

"Troner wants to bring in his own people, and Zach doesn't care for the mason," Margo explained. "So. Are you still in Monaco?"

He told her that he was. "When I heard you'd flown home, I decided to stay on for a day and visit friends before leaving for London. It's sunny and warm here—and I miss you."

She could hear music and laughter in the background and tried to imagine a warm sun and a turquoise blue sea, but the sound of rain kept intruding and ruining the picture. With an effort she stifled a sigh. "I miss you, too. Have fun," she added as cheerfully as she could, "and please don't worry."

"I'll give you the number of my hotel in London. Call me if you need me, okay? I'm going to be tied up for at least a week with the Herris people before I come home."

*And you'll be so nice to come home to.*

As the words touched his mind, Niell found himself wishing he could cancel his meeting in London and fly home to Margo. For a moment he actually contemplated this possibility—and then common sense rescued him. He'd worked hard and long to get Herris Company just where he wanted it. It would be insanity to do anything to jeopardize the final stages of the negotiations, and besides, Margo was capable of handling things herself.

"At least there's something I can do to help at this end," he told her. "I'm going to phone Luna and tell him you'll fax your plan views and finished drawings to him."

Margo was grateful for the businesslike note in his voice. It wouldn't do for her to get sentimental at this stage of the game.

"Thank you, please do that. I'm just about through with the mall revisions, so I'm going to start on the final drawings of the Villa d'Argento tonight."

She worked through the night, snatching a few hours of sleep toward dawn, and when she awoke, she realized that the sun was shining. Taking this as a good omen, she immersed herself in her work once more.

The drawings went well. When she finally had them and the plan views completed, Margo felt exhilarated with what she'd accomplished. She hopped in Niell's car and drove out to Carlin Business Supplies and, crossing her fingers, faxed her presentation to Luna. She'd done all she could, she told herself, and now all she could do was wait — and see how Zach was getting on with Troner's people.

As she'd expected, Zach was at the mall site along with the builder, the architect, and the work crew. "Work starts tomorrow," he reported when Margo drove up. "We're coordinating our schedules."

He introduced her to the subcontractors, and Margo was pleasantly surprised. From what Zach had told her about John Gifford, she'd expected a mason from hell. The reality was a pleasant-spoken middle-aged man who assured her that he was a team player.

"I've told Zach that I just want to get the job done the best I can," Gifford said.

"I'm sure that's what we all want," she agreed.

Zach made a noise like a snort, and glancing at him, Margo saw that a mulish expression had settled on his long face. A niggle of impatience touched her, and she stilled it by reminding herself that Zach no doubt had his reasons. Of course, it wouldn't hurt him to learn some diplomatic behavior. Otherwise, how could she leave him in charge and expand Sanders and Company—perhaps even to do business overseas?

The mall foundation was poured the next day. Margo's presence wasn't required, so she drove out to Pittsfield to talk to a bank manager who wanted to do a planting at the front of his building. This took some time, and when she returned home, she found Zach's pickup parked in her driveway.

"Margo, we've got problems," he called, striding to meet her as she stepped out of her vehicle.

266

"Gifford?"

Zach nodded grimly.

"What happened? Didn't he show up on time, or what?"

"Oh, he showed, all right." Disgust was thick in Zach's voice. "I just happened to check with the store where he gets his supplies. He's using shoddy materials, Margo. Probably skimming off the top and putting the balance in his pocket."

There was a sudden heaviness in Margo's chest. "Can you prove this?" she asked.

Zach shook his head. "He's too smart an operator for that, and he's smooth. But I've been around the business long enough to know when someone's pulling a fast one." Zach stopped short and looked hard at Margo. "Don't you believe me?"

He sounded so hurt that Margo wanted to put her arms around him and hug him, but at the same time a part of her mind was playing devil's advocate. Zach had never liked Gifford. Troner had hired Gifford over his protests. Was it possible that Zach's bias was making him see things that weren't there?

"I can't go to Troner just on hearsay," she pointed out. "Hang loose for a while, Zach, and see what happens."

"Are you saying I'm supposed to look the other way?" he demanded.

Margo struggled for patience. She reminded

herself that in Zach's shoes, she'd probably have felt the same way. But she was in charge, and she had to assimilate all the facts and then make a decision that would be the best for Sanders and Company.

The trouble was, she wasn't quite sure which decision she should make. She trusted Zach's instincts, but at the same time they needed Troner's good will.

"Gifford is Troner's choice," she said at last. "If I go to him with accusations I can't verify, he'll probably laugh in my face."

"We can quit," Zach shot back.

"That's not an option. We've invested time and money in this venture, and besides, Sanders and Company can't afford to get the reputation of walking off a job." Margo drew a deep breath and made her decision. "Let's just try to coexist with Gifford. If he's really crooked, he'll hang himself."

"Maybe. And maybe by that time it'll be too late." Zach glared at a point over Margo's head as he rasped, "I'll tell you one thing, Margo. I'm not working with any chiseler, no matter what you say. That's final."

He sounded so stubborn and self-righteous that Margo's patience evaporated. "Look," she snapped, "I'm not asking you to love the guy, just to work with him for a while. Will you please try to act professional in this matter? We have a job to do."

The words were out before she could think, and now it was too late to call them back. Zach's lantern-jawed face quivered with indignation and hurt.

"So now I'm not professional." He folded his arms across his chest and pushed his Red Sox cap back on his forehead. "You've changed since you went to Italy."

"I have not! Besides, we're not talking about me," Margo cried, but Zach ignored her.

"You've started to act like those big mucky-mucks you were telling me about—the ones who run that consortium that Kier introduced you to. Making a buck's all *those* guys care about, but I never expected that kind of stuff from you, Margo."

"You're talking foolishness," Margo said.

"Don't think so. You've been worrying more about those plans you're sending abroad than about our work here," Zach accused.

"I promised Luna I'd send him those plans." Nettled by Zach's mulish expression, Margo retorted, "If you'd handled things better here at home, I'd have had time to finish my work in Italy."

"So now you're saying I didn't do my job, is that it?" Zach's eyes narrowed. "Maybe I should just quit so you can hire yourself someone else."

This was an empty threat. Zach would never

walk out on her. All she had to do, Margo knew, was to tell him that she was sorry, that she believed him about Gifford, that she would do as he asked. But right now she didn't feel like smoothing down his temperamental feathers. Everything she'd said was the truth, and besides, Zach *had* to learn to be more flexible. He had to learn to see *her* side of a situation as well as his own.

The stony silence stretched out for a moment. Then Zach turned his back on her and strode away. As he reached his pickup, he turned to say, "I'd have stood by *you,* Margo."

Margo cursed out loud as Zach gunned his pickup's engine and peeled out of her driveway. She had to restrain a childish desire to jump up and down and scream. Instead, she stormed off to the house, rattled the stuck kitchen door till it opened, and slammed it behind her, scaring Traffy and Lady Hamilton, who were snoozing under the kitchen table.

If she couldn't convince Zach to work with Gifford, there'd be a nasty showdown in which Troner would almost surely take Gifford's part. Next morning Margo canceled all her appointments and drove to the mall site. As things stood, she wasn't sure whether Zach would even come to work that day, and it was with great relief that she saw his pickup approaching. But her relief was short-lived when she saw how Zach went out of his way to find fault with Gifford.

Not surprisingly, the mason complained to Margo. "I'm about ready to quit," he grumbled. "I can't do my work with this joker throwing his weight around."

Things couldn't go on this way, Margo knew. "I'll talk to Zach," she promised.

The prospect of another confrontation with her contractor plus an unusually busy day took its toll, and by evening Margo felt as if she'd been wrung out to dry. She had a headache that wouldn't quit as she was driving home, and to make things worse, it had started to rain again. Margo raced the raindrops into her house and saw her answering machine blinking. *Niell.* But the message was from the business supply store telling her that a fax from Italy had come in and was awaiting her.

A fax from Italy. Margo plopped down at the kitchen table with her heart doing a Gene Krupa number inside her.

The answer from Luna had come too quickly. It had to be a rejection, Margo reasoned. When Traffy jumped up into her lap, Margo buried her face in his soft, sweet-smelling fur. "I'm a coward," she whispered. "I don't want to find out that I can't work on that beautiful old place."

Traffy purred and patted her cheek with his paw. In the other room Margo could hear Lady Hamilton "talking" to Lord Nelson. The old re-

271

frigerator clicked in with a whir that could awaken the dead, the grandfather clock in the hall struck the hour. All the old, now-familiar, beloved sounds of home . . . but somehow they weren't enough.

Maybe Zach was right, Margo thought. Maybe she had changed, because right now she knew that she wanted to work on Luna's team so badly that nothing else really mattered. Nothing—not even the problem between Zach and Gifford—held a candle to the news that awaited her at Carlin Business supplies.

All the way to the business supply store Margo gave herself a pep talk. If it was bad news, she wasn't going to be disappointed. There'd be other opportunities, for Pete's sake. But once she was inside the store and she had the fax in her hands, she realized she was shaking so hard she could hardly make out what Luna had sent her. Not wanting to make a perfect fool of herself in public, she went back to the BMW and settled herself in the driver's seat before looking to see what had been sent.

There was a letter and several plan views. She scanned the letter first. "Yes!" Margo exulted. "Oh, *yes!*"

The letter told her that Luna approved of her presentation and wanted to have her on his team of landscape designers. He enclosed some plan views with the architectural drawings for the new

Villa d'Argento.

She wanted to pore over the plan views right then and there, but it was getting dark, and anyway she needed to be alone to savor the moment. In a sort of trance Margo took Luna's material home. Then she spread his plan for the restoration of the villa on her drawing board and took a good long look.

She couldn't believe what she saw. This couldn't be what the consortium wanted for the Villa d'Argento. Margo backtracked over the plan views, superimposed over the architect's blueprints, and felt sickened as she realized that there was no mistake.

Luna's plan called for having the main road shorn of all the old cypresses and holm oaks. In their stead Luna had drawn in neat laurel and boxwood hedges and stylish lamps that would illuminate the statues. Closer to the hotel, he had eliminated the fountain that cascaded down the slope. Replacing it was a new, oval fish pool presided over by a modern sculpture.

Margo's hands were shaking as she set down the plan views. There was no denying that what Luna proposed had a slick sort of glamor. Under his direction, Villa d'Argento would become a sleek, modern, stylish hotel. The only problem was that these plans went against everything she had felt in that lovely old place. The aura of tranquility, of nature, and a sense of history

273

would disappear completely.

She'd been hired to join Luna's team, Margo reminded herself. An entire vista was opening to her. That should have made her happy, but somehow the prospect made her incredibly miserable.

A scratching sound at the door told her that Lord Nelson wanted in. Distractedly Margo went to the door and opened it, and the big cat entered, rubbed himself against her. Automatically she bent down to pat him.

"Where've you been . . ." she began, but then her words trailed off in a gasp. The hand that had patted Lord Nelson was covered with blood.

# Chapter Eleven

Lord Nelson growled deep in his throat but allowed Margo to examine his wounds. When she saw how meekly he submitted to being put into the carrying cage, she became really concerned.

Lady Hamilton didn't help matters. As soon as she saw how badly her consort was wounded, she started to keen at the top of her lungs, and Margo had to shut her upstairs in her bedroom. It had started to rain harder, and water trickled down Margo's neck as she loaded the caged Lord Nelson into the pickup.

"Why can't you remember you live in a decent neighborhood?" she scolded worriedly as Lord Nelson snarled feebly and attempted to chew the bars of his cage. "One of these days you're going to run out of all your nine lives. You want Lady Hamilton to be a widow?"

Dr. Molinski said much the same thing. "This character must have a death wish. Better leave him here. He's either been in the mother of all cat fights, or he's tangled with a dog. I want to make sure there's no infection and fever." Then he advised Margo to go home and take two aspirins. "You look feverish yourself," he told her.

Weariness set in as she drove home, but that was the least of her problems. The kitchen door stuck again, and she got soaking wet trying to get it open. Once inside she discovered two inches of white powder all over the kitchen. Traffy had discovered the flour bin.

"Trafalgar!" Margo yelled and in answer was treated to Lady Hamilton's mournful caterwauls. Muttering to herself, she went upstairs to change. Lady Hamilton leaped off the bed as she opened the door, yowling her grief and abandonment. Margo took the distraught feline in her arms and tried to soothe her, but Lady Hamilton wasn't about to be consoled so easily. She jumped out of Margo's arms and began to roam through the house searching for Lord Nelson and wailing like a banshee.

In all the racket, Margo hardly heard the phone ring. When she lifted the receiver, Naomi's voice asked, "What's going on out there?"

Margo began to relate her cat's latest misadventure, but Naomi interrupted her. "I mean, what's going on between you and Zach? He was just over at my place, and he looked like he'd

276

lost his best friend. Maybe you were kind of rough on him."

"Rough on him!" Margo repeated, astonished.

"I can understand why you'd need proof about what Gifford's doing," Naomi continued. "Zach isn't practical, as you very well know. But he couldn't be dishonest to save his hide." She paused. "He's hurting because he thinks you're siding with Gifford against him."

Since when had Naomi been Zach's advocate? "That's not true," Margo protested. "I believe him, but I just can't go up to Troner and demand he fire Gifford. Why are you giving me a hard time on this?"

"Because I believe Zach has your best interests at heart." Naomi broke off to explain, "See, we worked on the books together while you were in Italy, and I got to know Zach a lot better than I did before. He's not one who lets down his friends. When Mom got sick and I needed a friend, Zach was always there for me."

It wasn't until she'd hung up from talking to Naomi that Margo realized she hadn't even mentioned Luna's offer to her friend. She tried calling her back but found the line busy and, feeling more unsettled than ever, went downstairs. Here she found that Trafalgar had returned to the scene of the crime and that white paw prints now led all the way across the living-room and into the woodbox where he'd fallen

277

fast asleep. Too dispirited even to start cleaning, she poured herself a cold cup of coffee from the morning's percolator, and reread Luna's letter.

But thoughts of Zach kept intruding. She told herself that she'd been right taking the stand she did. It was what had to be done if she wanted the job finished. Margo tried to drum up some righteous indignation by telling herself that she was only the designer, for Pete's sake, and that Zach was supposed to run interference for her with the subcontractors and make her life easier, not harder.

Niell had said that Zach wasn't the kind of contractor she needed, and maybe he was right. Margo knew that all this sounded perfectly reasonable, but when she thought of Zach's hurt face, she found that she had a hard, unpleasant knot in her stomach.

Then there was this decision she needed to make about Luna. So many decisions, and none of them clear cut. Restlessly, she turned away from the window and reached for the phone. If ever she needed advice, it was now. She knew what Niell would say, but there was another point of view that she wanted, as well.

Her grandfather answered the phone on the second ring. "Margie!" he exclaimed. "How are you, sugar?"

The rain, the day's aggravation, even the years

seemed to drift away as Margo curled up in a chair by the phone and let her grandfather's familiar voice fill her ears with soothingly familiar talk. Grandma Beth was at a church bazaar, Ez said, and he was in the kitchen sneaking an extra piece of her cherry cobbler. The weather was fine, and he'd spent the day pruning the boxwood hedges. The Johnsons' youngest daughter had gotten married to her high-school sweetheart. Yellow finches had built a nest on the south side of the house, under the eaves.

Margo could picture the house and the nest of finches. She closed her eyes and wished herself back in Taylor. Ez sounded content with himself, happy in his own skin. He sounded the way she'd used to feel herself.

"Ez," she said, "I need your advice."

While she told him about the Villa d'Argento, her grandfather simply listened. "Sounds like a grand place, Margie," he then commented. "To work on a place like that is something most folks'd give their eyeteeth to do."

"So you're advising me to do it?" Margo asked.

Instead of answering right away, Ez said, "Remember the time we were wondering on whether or not to put in a fence of forsythia?"

"Sure. Grandma thought it'd look great, but then you both decided against it."

"Forsythia looks pretty in the spring, all gold

and fresh like the sun. But then we got to figuring that the blooming season'd only last four weeks and that forsythia can look pretty ratty in the winter."

Ez paused. "Do what makes you happy, shug. I don't mean what makes you happy for today or even tomorrow, but for the long term. Now, tell me about Lattimer House. What've you done to it lately?"

As Margo answered his questions, she realized she'd neglected her property lately. At one time restoring Lattimer House had been the most important thing in her life. Now, because new and important matters had come up, it had been relegated to the back burner.

*Like Zach?* The question came out of left field and hit her a low blow right in her already aching conscience, and after hanging up the phone, Margo went to stand with her forehead pressed against the cold, damp windowpane. It was pitch dark outside, but she could picture the soggy, neglected garden. The weeds would be back and many of the annuals must have drowned. A month or so and the place would look the way it had before she tried to clean it up.

Enough, already, she told herself. Another minute of this and she'd start howling as loudly as Lady Hamilton. But the cat seemed to have settled down. At least, she'd stopped her awful caterwauling.

Maybe she was asleep with Traffy? When she found she wasn't, Margo called for her. There was no answer, so Margo went looking. Lady Hamilton wasn't upstairs, nor was she in any of her favorite hiding places.

Feeling a vague disquiet, Margo went down to the basement and discovered rain blowing in. Neat, wet cat prints led to the open basement window.

It was pretty clear that the distraught Siamese had gone looking for Lord Nelson. "But Lady Hamilton *never* goes out alone," Margo fretted. "She'll get scared and disoriented. And besides, she doesn't have any claws. If she runs into the animal that mauled Lord Nelson . . ."

She had to find the cat before she wandered too far from the house. Margo ran back upstairs and was hunting for her boots when she heard a knock on the door. Perhaps someone had found Lady Hamilton? Clutching her boots, Margo ran to the door and pulled it open to find Niell standing on the doorstep.

He wore a business suit with his shirt open at the collar and had a bottle of champagne tucked under his arm. He was carrying a single, perfect red rose in a froth of baby's breath. Rain glistened on his dark hair and eyelashes, and he was smiling at her surprise.

"Hi, there," he said. "Glad to see me?"

*He* was glad to see her, Niell knew. Days and

nights away from Margo had caused the act of missing her to solidify into an actual physical ache.

He'd never worked as hard as he'd done in order to get back to Margo. He'd worked on the Herris contract with such concentrated energy that he didn't have time for anything else. For the past week he'd hardly tasted what he ate, hardly seen anything or anyone but his work and his clients. He'd gone no place except to the conference room and to his hotel. Then on the last day in London, he'd stopped at Wartski's of London.

In Niell's breast pocket lay a diamond pendant in a black velvet box. When he'd first admired it, he'd fantasized about the look in Margo's eyes when she saw the perfect jewel, and on the taxi ride from Albany Airport—the closest international airport to Carlin—he'd continued that scenario. When Margo opened the door and found him standing there, he was sure she'd melt into his arms.

But instead, she was looking at him as if she'd seen a ghost. She appeared distraught. Her hair was wet, and there was a huge blob of flour on her nose, more on her shirt and jeans. Behind her, Niell could see that the kitchen looked as if a tornado had hit it.

"Ah, is everything all right?" he wondered as Margo grabbed at his arms, practically dragging him into the kitchen out of the rain.

"I didn't know — I thought you weren't coming back to Boston until the end of the week." Margo forced herself to stop babbling and added, "When did you get back?"

"An hour and a half ago. I flew in to Albany because I wanted to be here with you sooner." Niell tried to hug Margo and realized that there was something between them. He looked down and focused on the boots she was holding against her chest. "Were you going someplace?" he demanded.

"Lady Hamilton's lost. I've got to go looking for her."

So it was only some crisis with the cats. Niell felt himself relax as he soothed, "Let her alone, Margo. She'll come home by herself."

But Margo was already reaching for her poncho. "You know what a chicken she is. She's scared of her own shadow. When I found her in Boston, she was half dead with fear." Margo shrugged into her poncho and clapped a shapeless rain hat on her head. "She's gone looking for Lord Nelson, of course. Stay here and . . . and have a cup of coffee. I'll be back soon."

Niell managed to step in front of her as she was heading for the kitchen door. He put his arms around her and held her firmly. "Ease up," he said. "You're going too fast for me. Let's

283

take it from the top. What's that rascal gotten into this time?"

"Lord Nelson had another fight and tore himself up," Margo explained. Half of her registered how good it felt to be in Niell's arms, but half of her was already cataloguing the places a frightened Siamese could have got to. "I'll tell you the rest later."

There was no use reasoning with her. "Do you want me to look for the cat, too?" Niell asked in a resigned voice.

Her eyes shone with relief. It was, Niell thought, as if she were really looking at *him* for the first time tonight. "Would you?" she breathed. "She's small, and she could be anywhere. There's a poncho in the hall closet—No, wait," she blurted out as Niell opened the closet and several boxes crashed to the floor. "I meant to clean out that closet, but I haven't had time. The poncho is in the back there, behind the vacuum cleaner."

She was out of the door before Niell could speak. Gingerly he extracted the poncho from the closet. Though he had no desire to go back out into the rain, he knew Margo wouldn't rest until she found her cat and got it safely home.

If he didn't care for Margo—no, damn it all, if he didn't *love* the woman—he would never consider such a dim-witted move. Niell called up a rueful smile as he adjusted his plans. After they'd found the blasted cat, there'd be time to talk about the Villa d'Argento and her incredible good fortune in landing a job with Luna. Then they'd celebrate her good luck with champagne and the diamond pendant—and love.

Cheered by that pleasant prospect, Niell plunged into the rain. He could hear Margo calling for her cat some distance away. Shining a flashlight in the direction of her voice, he saw her wandering about the property. He began to follow her and immediately sank up to his ankles in mud.

"Is that you, Niell?" Margo called worriedly from the other end of the garden. "Are you okay?"

Who else would it be? Extricating himself from the mud, Niell asked, "Where do you want me to start looking?"

"Start with under the bushes. She's small and blends in with the background. If she doesn't want to be found, it's going to be hard to locate her."

"If she doesn't want to be found, why are we bothering?" Niell wondered aloud, but Margo wasn't listening. Grimly he began to investigate the sodden shrubbery.

"Have you found her yet?" Margo called from the distance.

"No!"

He sounded as if he were talking through

clenched teeth, and Margo couldn't really blame him. "I'm sorry about this," she said. "I'm just so afraid Lady Hamilton might stray into the way of a passing car and get run over. She hasn't got street sense."

The wretched beast didn't have any sense at all. Nor did he, Niell thought as a wet tree branch slapped him across the face. Water was trickling down the back of his neck, and his feet and legs were soaked. He made an effort to understand and sympathize with how Margo was feeling. She loved animals—that was one of the qualities that made her so adorable. Or at least he'd thought so until tonight.

"Look," he called, "the cat's probably hiding someplace, dry as toast, while we catch pneumonia out here. She'll come back when she's ready, Margo."

Instead of answering, she started down the driveway toward the road. Her flashlight made an arc of light in the darkness, and her voice grew fainter as she called Lady Hamilton's name. Swearing under his breath, Niell followed her.

"This is ridiculous," he exclaimed when he'd almost caught up with her.

She wasn't even listening. Niell saw the absorbed look on her face as she turned her flashlight onto the houses and yards of the neighbors. Probably, he thought, one of the busybodies in the neighborhood would call the police. "Maybe the neighbors have seen her," Margo said. "Will you help me find out?"

Gritting his teeth, Niell knocked on the Amberlys' door. The look Evan Amberly gave him was so lugubrious that he would have laughed if he wasn't so wet and disgusted.

"You're out looking for a *cat* on a night like this?" Amberly grumbled. "You've got to be kidding."

*I wish,* Niell thought. He could see Margo's flashlight bobbing up the wet street. A car passed her, perilously close, but she paid no attention. Niell hurried after her. "Are you crazy?" he demanded. "You almost got run over back there."

"He didn't even come close to me."

As Margo spoke, she stepped into a rut in the driveway which was slicked over with water, yelped, and fell forward on her knees. Niell caught her by the hands and pulled her up into his arms.

"Are you hurt?" he asked angrily. She shook her head. "To hell with this," he then gritted. "We're going back to the house."

"But Lady Hamilton—"

"Somehow she's not one of my priorities right now." He hoisted her into his arms and, ignoring her protests, carried her back up the slick road. When the kitchen door wouldn't open, he gave the door a shove that nearly took it off its hinges.

"Come in here before you catch double pneumonia," he growled.

Who was he to give her orders? But Margo suppressed her rising irritation when she saw how Niell looked. Rain had plastered his dark hair to his forehead. The too-short poncho had caused his trousers to be splashed with mud and water, and his shoes were a disaster.

"Let's have a look at your ankle," Niell was saying. His strong fingers stripped off her poncho and he knelt down to remove her sodden sneakers. "How does it feel now?"

"It's fine. . . ."

Her voice trailed off as a Siamese cat came padding through the kitchen doorway. Her tail was erect, her eyes slitted, and she was purring.

"Lady Hamilton!" Margo gasped.

She jumped out of her chair and knelt on the floor to cuddle the Siamese in her arms. "Where *were* you? You're not even wet."

"I told you she'd be safe and sound in the house." Niell retorted.

Margo gazed fondly down at Lady Hamilton. "I was sure she'd gone looking for Lord Nelson because she was worried about him."

"You're talking about a cat," Niell pointed out. "Cats don't have language or memory, so how could they worry?"

She didn't like his tone. He sounded unsympathetic, almost unfeeling. "How can you talk like that when you saw how she worries about her mate? And she does have feelings. She—"

"All right!" Niell was aware his voice had risen and lowered it. "Fine. She has feelings. Is there any chance that there's some coffee around that hasn't been buried in flour?"

Margo drew three steadying breaths. She reminded herself that Niell had just come back from a long, exhausting transatlantic flight. He had brought her a rose. *And* he had helped her look for her cat in the rain and the mud, and greater love than that had no man.

"I've said this before, but I'm *really* sorry about this," she told him. "Traffy upset the flour bin and I haven't had a chance to clean up. Why don't you sit down, and I'll get a new pot perked right away."

Niell reminded himself of the champagne, the diamond. With an effort, he forced himself to relax. "I'm sorry, too."

Once more he went to Margo and put his arms around her. He rested his cheek on top of her wet hair. "How about we start all over?"

She nodded mutely.

"Hello," he then said. "You can't imagine how I've missed you."

A slow, invasive warmth began to curl through Margo. When he ran his hands lightly over her arms, her skin tingled with warm goose bumps. "Oh, yes, I can," she whispered and raised her lips to his.

The phone rang. Instantly Margo's answering machine clicked on, and Zach's raspy voice invaded the kitchen. "Margo, made my decision. I don't figure I'm the right kind of contractor you need. I'll stay until you find someone to replace me, don't worry. I mean, we can still be friends."

Margo lunged for the phone receiver and shouted, "Zach? Za—" Reluctantly she replaced the instrument. "Oh, dammit, he's hung up."

"You mentioned you had something to discuss. Was it about Zach?" Niell asked.

Once more his tone made Margo defensive, but all she said was, "Let me get that coffee, and I'll tell you about it."
Niell fell silent, and as Margo set up the percolator and wiped the kitchen table free of flour, she felt that silence like a physical weight. She saw that he was frowning and felt a twinge of irritation, then reminded herself that Niell was tired—and wet because of her.

Margo massaged her temples, which had begun to throb. "It's been a terrible day," she sighed.

As she told him the story of her disagreement with Zach, Niell said, "Zach shouldn't have lost control. I understand that he felt frustrated, but

290

in business these things happen all the time. Changes have to be made. Employers bring their own people in. Plans have to be altered. Subcontractors bicker among themselves."

She didn't need a rehash of what she already knew, Margo thought. What she wanted was for Niell to put his arms around her and hold her close to him. What she *needed* was for him to sympathize and then point out options as he always did. She craved his humor and his support as well as his expertise.

"In a way it may be a good thing that Alloway wants out," he was continuing. "I know you could never bring yourself to let him go."

"That's cold!" she cried.

"Zach is a great guy, but right now he's not doing Sanders and Company any good," Niell interrupted. He hadn't meant to be so blunt with Margo, but sometimes straight talk was necessary. "Look, he should have offered to get proof about the mason's dishonesty instead of flying off the handle. He didn't handle himself professionally at all."

His voice was crisp, a lawyer's voice. Margo registered the fact that Niell was using the tone with which he negotiated billion-dollar deals with important corporations around the world. He was talking about Zach as though he were just a commodity.

"I know he's your friend, but friendship and

business seldom mix. I'm sorry if that sounds harsh, but can you really imagine Zach dealing with people like Cosimo Bartolomei and Luna? Let him go, Margo. You don't need a loser on your team."

There was a moment's silence punctuated by the bubbling percolator. Then Niell reminded himself that he hadn't traveled all this way to talk about Alloway's incompetence.

"And speaking of Luna, you've heard from him?" he inquired after a moment. At her nod he continued, "Bartolomei phoned me with the good news when I was in London. I thought we'd celebrate the restoration of the Villa d'Argento and the emergence of Sanders and Company as an international company."

His deep voice brought back so many memories. The feeling she'd had when she saw the Villa d'Argento for the first time, its sense of timelessness, its noble air of antiquity. "I need to talk to you about that," Margo replied. "But first let me show you what Luna wants to do to the villa."

She limped over to her drawing board, blew flour off Luna's faxed plan views, and pulled out copies of her own designs. She placed them side by side.

"Do you see how he's changed everything?" she asked.

Standing beside her, Niell frowned as he examined the two plan views. "I see what you mean," he then said, "but plans aren't carved in stone. The consortium will probably hate Luna's idea. They'll demand changes — at which time you could present your ideas again."

"Supposing the consortium approves Luna's ideas?" Margo stared down at Luna's vision for the new Villa d'Argento. "It's unconscionable, Niell. No ethical landscape designer or architect would ever alter the character of a place like this."

Niell knew that Margo was deeply troubled. He understood her feelings, even shared them. Still, a fledgling landscape designer didn't have the clout to call the shots.

"Look," he began, "I'm sorry that Luna didn't go for your ideas. For my money, they're far and away better than his. Still, the consortium is paying the bills, so they're the final authority." He reached out to take Margo's hands as he added, "They're not asking you to do anything illegal or immoral."

"I can't in good conscience accept this job as it stands," Margo said.

Sensing how she felt, Niell gentled his voice. "Don't be too hasty, Margo. For now you may have to compromise with Luna, but nothing is forever. Simply being on this project will open doors that neither of us can imagine. With Alicia Delfiori's backing, with Monchatto's recommendation, and now with some real experience behind you, you'll be able to write your own ticket."

Margo knew he was telling her the truth, but it was Niell's vision of the truth. She remembered Ez telling her to do what made her happy in the long run.

Both men were talking about the future; both wanted her happiness. But Niell wanted happiness as he saw it, while Ez was advising her to look into her own heart.

"If I restored the villa the way Luna wants to," Margo said, unhappily, "I wouldn't just be compromising. I'd be lying to myself."

"You've said that you want to create gardens of great beauty," he pointed out. "Once you've made a name for yourself, you can create those gardens. If you refuse this chance, there won't be another for a long time—perhaps never. Do what you have to do for now. You'll soon leave Luna standing in the dust."

They were using the same words but not talking the same language. Margo realized how much she wanted Niell to understand her reasons.

"I know that success is important," she told him earnestly, "and I really want to work on restoring the Villa d'Argento. I want it so badly I can taste it. But . . . but there are other things that are even more valuable to me, like my own self-respect. My . . . my integrity, if you will. If I worked with Luna, I'd hate the work, and I'd hate the way the garden would look in the end. I might win the battle, but I'd lose the war. I might be happy for the short term, but not for the long."

Niell just looked baffled, and Margo's heart sank. Whether they were talking about loyalty or about emotions or about Luna's approach to the villa, the difference between their way of thinking yawned as wide and as deep as the Grand Canyon.

"You've said yourself that I must do what I have to do. I've made my decision," she informed him sadly.

He felt her sorrow, but behind the sadness he also sensed a wall of obstinacy. "You're making a mistake," he said.

"Maybe, but I need to do what's right for me."

She'd made her choice, and nothing he or anyone else said would make her change her mind. Niell felt his own irritation rise. "So you're dead set on refusing to work with Luna?"

"I'm afraid so. And I should also be honest with you and tell you that I'm not going to let Zach go—not without a struggle, that is. His friendship means more to me than scoring points with Troner."

"In other words, you don't intend to take my

advice about anything." Niell struggled to keep his voice even, but hurt and indignation hardened it.

He looked and sounded as cold as the north wind—but why should she be surprised? Niell had never made a secret of his ideas and beliefs. She'd always known where he was coming from.

Niell wanted her to be a winner. Now that she'd disappointed him, he thought less of her. Perhaps he even thought her narrow and provincial. Margo steeled her spine and called on pride to override the ache inside her chest.

"We don't seem to see eye to eye on anything, do we?" Her mouth was dry as she added, "I know you've done a great deal of work on my behalf and that my decision has put you in an awkward position with the Italian consortium. Perhaps you want to sever your connection with Sanders and Company."

Disappointment . . . bitterness . . . betrayal . . . He didn't know *how* he felt anymore. "If that's what you want," Niell gritted.

It was the last thing she wanted. Margo had the sudden feeling that she was riding a runaway horse that was galloping her farther and farther from happiness and safety. But there was no turning back now, she knew. She'd put all her cards on the table and found that Niell liked none of them.

"Of course I insist on reimbursing you for all

the legal advice you've given me." Margo was proud that her voice didn't betray her turmoil.

She sounded distant. Indifferent. The diamond in Niell's breast pocket suddenly burned like a red-hot coal.

He matched his tone to hers. "As you wish." Then holding out his hand, palm up, he said, "If you'll give me the keys to my car, I'll be heading back to Boston. It's been a long day."

She'd forgotten she still had his car. Margo felt a knot the size of a grapefruit well into her throat, but she forced it down. "Sure. I'll get the keys. And thanks for letting me use your bimmer all this time."

The keys were in her pocketbook, which she'd thrown on the floor of the kitchen. She had to blow the flour off the keys before handing them over to him. He took them in silence, but as he opened the door, she added automatically, "Drive carefully."

His smile was neutral. "Thanks. I'll be in touch."

Margo heard his steps going away from her and stared at the rose and the bottle of champagne on the table. She felt close to tears.

"Better to find out sooner than later," she told herself. And then she added, "I have to think of the long term."

But for once Ez's saying didn't help at all.

## Chapter Twelve

Using yellow spray paint, Margo carefully marked the placement of the last burlap-wrapped plant. "Okay," she said, "that about does it."

"Let's get to work, you guys." Motioning to his crew to remove the plants from the grounds of the Pittsfield Omega Bank, Zach cautioned sternly, "Yo, Margo, don't *you* lift any of these plants. They're heavy. Didn't you say you have an appointment down in Springfield this morning?"

"With Bruce Varney, who owns the Springfield Corner Mall."

Zach groaned. "Not another mall."

Margo couldn't blame him. For the last few weeks they'd eaten, drunk, and had nightmares about the Mall at Mountain View.

After a long, soul-searching dialogue with Zach, Margo had requested a meeting with Troner and the other owners and had frankly told them Zach's concerns. The upshot was an investigation, which had revealed that Zach had been right about Gifford's shady ways.

With a new mason on board, they'd then worked hard to fulfill their end of the bargain. In the end, they'd even had to hire yet another mason. The additional man had put them in the red, but Troner had been satisfied, and the resulting publicity had been good for Sanders and Company. The surplus of job offers they now had made up for the losses they'd incurred with Troner.

Best of all, she and Zach were now a real team. They discussed things instead of flying off the handle or acting unilaterally. She didn't take on more than they could handle, and Zach had become less cautious about expanding their horizons. They'd both grown, Margo knew.

"Make sure you want us to take the job before you bid on it," Zach advised. "Don't take any wooden nickels, boss."

"I'll try not to." She gave his Red Sox cap a flick with her finger, and they grinned amicably at each other.

"Tomorrow's the fourth of July," Zach went on. "Feel like riding into Boston and watching the fireworks from the esplanade? I could pick you up and we could grab a bite to eat on the way."

"Nope. Tomorrow's the day I prune my annuals." Margo looked at her watch and added,

"And talking about eating out, did I tell you I'm meeting Naomi for lunch? She's got some business in Springfield, so we're having lunch at La Casa."

The interview with the mall owner took longer than Margo had planned. Naomi was already seated and studying the menu when she got to the restaurant.

"It's okay, I've already ordered for us," Naomi said in answer to Margo's apologies. "You look prosperous and professional except for that interesting yellow dye on your shoes. How're the mouse-catchers?"

"Fine. Traffy actually did catch a mouse yesterday, and Lady Hamilton went into orbit about it. And Lord Nelson's back to his old tricks," Margo reported. "He chased the Sheridan's poodle out of our driveway yesterday."

"Someday you ought to get that cat fixed," Naomi said darkly. "That'd settle his hash. Now, how about you?" Margo began to speak, and Naomi cut her short. "I mean, *really*. We haven't had time to talk in ages."

Margo looked down at her hands. There were calluses on her thumb and forefinger, and the backs of her hands were freckled from the sun. Designers weren't supposed to do any yard work—Zach lectured her about that frequently—but she still enjoyed getting involved with the tasks at hand.

"I've been kind of busy," she told Naomi.

"We live in a busy world. Even so, once in a while you have to slow down. Unless there's a reason why you don't want to slow down."

"Why should I—"

"Have you heard from Niell?"

Margo frowned at Naomi, who returned a look of sunny innocence.

"I mean, it's been, what, more than a month since you last saw him."

"Has it? I haven't been keeping track." Margo dug purposefully into her salad, adding brightly, "I had a good initial interview with that mall owner this morning. It looks as if we may be able to do business."

Naomi nodded approvingly. "I have to tell you, Margery Ann, I'm really impressed with Sanders and Company. And I hear you've decided to exhibit at next year's New England flower show. Now that'll bring you scads of new jobs."

"Maybe not. Zach and I agreed that we're going to slow down and only take on projects we really enjoy doing. It'll keep us a small firm in some ways, but a very excellent small firm. That's what we both want—for now, anyway."

"You know what works for you," Naomi allowed.

Having expected a lecture on upward mobility, Margo was astonished. But come to think of it,

Naomi had been unusually laid-back these past few weeks.

"Everybody's different," Naomi continued. "There are people who like to work on ten things at once, and there are others who are happier with one project at a time. Zach was telling me that Carlo Monchatto only designed a handful of gardens but that each one was incredibly beautiful. Nothing's wrong with that, right?"

Margo could think of nothing to say except, "Right."

"Are you sorry you didn't take on that Italian villa?"

The water Margo had been drinking went down the wrong way. As she coughed and choked into her napkin, images and memories invaded her treacherous mind: a warm spring day kissed with the scent of roses and salt, the rustle of the wind and Niell's deep voice.

"Not with Fabio Luna calling the shots," she replied. "It would have been a mistake. I told you a long time ago that there are two kinds of fish, Nao. The kind that paddle around in tide pools, like me, and the ones that swim out far into the deep ocean."

"Like Niell," Naomi murmured.

This time Margo was ready. "Exactly." She was proud that her voice sounded calm and relaxed as she added, "People like that enjoy challenge and achievement. Their arena is the world. People like me are better off in Hometown, U.S.A."

But while she was speaking, Margo was thinking about the friendly phone call she'd had from the Contessa Delfiori, who'd regretted her decision not to work on the Villa d'Argento. Alicia had insisted that Margo return to visit her soon at Delfiori.

A sense of sadness that was almost homesickness filled her, and she had to force herself to concentrate as Naomi asked, "But what happens when a big fish from the deep sea meets a small fish from the tide pool and they realize they love each other?"

Before Margo could answer, the waitress brought their entrées. "There has to be a mistake," Margo exclaimed. "Who ordered pasta primavera?"

"Veggies are good for you, haven't you heard?" Naomi said casually. "Zach tells me that you've been really quiet lately. Margery Ann, are you okay?"

"Zach should mind his own business," Margo retorted, but the damage was done. The pleasant, busy restaurant faded, and she felt bereft and cold. Nights full of painful dreams, days in which she always seemed to hear Niell's laugh, see him in every passerby . . .

"Zach's your friend, and so am I," Naomi reproved. "I wish you and Niell hadn't split up."

"We were too different." Margo put a bit of artichoke into her mouth. It tasted like cotton wool. "Listen, can we talk about something else?"

Naomi ignored this. "Differences are what make the world turn. *Chaucun à son goût,* or something like that. I can understand your taking a stand about the villa thing—I mean, this Luna sounds like a real creep—but that shouldn't have interfered with what you felt about Niell."

Was this *Naomi* talking? Margo blinked hard at her friend, who continued, "If the two of you were willing, you'd have been able to compromise. Now, Zach and me—"

She stopped short as Margo's fork clattered to her plate. "Are you telling me that you and *Zach* have a . . . a relationship?"

Calmly Naomi began to eat a piece of broccoli. "Actually, we started dating a while ago, when you were in Italy. We sort of agreed to disagree on things that didn't matter since we agree on the big issues."

"Like what, for Pete's sake?"

"Like what we're going to eat for dinner—I mean, vegetarian cooking isn't so bad. And like what we want out of life—which is, basically, a nice house and kids." Naomi's smile was uncharacteristically mellow. "Like the fact that

304

we're in love with each other."

Margo felt stunned. No, more than stunned. She felt floored. "You g-guys are in love?" she finally managed to stammer.

"When he's not being a stubborn jackass, Zach's a very sweet guy." Naomi was almost purring. "We've agreed that I'll handle the money and that he'll pick the house we're going to live in. It's a fair trade."

"You mean to tell me that you and Zach are—No, wait a minute," Margo moaned. "I'm hallucinating all this, right? Zach and you can't be getting *married?*"

"Well, not yet. Not for a while," Naomi said. "We have to do some saving first. Anyway, I didn't mean to get into all this. I just wanted to show you that you can compromise on anything if you want to. The important thing is you really have to want to."

Naomi paused. "I had to search my heart and see if I could live without Zach." She added softly, "I found I couldn't."

Could she live without Niell? Margo asked herself. Of course she could. She'd been doing it for five weeks and three days.

"Have you even talked to Niell since—well, since you guys decided to call it quits?" Naomi wanted to know. "I read about the big merger he pulled off between the Herris-Pruitt companies, but that was a while ago."

305

Margo shook her head. "We don't have anything to discuss. This isn't the soaps, Nao. You can't just say 'compromise' and solve the world's problems."

"How about Niell's bill?" Margo blinked. "I mean, have you paid him for all the legal work he did for your company? A big capital W, by the way. You can't be waiting for him to bill you."

The scorn in Naomi's voice raised Margo's hackles. "Of course not," she snapped. "I'm . . . If you must know, I was waiting for some time to pass. For the right moment to come along. Don't ask me when that'll be, either, okay? I'll take care of it."

But Naomi's question lingered in her mind long after the lunch was over. Margo went through the rest of the day—another interview with a prospective client, a site visit, a stop to make sure that the Black Knight butterfly bush she'd planted in a hummingbird and butterfly garden was doing well—with the question sticking like a burr at the back of her mind. The thought that she should contact Niell was what nagged her, and she knew that she had to deal with it or be haunted by it forever.

By the time she got home, it was late in the afternoon. Margo collected her mail and walked up the long driveway admiring her bright-hued annuals. The cats were outside in the rose garden—she could see Lord Nelson sprawled out on top of the stone sundial—and of course Lady Hamilton was by his side.

Margo sat down on a bench Zach had built near the fragrant rose garden and sorted through her letters. There were bills, an advertisement, and a letter bearing an Italian stamp. It was addressed to her in an unfamiliar, old-fashioned hand, and as Margo slit open the letter, she felt a quiver of awe.

"Oh, wow," she whispered.

Carlo Monchatto wrote in a courtly, somewhat old-fashioned English. He hoped that her health was good and then informed Margo that he had learned about her decision not to work with Luna at the Villa d'Argento. He wrote:

I myself have visited that villa as a young man, and I, too, have felt the atmosphere of the place. What Luna proposes to do is an abomination. You were right— morally justified—in refusing to work on such a commission.

Margo sat staring at the maestro's letter for a long moment. It felt as if the sun had come out of dark clouds, that birds were singing with the voices of angels, and that the world was a beautiful place.

She felt vindicated, joyful. She felt empowered. If she was ever going to have the moxie to phone Niell, this was the moment to do it.

Margo got up and went into the kitchen, where she dialed the number of Simons, Granville, and Kier. She did it quickly before she could change her mind, and asked the secretary for Niell.

"I'm sorry, ma'am," the woman said. "Mr. Kier no longer is with the firm. Do you wish to speak with Mr. Simons or Mr. Granville?"

Margo was so stunned that she could hardly speak. "No. No, thank you, that's not necessary," she mumbled. "Where—Do you know where Mr. Kier is working now?"

The secretary didn't know, and Margo hung up the phone receiver with an inexplicable heavy feeling in her chest.

She'd remembered that Niell's friend Barry had mentioned a Sacramento law firm that had been wooing Niell. No doubt Niell had decided to take the position. Or perhaps he'd decided to join a law firm in London or Italy or Paris. And why should she be so surprised? Niell being Niell, he must simply have decided that he'd outgrown New England and had gone to seek new opportunities and challenges.

Margo wasn't so sure why, but the thought depressed her totally. Perhaps until this moment she'd harbored the hope that someday she'd see his BMW driving down Peachtree Lane. Perhaps until this moment she hadn't truly believed that she'd probably never see Niell again.

"Wake up and smell the coffee, woman." Margo jammed her hands into the pockets of her slacks and tried to cheer up, but the silence in the house was deafening, and in spite of the July warmth she felt chilled to the bone.

Grandma Beth had always said that in times of stress, she needed to wash the kitchen floor. Margo felt no ambition in that direction, but when she looked out of the living-room window and saw her petunias in full bloom, she knew what she was going to do.

The long summer twilight was stealing down from the Berkshires, and soft mauve shadows softened the colors of the annual beds as Margo approached with shears and a basket. "I'm supposed to get you guys tomorrow, anyway," Margo told the flowers.

The petunias seemed too pretty to cut. Hardening her heart, Margo started to lop every other plant in half. "You'll thank me when you start growing like crazy."

Lord Nelson prowled over to rub his rough head against her shoulder. Lady Hamilton purred in her ear. Trafalgar was chasing a moth and batting it with his paws. Emma Amberly waved to her from her garden and called a friendly greeting.

Margo waved back. "I have everything I

want," she said aloud. "I'm very, very lucky."

She was happy with her work, her neighbors were mellowing and the warmth and peace of Carlin curved about her like a friendly hand. The house—her house—was becoming what she'd always wanted.

And Niell had what *he* wanted, which was the way it should be. He'd probably set the West Coast on its ears by now. Margo thought of the way he'd appeared that afternoon when they met with Bartolomei's consortium, knowledgeable, handsome, sure of himself. And then she remembered that moon-drenched night in the pensione outside of Rome.

She was only human, after all. For just a moment she gave in to the fairy tale. Margo closed her eyes and thought of that magic night, of Niell's lips on hers, his hands stroking her body as if it were a precious instrument. Of Niell calling her his love . . .

"Are you working or meditating?"

Margo's eyes flew open. No, she thought. He couldn't possibly be here. She stuttered, "Wh-why aren't you in California?"

Niell looked at her as if she were brain damaged. "Where am I supposed to be?"

He wasn't real. He was a mirage. Margo closed her eyes and counted to ten. But when she opened her eyes, he was still there.

He was wearing suit slacks and a white shirt

open at the throat, as if he'd torn off his neck-
tie and tossed it into the back seat. Set off by
his dark hair and those extraordinary smoke-
gray eyes, his face looked a little thinner than
she remembered. He was smiling, but there was
an odd, shadowed look in his eyes that she
couldn't read.

"I phoned you at your old office—"

Niell's eyes brightened. "You did?"

She had to get hold of herself. With an effort
Margo forced the quiver from her voice and
amended, "I wanted to know where—I needed
to talk to you about the bill for your legal
fees."

Her carefully modulated neutral tone took
Niell aback. When she'd first seen him, he'd
thought he'd seen welcome and delight in her
eyes, but perhaps that had been a trick of the
twilight.

"My, ah, bill," he repeated.

"Yes. You do remember that we had a business arrangement." Margo felt more sure of herself now, so she got to her feet. Her knees felt
shaky, but they held. "You helped us with
Sanders and Company," she went on. "I'm very
grateful, and I've taken an unconscionably long
time to reimburse you. If you'll tell me what
your fees are, I'll write you a check."

"Supposing my fees are higher than you're
prepared to pay?" He kept his eyes on her face,

trying to read it. He'd pictured that face so often in the past few weeks, vividly recalled hazel eyes that expressed all emotions and feelings. But today Margo's face and even her eyes expressed nothing. They seemed totally shuttered against him.

"I'm sure we can come to some agreement," Margo replied. She was determined not to quibble with Niell. Whatever he demanded, she'd pay, even if it meant taking on another job or two. "Can you give me a ball-park figure now so I'll know what to expect?"

Niell took a step closer to her and saw a flare of alarm in her eyes. He stopped and tried to remember the speech he'd composed while driving out to see her. But the words had left him, and his usual quick mind seemed to be full of sawdust.

"Margo," he began, then cleared his throat. "Ah, we need to talk."

"About the bill?"

"To hell with the bill." Niell took two quick steps forward and pulled her into his arms and kissed her.

Margo felt herself being swept into remembered arms, the same arms that had enfolded her in her dreams. The texture of his cheek against hers, the taste of his mouth—all of it seemed to release something in her so that the loneliness and the unhappiness melted like snow during spring thaw.

"Niell," she whispered. "Oh, Niell."

Their lips found each other's again. The warm July evening seemed to disappear, and they were lost, locked together in a golden chrysalis beyond time and space. Margo clung to Niell and ran her hands over his arms, his shoulders, his back. She knew that what Naomi had said was right.

Life without Niell had been a half-life in which everything and everyone seemed to move and operate in shadows. And realizing this, she knew that she couldn't keep living a lie. Come what may, she had to throw her cards back on the table once more.

"I love you," she told him.

"Thank God for that!" He started to kiss her again and then changed his mind to ask with uncharacteristic uncertainty, "You do mean it, don't you?"

When she nodded, he enfolded her against his chest and held her tightly against him.

"I never thought you'd come back," she murmured against his shoulder.

"I didn't mean to. I went back to work—to my world—expecting that I'd have no trouble forgetting you." Niell stroked back her hair to look down into her face. "I found that the game plan had changed."

When she breathed, she drew the scent of

Niell's cologne into her lungs. When she moved her cheek, she felt the softness of his shirt beneath it. *Home,* Margo thought. Aloud she asked, "How had it changed?"

"What had totally absorbed me before wasn't even a challenge anymore. The Herris-Pruitt merger, which was a big coup by any standards, meant less than nothing. Without you, everything was dust and ashes."

She sighed in deep satisfaction. "I know what you mean. Even my roses didn't smell as sweet anymore, and—But why did you quit your firm?"

He fielded the question calmly. "I decided it was the right time for a career move. I'm going to hang up a shingle in Carlin."

"You what?"

"Rupert Brooke is retiring," Niell pointed out. "The town has to have an attorney, and I'm the best I know."

The sky had begun to darken, and a pale moon had made its appearance. Warm wind tugged at Niell's dark hair as Margo stared up at him, searching his face.

"You, a country attorney?" she said, wondering. "You'd hate it."

"Says who?"

"You said! When your friend Barry moved to California, you said he'd never be happy as a small-town lawyer. Niell, please don't do anything drastic. You'll be sorry if you do."

"Not if you'll marry me." He leaned back to smile down at her as he explained, "You asked me what my fee was, so I'll tell you. I want it all, Margo. Your soul and your spirit. Not to mention your body, of course. I want the whole package."

She heard the words not only with her ears but with another deeper sense. It activated her heart. Margo felt as though something that had lain frozen and dormant inside her had come gloriously alive.

"Of course I'll marry you," she exclaimed happily.

He kissed her lips and the tip of her nose. "You're hopeless as a negotiator,. You're supposed to ask me what you get in return." Then he kissed her temples and the shadow of the dimple in her chin.

"Okay," she told him between kisses, "I'll bite. What's my side of the deal, counsellor?"

"Not much of a bargain. All you get is me. But I hope you'll take me because I can't seem to function without you."

Something in those words caught at her mind. Margo put up a hand, touching his lips gently, forestalling his next kiss.

"Niell, are you sure?" she asked quietly. "I know you're coming to Carlin because of me. You think that I could never leave Lattimer

House or the cats. But I couldn't bear it if later you regretted giving up everything and were unhappy. I'd rather give up the house and move with you to . . . to California or anywhere else you wanted. The cats will adjust."

But Niell only said, "Look over your shoulder."

The twilight had deepened, and a pale moon was rising over the mountains. "The last time we saw a moon like this, we were in Italy," Niell went on. "The moon's the same everywhere in the world, Margo."

Together they watched the full moon turn silver as it reflected the light of the sun.

"I used to think," Niell continued quietly, "that achieving—winning, if you like—was everything. That was the way I was taught, and I saw nothing wrong with it. But when I met you, the picture began to shift."

She started to speak, but he stopped her. "I'm making a speech, so listen. I began to alter my way of thinking before I was even aware of it. As far back as when I was working with you on your house, I found myself happy—even content. I liked the unhurried life, enjoyed the thought that I had *time* to repair a floor or build something with my hands. And when I missed my flight after your cat ate poison, I realized that being with you was more important than anything else. That's why I came to Delfiori—to be with you."

Niell paused. "I'm not saying that all of this took place overnight. It didn't. In fact, my conscious mind fought against what was happening to me. When you wouldn't take Luna's offer, I convinced myself that you were stubborn, unreasonable, even ungrateful. I interpreted your loyalty to Zach Alloway as a further demonstration of your obstinacy. I had to be away from you to realize how deeply you'd changed my life, changed me."

Listening to the music of his deep voice, Margo felt joy building up in her. Like effervescent champagne bubbles, happiness danced through her veins and into her heart. But she had to make sure.

"What if you regret this . . . this career move? The contessa once said that you were like a medieval cavalier and that the world was yours to conquer. What if country life bores you and the old dreams call you back?"

"I can't tell you that because I don't know," Niell replied. "Look at you. Right now here you are in Carlin, enjoying being a small-town operation. But who's to tell what'll happen if another Villa d'Argento—minus Luna—comes your way?"

"Dreams change, you mean," she murmured. "You're right, of course."

"I can't predict the future, Margo, and neither

317

can you. But if our dreams and goals change direction again, we can ride the crest of change . . . together."

"Together," she whispered.

Their lips came together tenderly, tasting the future. Then Niell said, "It's getting late. If you haven't eaten yet, I've got this idea. We could get together some bread, some wine, a couple of apples and spread a blanket in your rose garden."

Margo found that she liked the idea just fine.